Sanctuary

By

C. N. Martin

The United States Department of State
estimates that between **15,000 and 50,000** women and girls
are **trafficked** each year into the **United States.**

The International Labour Organization estimates **4.8 million
people, mainly women and children** were trafficked in the
commercial sex trade in 2016. More than **1 million children** are
victims of commercial sexual exploitation each year.

Chapter 1

Cédric was a diver almost as soon as he could put fins on his feet. He lived on Saint Martin on the French side of this island shared with the Dutch, high in the hills because he loved the view looking out onto God's palette of amazing shades of blues and greens that was the Caribbean Sea. His family had barely survived Hurricane Louis back in 1995 when he had just turned sixteen. He remembered huddling with his family in the middle of what was left of their living room. The roof had blown off. At one point, he looked up and saw the night sky filled with stars as the eye of the hurricane passed over, and he thought how beautiful it was before the backside of the hurricane delivered its second and fiercer rendition.

After Louis, he had plenty of work for a sixteen-year-old. It was during this time he got most of his diving training as a scavenger. He was on a salvage team that explored wrecks that had met their demise in the storm. In one yacht, he found two gold coins. He had fantasies of what it must have been like to be a pirate back in the 1700s when they ravaged the shipping lanes looking for Spanish gold and other riches. He gave one of the coins to his family, and it provided them with food and other essentials for a month. The second coin still hung around his neck; he had sworn that he would be buried with it. It had become a reminder of the night his father came home drunk from playing dominoes and tried to rip it off him for gambling debts. It was his mother, wielding her mighty frying pan, who saved him and his coin that night and put his father to sleep on the floor.

After that night, Cedric lied about his age to enlist in the military, where he spent two years. His wife Marie had also been in the Army for her own personal reasons. They met coming out of the service, got married and had a child, a special child they named Daniella. Cédric loved his work, the work of exploring the world that lay beneath the beautiful blue Caribbean waters, looking for treasure and retrieving things lost.

Things were quite busy again after Hurricane Irma, a Category 5 hurricane that hit Saint Martin ferociously in 2017. His family didn't fare as well in this hurricane as they had in Louis. There were many more deaths than were announced to the public, mainly because it was a tourist island and the economy depended on attracting visitors to fun in the sun on "The Friendly Island." There was a rush to minimize the damage, and the losses were expressed in soulful quietness and private grief – the kind of grief Cédric felt for his grandmother and his aunt. Auntie Viola had gone to stay with her mother and watch over her until the storm passed. They found the two women buried under the east-facing wall in the direction the hurricane had come from. Auntie Viola was lying on top of her mother, trying to shield her. Now she was watching over her mother for eternity.

What was to change Cédric's life forever happened about a month after the hurricane. He was out scavenging some of the boats and yachts that had gone down. He'd heard of a wrecked yacht situation where the owner had survived. Rumor had it that he had been smuggling liquor in the yacht's cabin. Divers knew these bottles can survive a long time on the sea bottom before they eventually hit something and break. And after the hurricane, liquor was a good commodity to have for trade.

He was searching the area between St. Barth and the Dutch side of Sint Maarten when he came across the boat at a depth of forty feet. Cédric swam down through the hatch into the cabin area he thought held the best promise for some riches, or at least a few bottles of alcohol, to help him better provide for his family.

He was stunned for a second, then he realized what he was viewing and threw up into his respirator. He had to leave quickly and make it up to the surface. Panting, in shock and gasping for air, coughing up water and vomit, he held tight to the side of his boat when he reached the surface. How could this be? He cleaned out his respirator and went back down, this time knowing what he would find. Inside the hull of the yacht were sixteen girls in similar early states of decay. From the looks of them and the clothes they still wore, they looked young, most looked under fourteen. They were chained together like the cargo of slave ships of past centuries that had been brought down by a hurricane, dragging its cargo of flesh to the bottom of the unforgiving sea. This modern-day slave ship had suffered the same fate. One young girl was about his daughter's age wearing nothing more than panties and what looked like a training bra, staring out at him; her wide-open eyes seemed to look into his soul, asking the question, "Why? Why did I have to die like this?" Around her neck was one of those dime-store necklaces with a stamped piece of metal so cheap it was already rusting it read *Tammy*. It was the

3

only identifying marker he could find on any of them. His air tanks were getting low, so he surfaced. Once back in his boat, he sat with his head between his hands, crying and throwing up into the gully of his small boat. He was clenching the necklace so hard out of his pain and rage that the metal was cutting into his hand, and blood dripped down his arm. Thoughts of his own daughter made him scream at the heavens. A Crusade and its Chief Knight Templar were born that afternoon.

Chapter 2

Cédric went home and the first thing he did was hug his daughter, Daniella, so tightly that it scared her. She looked up and saw tears in his eyes. "What's wrong, Daddy? What's wrong?"

"Nothing, honey, but something happened today that made me remember how much I love you."

Marie did not have a child's innocence. She knew that something was drastically wrong with her husband. She had never seen him look so upset and agitated.

"Sweetie, go outside and play. I want to talk with your father." Cédric sat, rested his arms on the kitchen table, and stared into nothingness. Marie sat next to him. "What is it? You found something today, didn't you?"

5

Cédric opened up his hand. There was the necklace still cutting into it.

"You're hurt!" She fetched some of the ointments she used to administer to Daniella's scrapes and bruises. Carefully and gently, she dug the bloody piece of metal from her husband's palm, sensing that somehow it was a sacred object. "This is going to hurt. I'm going to pour some hydrogen peroxide in the wound to clean it out." She made him cup his palm and poured the liquid into the depression. As it bubbled, the mental and spiritual pain he was experiencing far outweighed the physical pain Marie's medicine was necessarily inflicting.

Cédric finally looked at her. "Sixteen, Marie! Sixteen! I found sixteen young girls hardly any older than our Daniella chained together in the hull of a yacht." Marie gasped and covered her mouth with her hand. "They have all been there since the storm. It was clear they were prisoners being taken somewhere to be sold into the sex trade; they were sex slaves. They all had skimpy little outfits. The girl with the necklace — Tammy —" Cédric pointed to the bloody object, "her eyes were open, and she was staring at me. Her eyes were asking why, and what was I going to do."

Marie was the only woman Cédric had ever loved. Marie was also an experienced diver. She said, "Take me there. I don't want you to be the only person carrying this image in your mind and soul. I don't want to, but I need to see this; we need to see this together."

Cédric started to protest, but he knew it wouldn't matter. Marie asked a neighbor to watch over Daniella for a bit. Together they went to the harbor and Cédric's small boat, one of the few that had survived Hurricane Irma. He knew the seas like birds know the wind, and he steered the small craft to the exact spot where he had been earlier.

They strapped on tanks and together they descended. Once they reach the yacht, Marie went in to view the horrors waiting within, followed by Cédric. She knew instantly which of the sixteen young girls was Tammy, and that she would haunt her husband's soul and now her own for the rest of their lives. She looked at Marie in the same haunting way she had looked at her husband. After about five minutes, they backed out of the young women's coffin and returned to the surface. They crawled into the boat and sat across from each other, both crying. Marie's good heart also had been broken. Finally, she reached out and said, "Quick! We must pray! We must pray for their souls and for ours. The devil is afoot." They locked hands, and from their Methodist practice they remembered and recited Psalm 23 and the Our Father.

Cédric and Marie were both descendants of slaves. Parents, grandparents and great, great grandparents often told the children stories, passed on from one generation to the next, of what it meant to be a slave, and how they had ended up on these islands. The thing they had seen woke up stirrings of ancient relatives that lived in both of them. The pain they were now living felt new and very old at the same time, crying out both for their suffering to be heard, and crying out for justice.

Marie asked, "What are we going to do? Who should we tell?"

"For now, we tell no one. I need to think." She knew from their years together that he was a man who needed to sit with things, think them through, and feel them through before a decision would come from him. He had always told her when she pushed him for a decision, "My dear, God gave me two spiritual gifts – my head and my heart. Both must be searched and listened to before big decisions are made." This was one of those times.

For two days, Cédric walked the hills of Saint Martin deep in contemplative trance. At times he would sit on some outcropping of volcanic rock, staring out into the sea, looking at the spot where the fleshmongers had left their wares. Marie knew he needed to be alone. Around lunchtime, she would walk up to where her husband was, leave food on some rock he could either eat or leave for the animals, but she wasn't going to disturb him.

It was dark and cloudy on that second night, and his only companions were a few stars and Tammy, the young girl who now lived inside him. Around midnight, he walked back home. Daniella had been asleep for hours. He went to the kitchen table and motioned for Marie to come sit with him. He reached out, grabbed her hand, and looked directly into her walnut-colored eyes.

"Marie, my dear sweet Marie; they are our children now. In the hills in back of our home, we will build graves for them and bury them overlooking the sea. We will pray that their spirits find rest here, and also that their spirits guide us. I am going to bring in John, Ramus, Daniel and Thomas to help us." The four were good diving friends. "We will gather our daughters and bury them at night. Then we will start to do something about this. We cannot look away any longer. Everyone here knows that young girls from South America, Africa, and even Europe are often shipped through these waters as part of the sex trade. We will stop it; we will shut it down. Any young girls we discover in the process will come home with us. We will provide sanctuary and raise them as if they were Daniella."

"Why not just go to the authorities?"

"You and I both know what would happen. They would make a big fuss as they retrieved the bodies of the girls. Many words would be spoken and written, the cameras would click away, and the media would feast on these tragic corpses, and everyone would talk about how sad and awful it was. They might even put a buoy to mark to spot where the craft went down. Local people and even tourists would pay homage, maybe pray, throw flowers into the sea and take pictures. It would become a shrine for the ugliness that goes on right under our noses as we go about our day. It would become like the schools, churches, synagogues and malls in America with their shootings, their flowers, the tears shed and the media documenting it all and asking people stupid questions like, 'How did you feel when you heard about the shootings?' But little change ever occurs. Now and here, things will change."

"How?"

"We will hunt them like old man Rufus hunts the island iguanas. We will hunt these people who steal children, who sell their innocence. We will hunt them down, not to capture and give them to the authorities, but to destroy these soulless creatures. We will make it impossible for them to do this here. Both you and I have military training. Why do you think God gave it to us? Why do you think God saved my boat when so many others were destroyed? Why do you think God had us find this wreck? Why do you think God has burned Tammy's face into our souls – to make a circus out of their death, or to fight to make a real difference? My wife, we have been given a task, a mission. I'm sure others, some of our buddies, will help us. But for now, we have sixteen daughters to bury."

Chapter 3

John André, Ramus Duggins, Daniel Reyes and Thomas Nestor were Cédric's closest friends. Saint Martin being a small island, they had known each other all their lives and had always been there for each other's troubles. John and Thomas had helped Cédric dig out the bodies of Cédric's aunt and grandmother after the hurricane. Cédric was Ramus's best man at his wedding to Margaret Dupree, another childhood and life-long friend. It was only natural that Cédric and Marie involved these four and their wives, who were also all dear friends of Marie's.

Cédric threw the tarnished and bloody necklace on the table as the six sat around it, drinking a *Presidente* and sharing a loaf of the lemon poppy seed bread Marie was known for. "A couple of days ago, I found that sunken yacht we've all been looking for. It was supposed to be full of booze, but that was not its cargo. The yacht was a slave ship. In the hull below deck are sixteen beautiful little girls and young women chained together." The four friends stared at each other in disbelief, then stared back at

Cédric and Marie. This couldn't be true. But by the looks of anguish and despair on Cédric's and Marie's faces, they knew they were speaking the truth. A reverent silence filled the room. There's a reason these types of deeds are called unspeakable.

Breaking the silence, Thomas asked, "Where? Where did you find them?"

"East side of the island, about two and half kilometers off of Babit Point down about forty feet. I was over there investigating, looking for signs of that yacht wreckage. I saw a small bubble of oil break the surface, so I knew there was something down there. My tanks were about half full when I headed down. They're all chained together, attached to an anchor bolt in the middle of the main cabin. They're pretty well preserved for how long they've been down there."

Knowing his friend, Rasmus guessed, "You haven't called the authorities, have you?"

"No." Then, changing his wording to include the group, Cédric added, "And we're not going to. They would create a circus event using it for their own political advantage. These girls have been used enough already." The silence resumed.

Marie passed the sweet bread around again, saying, "We need your help to bury them."

Cédric added, "And we need your help to avenge them."

Everyone knew they were at one of those moments when what they said and did next would define them. It would mean either succumbing to one's natural fears and doing nothing, or else embracing courage like none had ever done before. They knew that the small house was being transformed into a sacred meeting hall, and the ideas and words they were speaking would pull them into the unknown, a dangerous unknown. They all knew Cédric was asking them to go to war with the slave traders.

Cédric stood and moved behind Marie, placing his hands on her shoulders. "Before any of you decide – for your decision may cost you your life – think about it, talk with your wives." He squeezed Marie's shoulders to let his friends know he was speaking for her also. "I will be seeking justice and letting these soulless creatures know they can't use our waters and islands for their trade. But for now, all Marie and I are asking of you is to help us retrieve our daughters, for according to scavenging laws, we have claimed them as our own. Help us bury them."

Thomas spoke up, "You can have my answer now. If they are your daughters, then as I'm Daniella's uncle, now I am theirs. Of course, I will help you bury our girls. And if this had been done to Daniella, I would help you avenge her and help reclaim her dignity. You invited me here because you knew my answer already." Thomas looked around. "You knew all of our answers." At which point, Daniel, Rasmus, and John stood up.

John added, "And you know our wives also stand with you and Marie. Family is family."

"Where are we burying our girls?" Ramus asked. In those few moments, a covenant, a holy covenant, was written and signed in their souls.

"I want to bury them up here on the hill behind our house. There's a flat area. It'll need a little work enlarging it, but I think it will be a good spot. The sun can warm them during the day, and at night, the cool trade winds can comfort them and take their spirits soaring."

John nodded. "A good spot, a very good spot. I'll get my Bobcat. I think we can have it flattened and enlarged by the end of tomorrow."

Rasmus, a stonemason as well as a diver, added, "I have enough forms and concrete to make their resting places, their burial boxes."

Cédric looked at them, smiling. "Thank you, my brothers! Thank you!"

Throughout the island were stone walls made by slaves centuries ago to mark out property divisions. Rasmus decided that he would embed stones from these walls on the outsides of each of the cement coffins.

Marie shared that her mother had often retold her great-grandmother's story about how slaves were buried on the plantation where her family had toiled. When a slave died, he or she would be thrown into a hole so as not to "waste" any wood on a slave's coffin. But if there was a special slave, they would be laid on a slab of wood to indicate that they had value. "The yacht where they are now is made out of wood, not fiberglass. I would like that we recover sixteen slabs to support them because they are special."

Daniel, who had a bit of a dark side, added in his own humorous way, "Let's get more than sixteen slabs. If something happens to me, I'd like to be buried on one with my nieces. I think I'm kind of special."

Marie, sitting next to him, patted him on his cheek. "You are, Daniel. You are very special."

"We'll get as much wood out of that ship as we can," John added, causing them all to reflect on the future they had agreed to.

Just about then, the *Presidentes* were finished, as was the poppy seed bread, and they all went out back and started planning out the graveyard.

"I want to retrieve them and bury them at night, to keep this from others for as long as possible," Cédric said. "We need to do this quickly before the authorities find out."

John looked at Cédric. "Brother, it's a small island. This won't be a secret very long. It'll be hard to hide sixteen new graves. But short term, we can use some of the blue tarps left over from Irma to erect a barrier from any curious eyes that might be watching."

Cédric nodded. He liked the idea. "I know, John. If there's one thing we know from living here our whole lives, it's that people are always watching. But if we get them buried in a proper graveyard in the proper way, people will understand, and most likely, the authorities will not want to be seen as graverobbers. We will also declare it a slave's graveyard, for that's what they were. Most of us on the island are descendants of slaves who would never dare to desecrate a slave graveyard. Marie and I have even talked of asking Pastor Eboune to come do a proper burial service for each of them and to bless the graveyard. Pastor would have the authority to declare it a slave graveyard. All of this should help to quiet things down if and when the authorities come snooping and wanting to claim them. We all know some of them are on the take."

Daniel, an expert underwater photographer, suggested that he and Cédric dive to the yacht to take photos. These would be important to document the spot, the boat, and the young girls whose lives were stolen from them for a couple of reasons: first, so the girls could be identified if, by some rare chance, family or parents ever come looking for them; and second, photos would help to keep the authorities at bay. Once the design for the graveyard was done, they all set about their tasks.

That evening they all sat around eating ribs from Mark's Place and fried rice from Rick's, for no one had the strength or energy to fix a meal. All except for Daniel, who had lost his appetite and parts of his heart from his day at the bottom of the sea documenting the horrors that lay below; he just sat on the ground that was to be the graveyard with his wife Gloria, talking about what he had seen that day. "God have mercy. So many of his precious creatures chained together in those raging seas. You can still see the fear and suffering on their faces. Chained together, having to watch each other die, wondering why their parents or anyone else weren't coming to save them. So much innocence." Gloria held him, knowing that the husband with whom she had started the day today was gone forever. Knowing old private wounds had been touched – maybe ripped open – for him.

"I hate God and I thank God for leading Cédric to that place. Those girls are not the only ones who lost innocence. My soul, too, has been ravaged. How could this be? What kind of God could allow this?" The pain in his eyes hurt his wife's heart. "Please don't leave me, please don't leave me! I don't ever want to be as alone as they must have felt." Gloria assured him she was going nowhere and tried to comfort him, though it didn't help. He would not find comfort for a long time.

Back at the dinner table, John, Daniel's best friend, said, "I should go be with Daniel and Gloria." As he rose, Marie put her hand on his shoulder.

"Stay, John. Stay with us right now. There's no way you, or even Gloria, can comfort him. No one can. You'll understand this soon enough."

Margaret, Rasmus's wife, Gloria, Daniel's wife, Alma, John's wife, and Rachelle, Thomas's wife, met early the next morning. Time was in short supply and they needed to complete their tasks before the whole island knew something important was going on and the authorities descended upon them. The women spent the whole day preparing the gravesites. By the end of that second day, just as the sun was going over the mountain, everything was finished. The fence they made from the blue tarps left over from Hurricane Irma helped offer some privacy from others, who by now must have been wondering what was happening on the side of the mountain. Rasmus and Cédric worked into the night, mixing and pouring the concrete for the girl's spirit homes – the above-ground graves that were the island custom.

Their graves looked beautiful with the stones from the slave walls embedded within the concrete. They were ready to retrieve and bury Cédric and Marie's daughters, whom they considered their nieces. They knew that when the blue tarps came down, their lives would be changed forever; they could only hope they were chasing a destiny written for them by the merciful God they all believed in.

Chapter 4

The moon was waning, and it would be three nights until the new moon. Pastor Eboune had agreed to perform blessings and burial services in strict secrecy for each of the sixteen innocents on that night. He, as an officer of the church, would also sanctioned it an official slave graveyard, making it harder for any authorities to come reclaim the girls to cover up the ugly reality of what was happening throughout the Caribbean.

They left that night in two small boats. They had chosen a route to offer the most protection possible from inquisitive eyes: a secluded beach to land on and a little-used path to carry the girls to their graves. Once they got to the site, Cédric led John, Thomas and Rasmus down to the yacht so they could have some moments to witness what the others had seen by now. The illumination from their underwater lights created a strange, surreal dimension to everything. The four men stared into the horror of that small room where the girls were still chained together, and the horror stared back, changing each forever.

Rasmus handed Cédric the bolt cutters, knowing it was he who needed to free them. Cédric went to Tammy and touched her face for the first time. He stroked her hair, kissed her on the top the head as he did Daniella when putting her to bed, closed her eyes and cut the chain that had sealed her fate. Then he gently carried her up to the surface and the waiting boat. The other men carefully pulled the chain through the shackles that circled each of the girl's wrists. John signaled the others to save the chain and shackles.

Thomas, because of his skills at dismantling ships claimed by the sea, set about the task of dismantling the craft and reclaiming its wood. As he was doing this, he came across a curious compartment. He motioned the others over and pointed. Inside the compartment were two more sets of chains and a pearl-handled handgun. John signaled the others to save these items also.

The plan was to leave the dive site around two o'clock, giving them enough time to return to the island and carry the bodies up the mountain before sunrise. When it came time for them to return to the island, they had eleven bodies in the boats. They all regretted the need to secure the remaining five in place until the next night, for by now, all sixteen had become part of their fiber and psyches, young faces etched in their minds and soul forever. Thomas had some slabs of wood ready to take back also.

In the boat, as they were heading back to their landing beach, Cédric asked John, "Why did you want to save the chains and shackles? I thought we'd leave that ugliness at the bottom of the sea."

"For conscience, my friend, for conscience. I want every person who visits the gravesite to see the reality of what these girls had to endure, and what killed them. You're right – there's a wickedness about chains and shackles. But everyone who sees them will see that ugliness. And I don't want us to forget it either."

Cédric nodded. "Good."

The women were waiting at the beach when the boats arrived, with dresses for the girls and sheets to wrap them in. Rachelle, a daughter of a minister, said blessings over each girl as they were prepared for their trip up the mountain. Once the eleven girls were wrapped in bundles, Cédric said, "We need to get going. We'll need to make two trips before dawn."

Marie looked at him. "Why two trips? There are ten of us."

"I'm not expecting you ladies to have to carry them. They're quite heavy."

Alma declared to Cédric, "We've all carried daughters before. We can each carry one and my John can carry two. Our ancestors carried heavier loads than these."

It wasn't long until there was a procession, each caring a child, with John carrying two over his shoulders. There was no conversation, but if you listened closely, you could hear prayers being whispered.

Upon arriving back at Marie and Cédric's, the girls' bearers laid them next to their concrete coffins. The men went down the mountain to take the boats back to their usual mooring places. John and Thomas walked back up the mountain again; John carried the chains, and Thomas a bundle of wooden slabs. They lifted each girl's body onto a slab of wood, symbolizing solidarity with their slave ancestors, and settled them into their coffins with the stars shining down on them offering blessings.

When morning came, they all sat exhausted. Marie and Margaret made a simple breakfast. The men took turns watching over the graves because the girls had not yet been covered with the concrete slabs that would protect their bodies from the animals that roam the area. The concrete slabs would not be placed and cemented on the tops of their coffins until after the services were performed by Pastor Eboune.

Daniella had been sent to the other side of the island to stay with one of her aunties during this time. Marie and Cédric planned to sit down with her and tell her everything after the sixteen funerals.

After breakfast, each found a resting place in the house and fell asleep, drained by the physical and emotional toll that was heavy on all of them. They all knew that they had another tough night ahead. In late afternoon, air tanks were refilled and preparations made to retrieve the rest of the girls and dismantle what was left of the craft.

As they were all eating, getting ready for the tasks of the night, Cédric put the pearl-handled gun on the table. "John, it was good that you wanted to save the chains and shackles, and that we found this with them. It will help us with the other tasks that lay ahead. It will someday hopefully lead us to the person who captained that boat that night." Everyone nodded, but they were too hungry and too tired to discuss the subject anymore.

That second night, the bodies of the remaining innocents were retrieved within a matter of hours. The wood had been removed from the vessel, leaving only a metal frame and motor to mark the spot. The women insisted on carrying the bodies up the mountain. Cédric carried the last girl, and his friends each carried a bundle of wood retrieved from the wreckage.

By three o'clock that morning all the girls had been placed in their graves, each resting on a piece of the slave wood taken from the wreckage. The women had dressed them the best they could on the beach before wrapping them in linen sheets. They wanted them to look like the little girls and young women they were, and not the sex slaves their captors were making of them.

The next night would be the new moon and the burial ceremonies with Pastor Eboune. They all went back to their normal lives as much as they could, except for Thomas. He was working like a crazy man, building the fence made from the slave chains to surround the graveyard. The chains looped through wrought iron stakes he had forged by hand, the shackles now hanging from the chains. Thomas used his welding torch to fuse some of the links together, forming a tall, rounded arch to form the entrance to the graveyard. Using his cutting torch, he created a sign for the top of the arch bearing the name he and John had given the graveyard: SANCTUARY. He wanted everything ready for his nieces' burial services. The site was still shielded with temporary blue tarp fences to shield the site from curious eyes. One young man, who approached using the disguise of delivering a pizza, was quickly turned back before he got close enough to learn anything. Thomas kept the pizza.

Chapter 5

Pastor Eboune showed up in time for supper on the night of the burial ceremonies. They all prayed together, and after supper, Daniel showed him the pictures he had taken at the wreckage site. They wanted Pastor Eboune to meet the girls and young women he was burying. As he wept and touched their faces on the pictures, he asked, "Was there any indication of who they were?" They shook their heads, having **decided to keep** the information about the necklace with the name "Tammy" private among the group, believing that information might help them as they tracked down the men and women responsible. He decided. "We will just call them what they are – Little Angels."

After supper and after Pastor Eboune had become acquainted with the girls, he put on his robes, gathered up his Bible and they all walked through the gate into SANCTUARY. For the next five hours, individual services were held for each girl. Prayers and blessings were made at each grave and Pastor Eboune ceremoniously sprinkled ashes and holy water on each body. By the end, anyone in attendance could have given the "ashes to ashes" speech performed at each gravesite. It wasn't until sunrise that the last of the concrete coffins was closed with cement, securely sealing the concrete slab placed on top. As the sun peeked over the ocean, Pastor made one more Sign of the Cross, offering a final blessing on the cemetery.

As the sun rose on a bright new day, the blue tarps came down. There, on the hill overlooking the Caribbean, was a new cemetery, dedicated to innocence lost.

Almost as soon as the blue tarps came down, rumors of what had taken place spread throughout the island.

That afternoon, the authorities led by Lieut. Col. Claude Fleming arrived at Cédric and Marie's home. Cédric warmly greeted them and they were invited in for coffee and lemon poppy seed bread. They sat at the table for two hours as Cédric told the story of discovering the wreck and the young girls and women.

"Cédric, we're going to need to know who these girls are," said Fleming. "We'll need to take their bodies for examination and try to get them back to their families." The cover-up had already started.

Cédric slid a large manila envelope across the table. "We took pictures from the wreck and of each of the girls that you can use for identification. But you and I both know that no one wanted them. They were probably traded by their families for a few dollars. If any parent comes looking, I promise they can have their daughter back, but otherwise, they stay where they are buried."

23

With Marie standing behind him, Cédric continued with a steely gaze into man's eyes, "Lieut. Col. Fleming, you are French. France was involved in the slave trade. I don't think you want to come to a slave cemetery and desecrate the bodies of those who rest there. That would not go over well with the people of this island. People are already starting to treat SANCTUARY as the sacred ground it is. Look for yourself."

Cédric saw through the window behind the official what Fleming could not. There was a small girl walking through the gates of SANCTUARY, one hand in her mother's and the other clutching a small bundle of wildflowers. The Lieut. Col. stood up and went to the window that Cédric was pointing at. Everyone in the room got up, looked, and then went outside. Thomas was there acting as a host, taking an island mother and daughter through the graveyard. He told them the story of the girl's deaths, and talked about how daughters needed to be protected, and how slavery still exists today. He proudly pointed out how the coffins were embedded with the stones that their slave ancestors had used to build walls. They heard him explain, "These poor girls were slaves, like our ancestors. They had been sold to slave traders and were being taken to be sold again when this tragedy happened. The fence is made from the chains and shackles that held them in bondage, first on their journey, and then at the bottom of the sea. They are just like the chains that were used on our ancestors when they were brought over from Africa and other places."

After a while, the girl and her mother, who had tears running down her cheeks, walked out the gate. The little girl turned to her mother. "Mommy, we need to pick more flowers! There's so many of them! They all need flowers."

As they walked past Cédric, Marie and their guests, the woman stopped in front of Marie. She took Marie's hand, and kissed it. "Bless you." Marie pulled the woman to her, and they gave each other a big long hug, as the young girl joined by hugging her mother's leg.

Marie cupped the woman's face with both her hands, and they looked into each other's eyes. Marie said. "Protect her, protect your precious. We must protect them all. We must protect their innocence until they feely choose to exchange it for knowledge. Protect her."

They hugged again, and the woman and her daughter continued down the hill. They heard the daughter already asking more questions. "Mama, why did this happen? Why do I need protection?"

"Honey, there's things about the world I'll have to teach you. But not today. Today we go pick flowers."

As they neared the bottom of the hill, a father with his son and daughter passed them, walking up the hill towards SANCTUARY. Cédric turned to Fleming and said, "I don't know whether you're protecting those who are involved in this trade – I hope and pray not – but you will not be taking our daughters. We have claimed them as our own; they are ours, and they also belong to the good people of this island and our ancestors. I think it's time you leave."

Just about then, a car drove up. In it were Cédric's and Marie's daughter Daniella, and Aunt Mimi, Marie's sister. Daniella got out of the car and ran to them. "Is it true, Mommy and Daddy? Is it true what they're saying about the girls in chains drowning and Daddy finding them?"

Cédric turned to Lieutenant Col. Fleming. "You'll have to excuse me. I need to be with my daughter. I need to introduce her to her sisters. The pictures are for you to keep. I hope they help, and as I said, if any of their parents come looking for them, I will help in any way I can."

Lieut. Col. Fleming began to leave, then stopped and turned, asking, "One more question. Did you find anything else on the boat, any identifying markers? A gun or anything like that?"

As Cédric was wrapping his arms around Daniella he looked at Lieut. Col. Fleming. "No sir, nothing else, but I've marked on the map where the wreckage is, or what's left of it. We took the wood from it; it was an old slave custom to bury a special slave on a slab of wood. Each of the girls is resting on one. The motor is still down there; maybe that will be helpful. I'm sure it has a serial number unless it was filed off." Both Fleming and Cédric knew that filing away serial numbers was a smuggler trick, a safeguard if they ever had to ditch the boat quickly.

Cédric, with one arm around Daniella, and Marie with her arm around her sister Mimi, walked toward SANCTUARY. "Yes, honey, it's true, and your mom and I have adopted them all. They're your sisters, but they also belong to the island."

"Mommy? So, they're my sisters that I'll never get to meet?"

"Yes, sweetie, maybe in heaven. But you can feel their presence in this place. It's very comforting and it's special."

Chapter 6

With Thomas's help, Cédric built a barrier near the bottom of the hill that Cédric and Marie lived on. Anyone wanting to visit SANCTUARY would need to park there and walk about a quarter mile up the hill. This offered Cédric and his family a small bit of security; anyone coming could be seen from a distance.

Early that next morning, a young journalist and a photographer from *The Daily Herald* showed up wanting to take pictures and interview Cédric, Marie and the others. The whole group was there, greeting the steady flow of people now coming to pay their respects. Cédric and John intercepted them, and Cédric explained, "Sorry, but you're not welcome here – at least not as reporters. No pictures, no interviews – but if you'd like to go back to your car and put away your cameras, note pads and your press credentials, you may walk through as citizens of the island. This will not be a sideshow; it is a graveyard, a slave's graveyard and needs to be treated with the respect that deserves."

"But Cédric, people need to know. They need to hear your story." The young reporter challenged him.

"I have no story. I'm a simple diver. And please look at the people already coming to pay their respects; they know. They've heard, and without your help. You must remember, we're a small island and most of us are descendants of slaves. Slaves did not have a newspaper, remember? We weren't allowed to read. But we did quite well using word-of-mouth. So, with all due respect, there will be no interviews, only conversations. No interviews!"

The reporter and her photographer left, frustrated that they could not cover the story in the way they had hoped.

It was a nice morning. Old and new friends showed up. Conversations were as numerous as were the tears as people walked through SANCTUARY and faced the reality that most all had wanted to turn away from and pretend didn't exist – at least, not in their small part of the world. Many talked about feeling the Spirits of their ancestors coming to this spot; it was as if they were coming to watch over it and guard it. Cédric had felt the same thing.

Later that morning, more toward noon than sunrise, Marie nudged Cédric and nodded toward the parking area. Parked at the bottom of the hill was a limo, and getting out of it was Ms. Dominique Bute, the woman who ran *El Capitan*, a legal brothel outside Philipsburg. The sun was high and bright, so she took out her parasol and opened it as she started up the hill. Her driver, an enormous island man blacker than onyx, walked about ten paces behind her, watching and on the ready. Nestled in her arms, she had a large bouquet of flowers. Marie and Cédric watched her climb the hill. As she passed close to their home, Marie stepped out in front of her with Daniella next to her and said, "Your kind is not welcome here."

"I'm not your enemy. I just came to pay my respect." The two women stared at each other intensely.

"Like I said, you're not welcome here."

Dominique looked at Daniella. "Sweet child, please do me a favor. Would you take these flowers and place them in the graveyard?"

Daniella looked up at her mother, seeking permission. "Can I mother? They're so beautiful."

"Yes, honey, but put them on the outside of SANCTUARY. I don't ever want her or anything from her inside this sacred place."

Daniella ran up to Dominique, who bent down and gave her the flowers and smiled. "Thank you, sweet child. You're so pretty. Put them wherever your mother thinks is best."

Ms. Dominique Bute then turned and walked down the hill. As she passed close to him, she stopped and looked over at Cédric. He saw strength, but also a great sadness in her eyes. He was drawn to them. Everyone there watched as the madam made her way down the hill and her driver opened her car door. She looked up the hill, first at SANCTUARY and then at Cédric again. Then she got in her car.

"Her kind are not welcome here," Marie said to her husband with the great intensity and then walked into the house. Cédric stood there, looking down the hill and wondering why a woman of her stature in her profession had come to his home and the gravesite.

Two days, later the man who had been Ms. Dominique Bute's driver stopped Cédric as he was leaving Carrefour Market. "Thank you for what you're doing." He stuck out his massive hand and the two of them shook. "Here, this is for you. It's very important; please do what is asked. Tell no one, even your wife." The man handed Cédric a manila envelope and quickly walked off.

Cédric had no way of making sense of what had just happened. He walked to his car, put his groceries in the back and the envelope on the passenger seat, and drove away. He drove down near the hospital and pulled into the parking lot, turned off the car, and opened the sealed envelope. Inside it was a plane ticket to Martinique for the next Wednesday.

There was also a note:

> We need to talk! I beg of you with every ounce of my soul that you come to Martinique so we can talk. As I told your wife, I'm not your enemy. As my friend told you, tell no one. Anyone who knows may be in danger. By the way, check out Francois Petit. He lets his friends use his daughter, as does he. If things are going to be cleaned up, it must start at home. P.S. Destroy this note after you've read it.

There was no signature, just a drawing of a small parasol.

Cédric sat there, reading the note over and over. He knew exactly who it sent it. Why did Ms. Dominique Bute want to talk with him? What did she want to talk about? Was it a set-up? Would he not return from Martinique? Why all the secrecy? But despite his suspicion, there was something inside him drawing him to her words. He could still see the sadness in her eyes, and it called to him. He decided he would go.

Chapter 7

Wednesday morning Cédric was on a Caribbean Airlines plane for the short flight over to Martinique. When he arrived, he was met outside the gate by Ms. Dominique Bute. He was surprised by her appearance; she looked nothing like she did in St. Maarten. There was none of the flair and color she always flaunted when she was on St. Maarten. She was wearing long black pants and a nice white blouse, and very little makeup; her beautiful almond-colored skin needed none.

She approached Cédric with a cautious smile on her face. She grabbed his hand and shook it, placing her other hand on top, holding him captive as if he might try to run at any minute. "I was so afraid you might not come. Thank you for coming! I rented us a car so we can go talk, and there are some folks I'd like you to meet." Cédric felt no fear. There was something calming about her voice but also hurried. It was clear there was much she wanted to share, and she felt the pressure of time.

As he got in the car, she again turned to him. "I was so afraid you wouldn't come, but I thank God that you did! We have so much to discuss and so much to do. I truly believe we can make a difference. I'm sure we can." Cédric had no idea what she was talking about. Maybe she was a crazy woman ranting, but somewhere in his heart, he knew he was supposed to be there. It wasn't much longer before they arrived at a beachside resort and settled down at a table on the restaurant's veranda, tucked away from the others and overlooking the Caribbean they both loved so much.

"I know you are wondering why I asked you here. I want to be your ally. I believe that, together, we can shut these people down," she said, meeting him eye-to-eye, clearly **totally** serious. In her eyes, he could still see the sadness, but there was also hope and excitement.

"Ms. Bute, you're a madam and you run a brothel. You *are* the sex business," Cédric stated.

"Please call me Dominique. All true, all absolutely true. But I run a brothel of women all who have chosen to be in this profession. They're not girls; they are women, all over twenty-one, who know what they are doing. I treat them well and look after them. This other thing is a plague. You were right to frame it as slavery. That's what those girls were – slaves. They were not sex workers; they were young slaves with vaginas. These are two different things. Yes, it may not be a great profession but..."

Cédric interrupted her, "Why? What is your real reason for wanting to help me and my friends? Does it have to do with the sadness that haunts your eyes?"

Dominique nodded with a raise of her eyebrows and a grim little smile. "You're very perceptive. Or maybe what you saw on the floor of the sea changed you forever; you have the same sadness in your own eyes. It comes from seeing things that no one should have to see. It comes from seeing or experiencing the devil's work."

"I want to know who you really are. I want to know why you want to help."

She reached across the table and patted his hand. "You deserve that. I knew that you'd want to know, so I came prepared. I came to tell you my story. After that, you'll know why I want to help. And you will know whether you will trust me."

Dominique called the waiter over. "Two margaritas for me and whatever the gentleman wants. And some appetizers, please – whatever you think is best. We'll be here a while." Cédric ordered a *Presidente*.

They made small talk about Martinique and Dominique's refuge there until the food arrived. After the drinks and appetizers came, she looked at Cédric. "I don't know my real name. They – my family – always called me Didi, but I think my name is Dominique. I can't really remember, and it doesn't matter. Names are just names; who we are is defined by deeds. I was born in Venezuela in a small village. I don't remember much about my mother and father, and for the longest time, I didn't really care to. I knew that there were four of us children. I had two brothers and a sister I haven't seen since I was eight years old.

"What I do remember is the day that my mother and father took me to two "gentlemen" who were in our village looking for young girls. You must remember that we were all very poor, living mainly on things we could grow or gather from the jungle that surrounded our village. The men had told my parents they were looking for young girls who could be taken to the big city and be trained to be servants or housemaids. They brought me to the men for I was prettier than my sister. I was always proud of that until that day, but after that, never again. I remember the men giving my parents what seemed like a lot of money. I can recall my father smiling, saying he could now get the cow he wanted; he always liked fresh milk. I can't stand milk to this day. For god sake he sold me so he could get a cow and some other things. I remember them walking away, my father not even looking back, just counting the money. My mother did look back, and there was a sadness in her eyes. It seems clear now that she knew what was **really** happening and what was in store for me.

"That evening, they took me to a hut on a beach. There was a boat in the harbor, but I would spend the night in the hut. There were four of them. The leader took me first; he wanted my virginity. Then for hours, the other three took turns over and over with me. They were drunk and laughing. I stared at the ceiling, crying, but eventually, I was filled with rage. I found refuge in my rage as they assaulted and desecrated my body, the part of me that defined me as a girl, someday a woman; they were out to destroy it. They laughed as I cursed God and my mother. Why hadn't she stopped what my father was doing? Why hadn't she protected me and my innocence? I was yelling for God and her to go to hell; that made the men laugh. I remember that when they were done, one of them said, 'There! She'll be ready for any man of any size that wants her.'

"They then went on to another girl, who had been watching in horror. Two of us were raped that night, the other three were left untouched they were to be sold as virgins. Me and the other unfortunate girl would be sold as common whores. They threw me a towel to put between my legs to help stop the bleeding. In the morning, as we were to get on the boat, they gave me this. It's all I have from my past life." Dominique picked up her purse from the floor and opened it, took out an envelope and drew from it a little necklace she placed on the table. It was identical to the one Tammy was wearing, except hers said, "Kitty."

A chill like he'd never felt before ran through Cédric's body. Dominique continued, "They put this one on me and the other girl that was used that night got an identical one. They were cheap little necklaces, and as we stopped at other beaches picking up other girls, the ones that were violated for the men's satisfaction were also given these cheap trinkets. After I was sold again, I never wore it. But I never threw it away. And I've never shown it to anyone else before. This trinket for my virginity and my innocence.

"Once on the boat, we were chained together like the girls you found. I was brought to St. Maarten where I worked in an underground brothel for underage girls. I decided early on that I would survive. I lived in my rage, and as men would crawl on me, I honed it into my tool for survival. I decided I would best them at their game, and I did. I did what was needed to raise my stature in their eyes, and in my free time, I studied. I taught myself – with help from some of the girls and ladies – to read, write and do math. I've kept records; I'll give you a copy of them to take with you before you leave. Through hate, I've risen to where I am now. I don't hang around with those who steal children, but I do know about them, what they do, how they do it. I also have some information about who they are. Remember, who I am today was born out of their perversions and evil.

"I wanted to tell you, Cédric, the day I heard about what you had done – not just finding the girls, but also creating SANCTUARY and giving those young girls a proper burial in a proper graveyard. I found new purpose in what I had been through. I knew we were to work together. When you gave them the respect and integrity their souls needed and deserved, something woke inside me. The best parts of my childhood were given back to me. Thank you. That morning when I heard what you had done, I got two things back: my belief in God and love for my mother. I went into the Catholic church and sat there seeing the sadness in Jesus's eyes, knowing his sadness had purpose – and now so did mine and yours. I also knew that my mother couldn't have stopped it. It wasn't her fault. I forgave her. I lit a candle for her and prayed for the first time since that night. The rage in me has been changed to determination; with each beat of my heart, I'm more determined and certain of what we need to do and can do.

"I know you're going to hunt them. The whole island knows. And people believe it is good. I'm going to help you. I'm going to give you all the information I can. I will reconnect with them and tell them I'm working against you and everything you stand for. I will curse your name and speak using every ugly word that we whores know to describe you and your friends. I will make them laugh, just as I did that night when I cursed God and my mother. But whenever you see the flag of *El Capitan* flying high, know that there will be a message and important information about them under this stone." She slid Cédric a picture of an area with a stone where one could easily sit. "I often walk the path on Butte Hill with my parasol; no one would be suspicious of me sitting on a rock looking out over the Caribbean."

Dominique reached across the table. "We can do this! We can shut these people down. I'm sorry I can't help you financially.

37

You'll need that type of help too, but I'll give you the names of others who can probably contribute money or help you raise funds. We have much to do."

They sat for two hours talking, Cédric asking questions, Dominique answering them; Dominique asking questions, Cédric answering them. A friendship and partnership that seemed as old as their heritage and as new as the morning sun was being forged with each word and smile they exchanged.

"You need to know about Alfred. You can trust him. I have two people in the world that I trust with my life. Now, with you, I have three. My driver and bodyguard Alfred is as good a man as you. He has a story, but that is his to tell, not mine. But what you need to know is that when I was sixteen, he was a young man and he saved my life. He was a big man even then and he was only twenty."

"He's a damn giant." Cédric threw in.

Dominique chuckled. "That he is, in many ways. When I was sixteen, a crazy man came to the brothel, if you could call it that. It was a pimp with a house, and three of us girls working there. He called his brothel 'Young Love'. Alfred was working there as our protector. I was sent into a room to pleasure the crazy man, because to the pimp, his money was as good as anyone else's. Alfred sensed something was wrong, and he posted himself just outside the door. The man paid extra to tie me to the bed. He then took out a machete, and when I saw it, I screamed. Alfred rushed in the door, and just as the man was going to split me in two, Alfred pushed him aside and stuck his own knife in the man's stomach. The machete flew out of the man's hand and landed on my arm; I still have the scar from it. There was blood all over, but in the end, the crazy man was dead, and I lay on the bed with my arm bleeding. Alfred cut me free with the machete and wrapped a towel around my arm. Just then, my pimp came in screaming, 'What the hell? What's going on?'

"Alfred hated him. He was mean and violent to us girls. Alfred later told me he figured since he'd already killed someone, why not make it two? So, Alfred took the machete and ran it through my pimp's tiny heart. Then we looked at each other, and he said, "Now what the fuck do we do?" I started laughing and he did, too. But then I took control, and by the end of the evening, everything was cleaned up, and the two men's bodies were disposed of where they'll never be found.

"Thank God the two other girls were out working a party. When they got back, we acted as if everything was normal, only there was no more pimp. After a while, the two girls left, and Alfred and I moved on, too. We have been together looking out for each other ever since then. Alfred has a sister who runs a fruit stand selling mangoes, pineapples, tomatoes, sweet potatoes, spices and other things. It's just down a mile west from *El Capitan*. She is the other person I trust with my life. Start buying your fruit daily from her. Become a regular of hers. You can see the flag of *El Capitan* from there. If you need to leave me some information, put it in a pineapple, bring it to her, and tell her that when you got home, it was rotten. She'll take it, give you another one, and get the information to me through Alfred. This is what I've come up with for our communication system. Don't tell anyone on your side."

Cédric was struck with how well-thought-out everything Dominique did was; she was truly brilliant and resilient. And now Cédric knew why he had instantly liked Alfred.

Then Dominique smiled in a way that lit up the whole beach. "Well, now that this part is over, I want you to meet two young ladies that no one else from St. Maarten except Alfred has ever met. They're my daughters. They don't know my history; they just know that I'm their mother. They've lived on this island all their life at a boarding school, and I visit them when I can. I bought them when they were seven and eight at a virgin auction. I wish I could've saved more, but that was all the money I had at that time. Ever since, all my money has gone into caring for them and their future. I'm so proud of them! They leave tomorrow for Paris to study and set up their lives there. Cédric, my friend – I hope you don't mind if I call you that – I want you to meet my daughters, Frieda and Esther." Dominique motioned over to two proper young women in their late teens who been patiently sitting at a table on the other side of the restaurant. They got up, smiling, and walked over.

"Frieda, Esther, this is my good friend Cédric. He is one of the best men I know. I wanted you to meet him before you go to Paris. Come, let's all have lunch. Our business conversations are done."

The four visited over a delicious lunch and sat talking for the rest of the afternoon. Cédric played his role well, speaking highly of Dominique and telling the girls what a wonderful asset she was to St. Maarten. In a joke designed for him and Dominique, he said to them, "Your mother has put out more for our island than you'll ever know." The young ladies smiled proudly at their mother. Dominique reached across and patted Cédric's hand. "My funny old friend, but you are so right."

As afternoon was fading toward evening, Dominique told Esther and Frieda she needed to drive Cédric back to the airport, and that she would be back soon. She had planned to spend the night with them and send them off to Paris in the morning.

As she started up the car with Cédric in the passenger seat, she said, "Now you can see why I can't help you financially. Everything I've ever made goes into taking care of my girls and providing for them the best I can."

When they got to the airport, Dominique parked the car, planning to see him off. Once outside the car, Cédric turned to her and said, "Dominique, my friend, now my ally, I'm going to say something to you that I've never said to anyone except my wife, my daughter and my mother: I love you, you're a wonderful woman. You're the strongest woman I've ever met. Stay strong; we'll need it. Thank you for your story and for letting me meet your beautiful daughters. I'm sad that we will not be able to meet like this again, and I look forward to a day in the distant future when we can."

Dominique had tears running down her cheeks, as did Cédric. "I was going to walk you to your check-in, but I need to say goodbye before I break down; I still need to be strong. We have much to do. Goodbye, my friend." As Cédric walked away Dominique stopped him, adding, "Don't forget Francois Petit. He's not part of them, but he's a bad man, as are his friends. And don't trust Lieutenant Col. Fleming; he's owned by the drug cartel."

"Thank you for the confirmation. I already suspected Lieutenant Col. Fleming was dirty by the visit he paid to us."

"Please be careful!"

"And you."

On the plane ride home, Cédric opened the packet of information Dominique had given him. Inside he found the envelope she had taken from her purse with her "Kitty" necklace in it. It would go in the box where Tammy's was kept. Then he started to read.

Chapter 8

For two weeks, Cédric studied everything in the packet of information that Dominique had given him. Then he destroyed it; it would be dangerous for her and for him if it was found by the wrong people. The French Coast Guard had salvaged everything they could – which was little – from the wreckage of the slave ship. He suspected, however, that Fleming might have allies who were not above searching his home for information if they could get away with it.

One evening Cédric called together his friends and their wives for barbecue, which had become their ritual whenever there was business to discuss. Rasmus was excellent at barbecue; he had worked at Mark's Place in his youth, where he honed the skill. He used Marie's special secret-recipe barbecue sauce that everybody loved. Just as Marie was known for her sauce, Margaret was known for her rice and peas, and Gloria for her cornbread. When they came together like this, it wasn't just a meal – it was a feast.

After enjoying dinner, they sat around sipping on *Presidente* or Marie's lemonade. Daniella and a friend were playing in the yard. Cédric asked the group, "Francois Petit – do any of you know him? I don't."

Thomas answered, "I know of a man by that name who lives in the area of Middle Region, but I know nothing of him. Why?"

I have it from a very credible source he is incestuous with his ten-year-old daughter, and he lets his friends use her little body too." There was silence.

"I know what I want to do, but I want to hear from the rest of you. He's not exactly the kind of man we have decided to hunt, but I want to hear your thoughts."

Daniel immediately spoke up, "I beg to differ, my friend, I beg to differ. He is exactly like the men we've decided to hunt. If this is true, his daughter is as much a slave to him and his friends' desires as our girls would have been if their vessel had not gone down in the storm. I say we hunt him. If your information is as reliable as you say it is, we hunt him. We get as much information from him as we can, and then deal with him as we must. But we must make sure the information is accurate." The others seemed of like opinion, especially the wives.

"And his daughter?" Cédric asked.

Marie spoke up, "Like we said, we will raise her as our own. She'll need a good home."

They all knew that they were deciding more than the fate of Francois Petit and his daughter; they were committing themselves to their own fate. If they did this, they would be signing the covenant they had made with each other and the girls that lay in SANCTUARY. They would be signing it with blood.

"And who will get the information from him? We all know what that means. Let me ask it bluntly: who will torture him?"

Daniel stood up and declared, "I will!" Tears ran down his face and his lip quivered. Gloria had tears in her eyes, too. She knew what her husband was about to say.

"I will do it. What you don't know, my friends, is that when I was a child, my father and his friend used me in the same way Francois Petit uses his daughter. Thank God my father got cancer and died, so that it only went on for a year. But still, it is part of who I am. I have deep anger inside – rage, I will call it – that will give me strength. I will have no qualms doing to these men or others what needs to be done. I know as well as you do – maybe better – what we're dealing with. When the devil has had his way with you, part of him gets inside you. It changes you. I do not wish this work on any of you, so I will do it."

Cédric looked around the room. "So, it is decided." Nothing more was ever spoken about what Daniel said that night. None were surprised when later that night, he and Gloria got up from the table and walked up to SANCTUARY to sit for a while just inside its gate, seeking the peace that came to all of them whenever they walked about the graves.

The ten friends started subtly investigating, learning everything they could about Francois Petit. He owned a trash hauling business that had been quite busy since Irma. The friends he hung around with did the same work.

Rasmus hung around Petit's neighborhood; he had an ability to blend in and not be noticed. One night, he was peering in the window of Francois's home when he saw first-hand what would seal Francois's fate. Francois's ten-year-old daughter Monique was lying nude on the bed, posing in suggestive ways as Francois took pictures of her. Rasmus heard him say, "I can get good money for these. You have no idea how much money we're going to make from these. So many men think you're pretty and like looking at you. And when I take pictures of you with my friends, we make some real money." He was talking to his daughter as if they were doing a good thing together. She was quiet, saying nothing, just smiling – a plastic little smile – as he clicked away with his camera.

A week later, Daniel called Petit, saying he had some trash from Irma he needed removed. He gave an address for a remote part of the island near a beach, and a time was set up.

John was there within a minute after Petit had stopped his truck. Before the trash man knew what was happening, John knocked him out with a baseball bat. Daniel quickly secured zip ties around his legs and wrists, and they loaded him into a boat, covered him with a tarp, and Daniel motored out to sea with his prisoner. On shore, John pulled a baseball hat low over his face, got into Francois's truck, and drove away to park it on another part of the island.

Once out to sea in an area where traffic was rare, Daniel secured one of Francois' wrists securely to one side of the boat, cut the zip ties that held his wrists together, and stretched his other arm out, attaching it to the other side of the boat, so both hands were hanging over the gunnels of the small craft. Daniel watched Francois as he came to, thrashing, swearing and wondering what the hell was going on.

"Francois, we know what you do with your daughter."

Petit's eyes lit up with rage. "Fuck you! What I do with my daughter is none of your business."

"But it is *your sick business*; you sell nude pictures of your daughter. How disgusting."

They glared at each other. "Francois, we can do this the easy way, or we can do it the hard way. I want to know the names of your friends–the ones that you let use your daughter. And I want to know whether you used any of their children."

Petit defiantly spat out, "Fuck you!"

Daniel reached over with his tin snips and slowly cut off Petit's baby finger as he screamed. It fell into the sea and blood from the stub followed it into the water. "Nine more to go. Then I cut off the real prize." Daniel grabbed Francois's groin. By the fourth finger, all Francois's defiance was gone. Amid tears and screams of agony, he coughed up the names of his perverted associates. Daniel went over the list many times, making sure the information was correct. Every time he raised his tin snips, Francois cried and begged for mercy – which there was to be none of – saying how sorry he was and spewing out the same three names over and over. By now, the sharks that Daniel knew hung out in this area were circling the boat. Once he had all the information he needed, he quickly killed Francois Petit and dumped his body over the side of the boat.

Then Daniel motored back to shore and waded into the water, washing himself off and cleaning the boat. He was glad his method of interrogation and body disposal left minimal blood or other evidence in the boat. It was an easy clean-up job.

About that same time, Marie was visiting Monique, Francois's ten-year-old daughter. "Honey, I'm sorry to say there's been an accident, and your father will not be coming home. You're going to come live with us now. Monique put up little resistance; she was used to being told what to do. As Marie gathered up Monique and her things, Cédric and Rasmus looked through the house. They found the sex toys that had been used on the little girl, judging from the pictures that they also found. They found three shoeboxes of pictures. In many of them, Francois was sexually penetrating his daughter or someone else was. They took the pictures and planned to give them to the police if there was an investigation. They agreed that if after three months there was no need for the photos, they would burn them in the fire pit. They hoped Monique would never have to look at them again.

Within a week, the three other men named by Petit, who were identifiable in the photos, met the same fate. They had provided no more new information despite their torture. Surprisingly – or perhaps not surprisingly – no one seemed to miss the men.

Monique made no fuss about moving in with the Beaujon family. They moved another bed into Daniella's bedroom, and the girls seemed to be pleasantly curious about each other. The second night, Monique approached Cédric after supper and whispered something to him. "Honey, I can't hear you; what did you say?" She whispered it again, still too softly for him or Marie to make out. "I'm sorry, honey, I still can't hear you. You'll need to say it louder."

She looked at the floor and asked, "When do you want me to come to your room tonight? Daddy always wanted me to come before he went to sleep."

Cédric bit his lip to calm himself. "Honey, you don't come to my room. We don't do the things your father asked you to do. You won't ever do those things here. You're safe now."

Marie picked her up and settled into the rocking chair with Monique on her lap. She sat rocking Monique for a long time, for her own comfort as much as for Monique's. That next week, Marie took Monique to a social worker she trusted who worked with abused children. She told her Monique's story and asked for her help.

Marilyn Couture was a social worker at the Mental Health Foundation on St. Maarten. She agreed to help, saying, "I know what you're doing; many on the island do, and many of us secretly and not so secretly support you and the necessary work you're doing. I will be glad to help, but I will come to your house and see Monique there. That way, I can also teach you and your friends about what to do with these children. If you're successful, more will come to you. I know this. We'll all need to work together to help them. There is more need than you know."

After that, Marilyn came regularly to the house to meet with Monique. Each time she visited, she also sat for a while with Gloria, Marie, Margaret, Alma and Rachelle, teaching them what she had learned about how to connect with and care for abused children. Sometimes, as needed, the men would be brought into the conversations.

After about four months, they all felt good as Monique showed signs of coming back to life. She and Daniella played well together. Daniella loved having a younger sister, and she seemed to be the best therapy for Monique. Daniella noticed that Monique hatred cameras and refused to allow anyone to take her picture; the little girl didn't have the words to explain it, but she would never again allow her spirit to be captured in a photograph. Not even, it turned out years later, at her wedding.

Strangely, the police never came to question any of them. It was as if the men had vanished into thin air, and no one cared.

Chapter 9

Things seemed to change around the island. There was talk that some questionable families had moved off the island, especially after rumors about what happened with Francois and his friends circulated. There seemed to be an air of hope taking root among the natives of Saint Martin. Pastor Eboune was happy because church attendance had increased.

Every day, people from both sides of the island – French and Dutch – were stopping by to pray and place flowers on the graves. SANCTUARY had become sacred ground. It was a place where the horrors of what the islanders' slave ancestors had gone through melded **together** with the horrors that still existed in today's world. SANCTUARY, that tiny patch of sacred ground, seemed to transform suffering into dignity, pride, and a new and intense sense of purpose for all who visited it. It was also becoming a cause.

One day as Marie was standing at the window, she saw a young white man about thirty years old walking up the road. He turned off the road, walked up the driveway, passed the house and went into SANCTUARY. He walked around, touching each grave.

Cédric was gone on a salvaging job, so Marie walked up to the young man. "Can I help you? Are you a tourist?" They weren't **particularly** fond of tourists who wanted to come see SANCTUARY. That was true for almost everyone on the island. Even the taxi drivers who made their living giving tours of the island weren't telling those who got off the cruise ships about SANCTUARY.

"No ma'am, I'm not a tourist; never been one, never want to be one. You'll never see a camera around my neck and I've never taken a selfie. I don't take pictures of life, I live it. I've been living up in the U.S. Virgin Islands. That's where I heard about what's happening down here."

Marie was surprised. She knew that the story of the slave ship had spread to some of the nearby islands like Saba and St. Barth's, but way up to the U.S. Virgin Islands? That surprised her.

"I'm looking for a 'Rick' fellow or something like that. I'm not really good with names. He's supposed to be the guy who found that slave ship."

"Cédric is his name." Marie responded.

"Yeah, that's right, Cédric. But that's what I said – I said Rick." He laughed, "Do you get it?"

Marie very politely smiled. "Yes, I get it. How can I help you?"

"Well, I want to meet him. I want to offer him my help."

"Well, that's nice of you, but he's not here. And I don't think he'll need your help."

"Ma'am, with all due respect, he's going to need my help and more. He's kicked the hornet's nest. Is it because I'm white? Are you racist?"

"Of course, I'm racist. I am, all of us are. I don't care what anybody says, we all see color to some degree. And if your heritage is one of bondage, of course, you see the color white differently. But what do you mean about 'he's kicked the hornet's nest'?"

"Nice to hear you say that. I agree we're all a bit racist, it's just what you do with it that matters. But these kids that he brought up from the ocean's bottom, they weren't all black, were they? This Rick fellow saw children, not color."

"No, only three of them were black. The rest of them seem more Spanish, from South America, we guessed."

"Oh, so you're one of them."

"Yes, I'm Cédric's wife Marie—or Rick as you call him."

Feeling excited, he stuck out his hand. "I'm proud to meet you, Marie, very proud. From everything I hear, it sounds like you're good people, real good people. My name is Sam Dresser. I'm originally from Texas. I'm from the Amarillo Dressers, not related at all to the Houston Dressers, but that probably doesn't mean much to you."

"Nothing. It means absolutely nothing to me, but now I know why you talk so funny – you're a cowboy like I've seen in the movies?"

"Yes, ma'am, I'm from a small ranch up in the Panhandle. Well, small by our standards; the ranch is about the size of your island. And I must say, to me you're the one who talks funny."

"Okay, so we've established that we both talk funny. What is this about the kicking hornet's nest?"

"Well, you might say I'm in the same business as your husband. I had a sister who was abducted when she was a young girl by one of them pedophiles. They found her after six weeks. They were all surprised she was still alive. But it changed her; I guess you could say it changed me, too. A year after that happened, I join the U.S. Navy and became a SEAL. They trained me good. I thought I'd be staying there for life, you know – all that "Hoo-yah!" and all that stuff. Well, I got a call from my folks one day; my sister had killed herself. I never really saw it was her killing herself, it was that pedophile who had killed her, only it took years for her to die. I left the SEALS and I've been hunting them ever since. Sometimes some of my old buddies help me."

"That's very sad, but what about this hornet's nest?"

"I was getting there, ma'am; we Texans like to tell a story. Well, I was up in the Virgin Islands, tracking this pedophile. When I found him, I was having a "talk" with him – finding out about his friends and stuff like that – when he said, 'You're one of them, aren't you? You're one of them from down in Saint Martin, aren't you?'

"You can imagine my surprise! I had no idea what he was talking about, but I was interested. Well, he, me and my knife talked for a while. He told me about everything that he had done, but he also told me from his hate – still thinking I was one of you – that we were going to pay. He'd heard it in his circles that the people who provided the young girls for him were going to make 'those people' pay, and soon. Well, after that, it made sense for me to come down here and help you folks out. If it's true, you're going to need my help. By the way, it's a beautiful graveyard, kind of peaceful. I think my sister would have liked to be in a place like this instead of with all our old relatives."

Sam looked at Marie. "You got military training, don't you?" It was a statement, not a question.

Marie was surprised by his correct assessment. "Yes, two years in the Army. How did you know?"

"Well, ma'am, it's the way you carry yourself. How you were watching me from your window ever since I was about a quarter mile away. And how you didn't come out to greet me until I had my back turned and you would've had the drop. They trained you well."

Marie was quite impressed with how observant this little man standing no more than 5 foot eight was. "Where do you live now?" she asked.

"I live on a boat. I anchored over there off that nudie beach. I always like hanging around nudists; you don't have to worry about hidden guns! I can always see what they are packing." Sam laughed, "You get it."

She was surprised how quickly this strange little white dude was kind of growing on her. Marie smiled, "Yes, Sam, I get it."

"And these nudies are pretty much good people. Most of them just like the sun and hanging around without any clothes on. You know these *petties* – I like to call them *petties*; I never did like the word "pedophile". It sounds like something an angry dog or cat owner would do with their pet if it had wet on the carpet one too many times, you know, Pet-e-File or File-e-Pet or somethin' like that. Well, anyway, petties don't like the sun; they prefer the dark. They are kind of like sexual vampires; they hide during the day and come out at night to feed on things that are young, fresh and innocent. Nope, never found one pettie that was a nudie or naturist, as some of them like to call themselves. But I prefer *nudies*, got a nicer ring to it."

Marie now started into a regular conversation with the stranger. "I had many friends who worked over there at Club O before the hurricane. I agree, they're basically harmless, and I heard they tip well. That would've been a long walk from there to here."

"What's the name of your boat?" Marie was gathering information.

"It's called *Justice*. When she was a young girl, my sister wanted to grow up and be a judge like our grandpa. She would always go on and on about justice, and how it needed to be served. After those six weeks she spent with her captor, I never heard her mention the word again. I don't think she saw the world as just anymore, after she suffered those six weeks and he got off on a technicality. At least, until I caught up with him."

"It's a good name, a good way to honor your sister. How did you get over to this part of the island?"

"Yes, it is a good name. I walked over, ma'am. I like to walk. I also like to run and swim. There is an island out there that's pretty fun to swim around. I saw a big beautiful turtle the other day as I swam around the island. You got to remember I'm a former SEAL; I could swim from sunup to sundown. I've got friends who could swim around your entire island and hardly be tired. I'm a little out of shape, but in my better days, I could have, too.

"But, anyway, I'd sure like to meet your husband. Would you mind if I come back to meet him and talk with him? I truly believe he could use my help. I'm not a bad man to know."

"Well, he'll actually be back here in about an hour. So, if you want, you can stick around."

"I'd like that. I hope you don't mind if I go back to the graveyard and pick up a bit. I saw some weeds and some of the flowers people left are pretty much gone. I'm a believer that graveyards should be kept up nice."

"Feel free. There are some clippers by the side of the house. We usually clean up SANCTUARY about once a week; tomorrow would be the day. But if you want to do it now, that would be a nice thing. I'll bring you some lemonade."

It was actually closer to two hours before Cédric returned from his dive. By then, Sam had SANCTUARY spruced up and looking nice.

When Cédric came walking up the hill, Sam and Marie were sitting at the outside table, sipping lemonade and talking about everything under the sun.

Marie caught sight of him and announced to Sam, "Here he is; here comes my husband."

"He's a handsome lad. You must've taken a fancy to him right away. But he's got pain in his eyes. He's still hurting and haunted over what he found."

They walked to meet Cédric, and Marie said with a smile, "Honey, this is Sam Dresser. He's from the Amarillo Dressers, not to be confused with the Houston Dressers. You have to excuse the way he talks a bit funny; he's a cowboy."

Sam stuck out his hand. "Sir, it is an honor to meet you, a damn right honor! And I must say your wife makes the best lemonade I've ever tasted."

Cédric stared at him for moment, then looked at Marie, who smiled. Looking back at Sam, he asked, "Are you a tourist?"

"No, sir. As I told your wife, I am no tourist. Don't like them much; they're kind of like summer mosquitoes, always buzzing around, always being a nuisance. No sir, getting down to the fat of the matter, I'm a hunter. I hunt the same things you hunt, and I've come here to help you."

"Thank you, Sam, but I don't think we'll need any help."

Sam looked at Marie, "He's a racist too, isn't he?"

"Yes, he is, Sam, but I'm more racist than he is. He trusts some white people I don't. I like you; I don't trust you yet."

"Fair enough, Marie, fair enough. Trust is something that's got to be earned."

Cédric coughed, breaking up their little conversation about race.

"Honey, Sam says he heard about you while hunting a pedophile up in the Virgin Islands. He says there's rumors up there that the people who trade in young girls don't like what we're doing down here. Rumor has it they are coming after us; particularly you. Some guy put a price on your head. It's not much – $10,000 – but still, for some folks, that's a lot of money."

Cédric's ears perked up; this was important. Three days ago, the flag was flying high at *El Capitan*, and when he picked up the message, it was a similar warning. Dominique had warned there were rumors of people coming to "cut off the head of the movement" that had started in Saint Martin. The first thought that came to Cédric's mind was a question, *'Is he a clever assassin?'*

"Sam, I'm going to have to ask you to leave. But if you would leave your passport with me, I would like to check you out."

Marie was a little taken back at her husband's abrupt and somewhat rude request of Sam. She was clearly going to say something when Sam interrupted her, saying, "Marie, it's no bother. He has to check me out."

Sam turned to Cédric. "So, you've heard the rumors too?" Sam slowly reached into his back pocket with two fingers, turning so Cédric could see there was no danger, and drew out his passport and handed it over. Moving his gaze to Marie and then back to Cédric, Sam said, "Marie, your husband has heard rumors and worries that I may be an assassin coming for him or even for all of your family. He's doing exactly what he needs to do. So, I'm just going to walk down the hill now with my hands on my head so you can see that I mean no harm. Cedric, please check me out. Your wife knows where I'm staying. If I check out, get in touch with me. And thank you very much for the lemonade." Then Sam laced his fingers across the top of his head and started the walk down the mountain. He kept his hands atop of his head until he was out of sight.

"Is what he said true? Are there rumors?" Marie was quite serious now.

"Yes, I learned about them a couple of days ago. But I didn't know that there was a price on my head. I want us to get everyone together. But let me first check out who this guy is; see if he is the real deal." The mood had changed drastically.

The next day Cédric stopped at the fruit stand, telling the young woman how the pineapple he'd bought the day before was rotten. She apologized, took the one he was holding, and gave him a new one. One without a note tucked inside of it.

Cédric had written,

> Visit from American, a Sam Dresser
> from Amarillo, Texas, says his sister
> was subducted by a pedophile, ended
> up killing herself years later. Says he
> was a Navy SEAL. Says he's a hunter
> and wants to help. He told me about
> the same rumor you had. Need to

know if he's real deal or a possible assassin. If you have any connections with the Dutch police, please check him out. If you can get a picture of him, I have his passport."

Two days later, the flag at *El Captain* was flying high again. Cédric went to the drop-off place. He opened Dominique's note:

Seems to be the real deal. What you say about his sister is true. There was a Navy SEAL named Sam Dresser who dropped out for personal reasons. My contact gave a description of him and ended with, "he is suspected in the death of two possible pedophiles. Never enough information to pursue charges." Included was a picture. Be careful. These are dangerous times.

Cédric felt some relief. The information was consistent with the visitor's story and the photo matched the man Cédric had met. Back at home, he asked Marie where he could find this guy, telling her he seemed to check out. "We'll have him over with the rest of the folks for supper tomorrow."

"He's living on a boat over on Orient Beach, it's called *Justice*, in front of what's left of Club O. He says he likes to be around nudists because you can tell easily if they have a gun or not — as he said, "You can always see what they're packing." Cédric cocked his head a bit and lifted an eyebrow as if to say, *he's got a point there.*

The next day, Cédric went down to the beach and waved. Sam appeared on the stern of his boat, waved back, dove in and swam to meet Cédric. He came walking out of the sea nude. "I'm not packing, as you can see." Sam smiled. "So, I checked out."

"Pretty much; two charges that didn't stick?"

"There's a lot more sir, those two were messages that needed to be sent. So, they needed to be public."

"I'm inviting you to come to supper tonight. We'll barbecue, and I want you to meet the rest of my diving friends and their wives."

"Great. I'd love to and I love barbecue! Yours down here is almost as good as what we have in Texas. What can I bring? I can make up some of my special barbecue sauce if you'd like."

"You're on Marie's good side – don't mess it up by bringing your own barbecue sauce! She's as tough as either of us! Just bring yourself. I brought your passport to give it back to you; I see you have no place to keep it, so why don't I just give it back to you tonight?"

"That's okay – I can take it now. What time tonight?"

"Around six o'clock," Cédric said, handing him his passport. He watched as Sam waded back into the sea and swam out to his boat with one arm raised above his head, keeping the passport high and dry.

A little before six o'clock that night, Sam came up the road and climbed the driveway hill carrying two giant 40-pound bags of lemons. Arriving at the house, he set the bags on the porch.

Marie smiled at him. "Nice to see you again, Sam."

"Nice to see you, ma'am. I didn't know how many would be here tonight, so I stopped and just got a load of lemons over at that froufrou French grocery store down near Grand Case."

"You walked all this way with those things on your shoulder."

"Yes, ma'am."

She smiled. "Strong shoulders. You must have been a slave in a former life."

He chuckled. "It would've been an honor, ma'am. Most of them had more dignity and spirit than those they worked for."

"You mean who owned them."

"You're absolutely right. I apologize. But it is such a disgusting thought; I guess it's part of my racism – cleaning up the ugly truth. But as far as that former life stuff goes, I don't quite know if I believe in it. Heck, I don't even know if I believe in this life."

"Yes, it is your racism. But at least you'll own it, Sam. Thanks for the lemons; this will be more than enough. The others aren't here yet. They went on a dive this afternoon. Why don't I go get us some pitchers and we can start squeezing the juice from these beautiful lemons?" She walked back into the house and came out with four pitchers. "We need to fill each one up about a third with lemon juice."

Sam took out the knife strapped to his leg and cut the lemons in half and squeezing the contents into the pitchers. Marie noticed that one of Sam's squeezes got most of the juice out. *His hands must be damn strong*, she thought.

Just as they were finishing, Cédric and the four couples walked up the driveway.

"That's quite a group you got there. Clearly strong men and strong women." Sam said to Marie. "Quite a group."

Marie was impressed but not surprised with how quickly Sam seemed to read the group. Introductions were made when they arrived. Marie noticed Sam and Daniel locked eyes for an extra second. Everything was ready for supper, and they all sat outside eating and talking as Daniella and Monique played off to the side. "I fed them earlier. They were hungry and I thought we'd need to talk."

Cédric said, "Sam, I've already told them about you how you're from the Amarillo Dressers, not to be confused with the Houston Dressers. You tell them the rest."

Sam sat for a moment, picking at the ribs, rolling them in the rice and beans. "Thank you, Cédric, for making that clear with your friends. I'm a hunter like the rest of you. I heard about you up in the U.S. Virgin Islands from a "pettie" I had caught. He was sure that I was one of you, which I considered a compliment after I heard more about you. He said that the guy who owned the boat that Cédric found was angry at what you done with the girls. He had wanted them to stay buried in the sea. He's planning to hunt you folks, especially Cédric. As we say in Texas, he's out for payback, and he's making a plan with his men. I came down to be of help. They particularly want Cédric – something about

64

cutting the head off the beast. What you're all doing down here's too important to let him win. I have skills. I think can be of help to you."

Sam said if it was up to him, they wouldn't be sitting outside right now. There was an easy shot at the group from up on the hill, if a shooter wanted to take it. He said he'd already gone up and checked it out earlier. "If they're sending a professional, that's where he'd be shooting from." He said he lined the bushes up there with cans and other things that would make noise if someone was snooping around; so, if they heard noise, take cover. Everyone listened to him intensely; everything he said made sense. "You are good people. You'll kill when and if you need to, but you're not killers, except for him." He looked to Daniel. "You've been bit by the devil, haven't you? You're the one who gets information in any way you have to. You knew we were kindred spirits the moment we looked into each other's eyes, didn't you?"

Daniel looked at him and smiled. "I do what's necessary."

"As do I, my friend, as do I. I've been bit by the same devil."

Everyone stared at the both of them, watching them communicate with a look. They were connecting with each other in a way that neither of them could bond or connect with the others. Sam just reached over and stuck out his hand. Daniel reached out and took it. "Feels good not to be alone."

"Yes, it does, brother, yes it does."

Cédric spoke up, interrupting them. "I've heard the same rumors. I think we'll need to arm ourselves."

"Well, well! I may have just what you folks need. My boat is loaded. Any of you need a grenade launcher?" Sam interjected.

Thomas laughed, "You damn Americans; you don't go anywhere without your guns!"

"Well, at least not us Texans or us SEALs. And, I might add, they'll come in handy. These folks are not going to be coming at you with pitchforks and machetes." The rest of the evening was spent eating, talking and strategizing.

The next morning Cédric and the other guys went out to Sam's boat, and each picked out a weapon to carry on their person, if it came to that. Each man also picked out a long-range rifle. That was the last they saw of Sam for a bit; he seemed to have blended into the jungle of the island, none having any idea where, until a week later.

Chapter 10

Cédric was working in his yard getting ready for a dive later that day, when two shots rang out almost simultaneously. Cédric took one bullet in the arm. Marie rushed to him, ushered him speedily into their car, and sped to the hospital. The emergency room doctor told Cedric how fortunate he was that it was a through-and-through, missing the bone completely and only ripping up a bit of muscle in his left arm. He should heal completely, but he would have a nice scar.

Following protocol, the hospital called the police to report the gunshot wound. In short order, into his room walked Lieut. Col. Claude Fleming. "I told you to let this thing go and leave all investigations to us."

Cédric, wanting to give him a message he knew what was going on, said, "Lieut. Col. Fleming, this is about young girls becoming sex slaves. This has nothing to do with drugs. The two things need to be separate. You don't leave dead slaves on our island and expect us to do nothing. In the case you're concerned, it was just a scratch. Doc says I'm going to heal up completely. Thanks for stopping by." Fleming left, and Cédric told a patrolman the details of what happened.

The doctor stitched and bandaged Cédric's wound and sent him home. By noon, Cédric and Marie's house was overflowing with gifts of so much food they called Pastor Eboune and asked if he could distribute it to those in need.

The police investigation solved the mystery of what happened to the second shot Cédric and Marie had heard. They turned up the body of the assassin on the other side of the mountain, nailed to a tree with the sign:

"YOU CAME FOR HIM, NOW WE COME FOR YOU.
STAY OFF OUR ISLAND! STAY AWAY FROM CHILDREN!"

A picture of the sign and the story of Cédric's attempted assassination was on the front page of *The Daily Herald* the next day, and it was snapped up by the other newspapers throughout the Caribbean.

Three days later, a note was slipped under Daniel's door. "Meet me at Jimbo's 6:30. Dinner on me." When Daniel got there, he found Sam Dresser already seated over in a corner, right next to the noisiest part of the little river that ran through the restaurant. On the table lay a newspaper folded, so the picture of the sign found with the assassin was showing.

Daniel sat down. "A bit showy, but I like it."

"How's our friend doing? You have to tell him I'm sorry he had to take one, but I'm also glad I saw the villain when I did." Sam had been up in the hills and spotted the assassin aiming toward Sanctuary. Just as Sam was squeezing off a round, so was the assassin. Sam's bullet arrived just in time to throw the assassin's shot off by just a hair. If Sam's bullet had arrived half a second later, Cédric would have been a dead man; but as fate would have it, the assassin died that day. Maybe it was the ancestors, the ancient ones, that helped Sam spot the assassin when he did, for there was a small sound like the crack of a twig that swung Sam's attention in the assassin's direction.

"We are too. He's okay. Got him in the fleshy part of his arm, a through-and-through. The man's blessed – it wasn't even his good arm! He'll be fine, but it's going to take some rehab to get the arm back to strength; doc says it'll only ever come back to about eighty percent. But again, it's not his dominant arm."

"It was just the one. Did the police figure out that he's from Dominique, and part of a gang?"

"Yes, he's a very bad boy from Dominique with quite a record."

Sam looked at him. "Do you want to send a message?"

Daniel smiled. "I thought you'd never ask. When do we leave?"

"After supper. I've already been over there checking things out with a SEAL friend of mine. He's still over there keeping a watch on things. You'll like him; he's been bit by the same snake."

"I'll call Gloria. What should I tell her about when I'll be home?"

"In a day, two days tops. It should be a quick operation."

Two days later, there was a picture of four dead men in the newspapers. The picture had been taken over on Dominique. The four gang members had been gutted and nailed to trees, just like the man who tried to assassinate Cédric. The sign above them read:

DON'T PROTECT OR WORK FOR
CHILD SLAVE TRADERS.
THEIR DAYS ARE NUMBERED.
IF YOU DO, THIS WILL BE YOUR FATE AT BEST.
STAY AWAY FROM SAINT MARTIN!

Chapter 11

Things were quiet for the next two months. The flag at *El Capitan* flew low and Cédric was healing well. It was carnival time on the island. There were parades and dancing and much celebration. People were nervous, but also proud of what was happening. Most graves in SANCTUARY were often covered in wildflowers. People were still periodically bringing Cédric and Marie food, and whenever they did, it was always too much. Marie would call their friends to come over and enjoy it with them.

Sam Dresser was not to be seen or heard. His boat *Justice* was gone from its mooring out in front of what was left of Orient Beach, but the ten all believed he was around somewhere and would show up sooner or later.

Carnival time always meant parades. One day Marie was standing on the sidewalk watching the parade and eating ice cream with Daniella and Monique. All the colorful dancers were prancing and dancing their way down Front Street. The group of dancers from *El Capitan*, always quite lavishly dressed in skimpy outfits, came dancing by. They were led by Ms. Dominique Bute, colorfully dressed and spinning her parasol. When she saw Marie in the crowd, she walked up to her and scolded, "Look at the danger you have brought to our island! Shootings and people nailed to trees. Shame on you! Shame on your husband! He seeks just to be famous and have people look up to him as he sits on his high horse."

Rage boiled up in Marie and she spit in Dominique's face. "Move on, whore! Move on! I don't want your kind anywhere near my daughter! Even in all your pretty dresses, you're nothing but a cheap whore."

Dominique wiped the spit from her face, haughtily proclaiming, "I'll have you know I'm certainly not cheap!"

"But you're nothing but a whore! It's because of people like you these girls are dead. Move on, whore, move on!" Suddenly, a tomato came sailing from the other side and hit Dominique in the back. The thrower shouted, "You heard Marie. Move on whore! We don't want you here!" Others yelled the same chant, some throwing fruit. Alfred came up, wrapped a coat around Dominique and ushered her and her ladies out down a side street to cheers from the crowd. "The whores are leaving. Stay away, you whores, stay away from our men and children."

Marie stood proud until she looked down at Daniella, who was trying to comfort Monique. Daniella carefully scolded Marie, saying, "You scared her when you spit in that lady's face and said those mean things to her. You scared her bad. That wasn't a very Christian thing to do."

"But she's a bad lady. She's part of the whole reason why your father is in danger. And she came up to me; she started it." Marie could feel herself making excuses, something she had told her daughter never to do. She always taught her. "An excuse is just a guarantee that you'll make the same mistake again." And here she was, making excuses for the way she had treated Ms. Dominique Bute.

"But Mother" – Daniella had never called Marie *Mother*, always *Mommy*, even though she was older now – "haven't you always told me we're all God's children? Plus, they always have such beautiful costumes and dance so well. You really scared Monique. She told me her father used to spit on her and call her the names you called that woman. Can we go home? I don't feel like doing carnival anymore. It's best if I get my sister home."

All the pride that Marie had felt about standing up to the notorious madame was gone, replaced with shame. She grabbed Daniella's hand and reached out for Monique's, but Monique would hold only Daniella's hand. Now that her conscience had returned, she could see on Monique's face she, with her words and actions, had sent her back, at least for the moment, into the home from which she had been rescued.

When they got to the car and the girls were sitting in the backseat, Marie turned to them. "That lady said some mean things about my husband, your father. But what I did was wrong. What I said to her was mean. I was wrong. I shouldn't have done that. Monique, I'm sorry that I hurt you. Do you want to talk about it?"

Monique was quietly looking at the floor. She just shook her head. Daniella frowned at her mother and held Monique's hand. It was clear that they were not going to let her off the hook. Marie turned and drove home. That night she fixed macaroni and cheese, Monique's favorite meal.

After they went to bed, Marie joined Cédric, who was out on the porch reading the newspaper. "I had an incident this afternoon."

Cédric put the paper down; it was clear from her tone she had some things to say, and his job was just to listen. "Yes, what was it?"

"We – Daniella, Monique and I – were at Carnival, and the dance troop from *El Capitan* came dancing by. That Madame who runs it came up to me and started blaming me, saying how unsafe we have made the island. She talked of the shootings and the man nailed to the tree. She was quite mad, especially at you. She was cursing you out. I got mad, and I spit in her face and called her a whore. I told her to move on."

As Cédric sat there listening, everything inside him wanted to tell Marie Dominique's story, and how actually it was Dominique that had first warned him about the assassin, and how he was in danger. "What happened then?"

"I kept calling her a whore and telling her to move on. Someone threw something at her, hitting her in the back. Then the crowd started calling her a whore and telling her to move on. Soon many people were throwing things at her. That man who is always with her came up and put his jacket around her and whisked her and the ladies from *El Capitan* off and down one of the side streets."

"Doesn't sound pretty. Sorry you had to go through that." Trying to be empathetic.

74

"No, the worst part is that the girls were with me. They witnessed the whole thing, and they were not upset with the madame, but they were very upset with me. Daniella actually called me *Mother* – not Mommy, *Mother*."

Cédric eyes opened up wide. "She's never called you that before."

"No, but it got the message across! She gave me the speech about how we're all God's children. Shit, she was using my own words against me! But the worst part was Monique's reaction. Daniella told me that Monique's father used to spit on her and call her a whore. I damaged her again, and she doesn't deserve or need any more trauma like that. She didn't even want to hold my hand, just Daniella's. I was so angry I had stopped being a mother and sunk to that woman's level. Monique will probably be hanging around with you for a while more than with me, and truthfully, I can't blame her. I don't like myself much right now."

Cédric stood up, pulled his wife to her feet, hugged her and held her tight. He so wanted to tell her that Dominique was a proud mother, just like her, and that she had obviously created the confrontation on purpose to hide her involvement with Sanctuary. He thought to himself, "Honey, you would so much like her; she's so much like you." But instead, he whispered to his wife, "She's just a whore."

Marie pulled away. "We won't be using that word in this house anymore. And my daughter is right, she *is* one of God's children, and I should treat her like that. I was thinking about it; that's how our masters looked at us centuries ago – like we weren't people, just property, just pieces of meat. That attitude was dangerous then, and still is. No, I owe her an apology. I'm going over to *El Capitan* tomorrow and apologize."

"May I make a suggestion?"

"What?"

"Why don't you send her a letter of apology? I don't really think you should be going over there. And a letter would be something that she can keep and look at again and again; it may have more impact on her the just hearing the words once. I'm sorry. And truthfully, I don't want you around that brothel. You're so darn pretty, someone might see you and think you're working there."

Marie smiled for the first time since the incident.

The next day, after the girls had been sent off to school and Cédric was out on a diving job –hooking up equipment to some yachts sunk in Irma so they could be pulled out of some of the harbors – Marie sat down with paper and pen.

Dear Ms. Dominique Bute,

> I'm writing this letter of apology for the way I treated you and the things I said to you the other day at Carnival. You were just giving me your opinion, which you're entitled to. Instead of listening to you, I became angry and behaved horribly and said horrible things. There is no excuse for the way I acted. I repeat, there is no excuse for the way I acted and treated

you. I apologize for spitting in your face. You did not deserve that; no one does. I repeat, you did not deserve that. That was me being childish. The nasty things I said to you I will not repeat, but please know that I sincerely apologize for saying them.

I take responsibility for raising up the anger of others and supported them directing it at you. I'm glad your man was there to get you safely away from me and the others.

As my daughters reminded me, "We are all God's children and deserve to be treated with dignity and respect." If I see you on the street someday, you'll not need to be afraid of me. I look forward to the day when I can apologize to you in person.

May God watch over you and the ladies at your establishment. I'm sorry for any pain my actions may have put them through, also.

Sincerely,
Marie Beaujon

That afternoon when the girls got home from school, Marie sat them down. "Your mother had homework to do today, and I want to read it to you. I want to thank you for helping me be a better person." She then read the letter. It was clear that Daniella approved; she smiled when it was done. Monique listened intently, but she was still detached.

She was emotionally hiding under her bed, tucked away in the corner as she used to do when her father would scream angrily at her, yelling those nasty names at her. Many nights she stayed under the bed until he had left for work the next morning; he had a hard time getting to her and dragging her out from under the bed with his bad knees, especially when he was drunk. But there were some nights when he would call one of his friends for help, and together, laughing, they would pull her out from her hiding place. Those were especially bad nights.

Daniella told her it was a nice letter, then asked, "Mommy, when are you going to deliver it?"

"Tomorrow, sweetie. Your father said he'd drop it over there when he goes to that fruit stand where he gets us those good mangoes and pineapples. How about if I fix you guys some more mac & cheese to celebrate?" Monique took two more weeks and a couple of therapy sessions to crawl her way out from under the bed. Marie knew she was back when they were in the grocery store one day, and Monique grabbed her hand and they walked together.

A couple of days after the letter had been delivered, the flag at *El Capitan* was flying high.

Cédric went to the exchange spot and found a note there.

> Sorry for what I put your wife through
> at Carnival, but it earned me some
> good credibility with the people I'm
> trying to get closer to. It was a good

letter. It's clear you married well. No need to respond, I just wanted to let you know it was a good letter and I'm sorry for having to involve your wife in that way."

That night when Cédric got home, there was a small box lying on the kitchen table. "Her man delivered it this afternoon," explained Marie. Inside the box was the letter Marie had written, torn up into very small pieces. From the looks of the envelope, it seemed like the letter had never been read. With it was just a small note:

Never speak or send me any letter again!

Signed,
The Whore

Cédric just looked at her and shrugged. "I guess your letter wasn't well-received."

"I don't even think she read it, from the looks of the envelope."

"You're probably right, my dear. I bet she can keep a grudge for a long time. Like maybe forever. Yeah, I think if you see her, you might want to just cross the street."

Chapter 12

A year had passed since the burial of the young girls up in SANCTUARY. Pastor Eboune celebrated a special ceremony and over 400 people showed up. But in terms of hunting those who traded in underage flesh, things were quiet.

Then one day, when Cédric stopped by the fruit stand, he noticed that the flag was flying high at *El Capitan*. Tucked under the boulder was the note Cédric had been hoping would arrive someday:

> The pearl-handled revolver belongs to José Zavaia. He's a Columbian, but he lives on the island of Trinidad. I think he can provide you with lots of information. You can identify him by the large tattoo on his arm of a naked woman lying under a palm tree.

This was the first real information they had received since the assassination attempt on Cédric's life. He could feel the excitement. This José Zavaia had probably been piloting the yacht the night it went down. He would be the person directly responsible for the death of Cédric's sixteen daughters. They were going to give this man special attention. As he was heading home to tell Marie and make a call to gather everyone together, Marie called.

"Cédric, we have another daughter. Someone pulled up to the bottom of the hill, let her off, and sent her walking up the hill. She has that same hollow look as Monique did when we first met her."

"I'm 10 minutes away. I'll be right there!" Cédric was usually a slow, cautious driver, but he was there in five minutes, passing cars left and right. Marie stood in the yard with the young girl, who was wearing a tattered green and red sundress. Her hair looked like it hadn't been combed in months. Her dark brown eyes were sunken, and she looked emaciated. Pinned to her dress was a letter. Marie unpinned it and handed it to Cédric.

> This is my daughter Juliana. My husband died years ago, and my new man has been sexually and physically abusing Juliana for two years now. I never told him no. I know I'm a horrible person. Juliana stopped talking about six months ago. I can't tell you who we are, because I know what you do to people like us, and maybe we deserve it. We don't live on Saint Martin. Please give my daughter a home at Sanctuary. She needs more than I can give her, and

I'm afraid my man will let her die or even kill her. I don't mind if he kills me, but she deserves better, and she still young enough. She's only twelve. Please give her Sanctuary.

Cédric looked at Marie, who was already on her knees, stroking and cleaning the young girl's face. "Hi, sweetie, we're glad you're here. You've got some dirt on your face; let me clean you up." Marie's face was glowing like a new sunrise as she met her new daughter. Cédric watched his wife's gentle compassion in action as Marie cleaned the young girl's face. This little girl was broken by who knows what. "What's your name, sweetie?" The young girl just stared ahead, looking somewhere or nowhere, past Marie and her kindness.

"Her name's Juliana," Cédric answered Marie's question. "She stopped speaking about six months ago. We need to call Marilyn. We're going to need her help."

Marilyn was there within about 20 minutes, reading the letter. "The poor woman probably used the last drops of motherhood she had left in dropping her off here."

"She hasn't talked in over six months, and she looks so skinny. Are we equipped to help her?" Cédric asked.

Marilyn looked at the two of them. "She's going to be a handful. To be honest, she may not make it; her decisions not to eat and talk have to do with her giving up on life. Some children see death as a solution, not a problem. They seek that final release from a world that hasn't shown them much love, if any. That's probably what scared her mother. But in my opinion, Sanctuary is her best hope. You know our social services system is already overflowing. She would never get the help she deserves or needs. If you're going to keep her…"

Marie interrupted, "Of course we're going to keep her. There's never been any question about that." She looked at Cédric, "Aren't we?"

Cedric calmly replied, "Never been any question, but we're going to need Marilyn's help."

"Absolutely," Marie agreed.

"Don't worry, you two. I'll just add a couple of extra hours onto my visits with Monique and see her then." She needs the kind of love you two and your friends have plenty of. But also, I think living with the girls will be some of the best medicine for her. She has to learn how to be a person and a child again. You can help her be a person again. They can help her be a child again."

Just about then, Daniella and Monique came walking up the driveway from school. "Hello girls, come meet your new sister! Her name is Juliana. She doesn't talk, but she listens well." Marilyn nudged Cédric; Juliana, who'd only stared straight ahead, turned her head slightly and glanced over at the girls.

Daniella, whose heart was as big as the night sky, ran up and grabbed Juliana's hand, saying, "Hi Juliana! You come with us. We're going to go play."

"Remember, honey, Juliana doesn't speak."

"Okay, then we'll just draw pictures." Daniella, who was probably the best therapist in the house – maybe the whole island

– just tugged Juliana's hand. "Come on, Sis, let's go draw." Daniella looked at Marie. "Mommy, can she speak at all? I got so many questions I want to ask her, and I'm sure Monique does, too."

"I don't know, honey, I don't know. She's just been here a short time. I think we'll have macaroni and cheese tonight."

Both Monique and Daniella jumped up and down with excitement. "You're going to love my mom's mac & cheese. It's the best!" Monique said. It was the first time Monique had acknowledged Marie as her mother. Marie bit her lip and a tear ran down her face. Juliana's therapy had started. It was to be found in the two girls: their acceptance of her, broken as she was; their unconditional love; and their excitement at having a new sister.

"Mommy, is she going to be meeting with Auntie Marilyn?" Daniella asked.

"Yes, honey. In fact, she's going to meet with her tomorrow."

Monique, who was standing next to Juliana, turned to her smiling. "Oh, you're going to like Auntie Marilyn! She's a very good lady. She will help you find your voice, then you'll share with her that stuff, it's not fun, but it does help. You're going to like her. Come on, let's go draw!" Daniella and Monique kept talking to Juliana, not caring whether she answered or not. The door banged behind the girls as they headed into the house together.

Marilyn was smiling. "She'll be okay, but when she does start talking, the things she's going to be saying won't be nice. Don't be surprised if she swears a lot. If and when she does, it'll be a test, and if you shut her down, she may give up. She's got to be strong – real strong; to be silent for six months isn't easy. Somewhere it's tied to her survival. She would probably say things and then get beaten for it. As soon as I can, I'd like to get her to the hospital. If you noticed her baby finger, it's clear that is has been broken. There's something about her arm– it doesn't look quite right either. I wouldn't be surprised if x-rays tell us that she has had a few broken bones. But we won't do this until we have some type of relationship and she feels at least somewhat safe. She must be terrified."

A bit later that evening, as Marie was cooking up some macaroni and cheese for the girls, Daniella looked at Juliana's picture and exclaimed, "Oh my gosh, is that good! Show my mom!" Juliana shook her head no. "Do you mind if I show Mommy?" she asked. Juliana didn't say anything, so Daniella took that as a 'yes' and brought the paper over to Marie. The picture was of angry seas crashing against a rocky island, and the detail was superb.

"Sweetie, this is fantastic! You're an artist! An absolute artist!" And she was.

Monique wanted to see, and she too thought it was great. "This is so beautiful we've got to put it up on the fridge! Would that be okay with you?" Juliana shrugged her shoulders as if she didn't care, but at least it was a response. Monique immediately taped it up on the fridge.

Daniella laughed, "Don't anybody say anything to Daddy! Let's see if he notices it when he comes in." About 20 minutes later, Marie called Cédric for supper. He came in, washed his hands, and then went to the fridge for some lemonade. He opened the door, then immediately closed it again as his brain registered the picture he has just glimpsed. He looked at it carefully, then up at Marie, and then at the girls. "This is fantastic! This is absolutely fantastic!" The girls were giggling.

He looked pointedly at Daniella, who said, "Nope, Daddy, not me."

Then he looked at Monique. "Nope, Daddy, not me."

Then he looked at Juliana, and as she stared straight ahead, the two other girls excitedly bragged about their new sister. "Yes! Juliana drew that! Isn't it wonderful?"

"It's more than wonderful! It's fantastic!" Cédric stooped a bit to look at the fine details of big waves crashing against a rock as dark, angry clouds circled above. He knew it was about Juliana's insides, as did Marie, but they just kept talking about how they liked all the details and the beauty of the drawing. It was not a time for therapy; that would happen with Marilyn. This was a time to show care and appreciation of her talents and of her way of teaching them what was going on with her.

That next Saturday, Marie came back from town with Daniella and Monique. The girls were all giggly. Juliana was sitting quietly on the porch, where she spent most of her time, as if she was waiting for her parents to come back. The two girls couldn't hold their excitement anymore. "Can we give it to her, Mommy? Can we give it to her now instead of after supper?"

Marie gave in. "Okay, you can give it to her."

The two girls ran over to Juliana, big smiles on their faces. "We got you a present, little sister, we got you a present! Monique saw it – it's just perfect for you." They put it on her lap as she stared at them as if she didn't know what to do with it; could it be she'd never had a present before? "Open it! Open it." After a bit, Juliana figured out that it was for her, and she pulled the strings and slowly opened the package. Inside she found a sketchbook and a set of colored pencils. She looked at it, then looked at her sisters. "You can draw every day! Isn't it perfect? You're so good, you can draw every day and put a new picture on the fridge!" Monique bubbled.

Juliana took the book, went to the kitchen table, and started drawing. It was another angry sea crashing against an island, but this time there were some trees on the island, not just bare rocks. The other two girls sat around her, watching. When she was about done, Monique asked, "Are there any people on the island?" Juliana shook her head no, but it seemed like the first real bit of person-to-person conversation she had made, and it happened by the girls being interested and curious about her picture.

Chapter 13

José Zavaia had been the man piloting the slave ship when Irma hit. He was as evil as they came. He and his crew had anchored the yacht over near St. Barth's, hoping to wait out the monster. The girls were terrified and screaming, but the fear of sixteen young innocents being tossed back and forth, the shackles cutting into their wrists, meant nothing to him. In fact, he quite enjoyed it; it was music to his ears. He just kept laughing, joking with his crew, encouraging the girls to scream louder – until suddenly, he heard a loud, ominous splintering sound. The anchor chain ripped from the yacht, causing a crack between some of the wood planks while tossing the boat into the center of Irma's fury and throwing his crew members overboard.

He yelled at the girls to shut up. He needed to think. Quickly, he put on a life vest. Even though there were more stowed under the seats in the bow and stern, he left them there; he had no concern about the survival of the girls. He tied rope around his waist and secured himself to the steering column with it. Then he sat in the Captain's chair, clinging to the wheel, hoping not to be tossed into the sea like his crew had been. The girls were screaming at him, begging to be set free. That would not happen. He prayed for his life, but God was too busy to listen to him; He was down in the small room with the young girls, trying to comfort them and tell them that soon they'd be home and their suffering would be over.

The yacht quickly drifted away from St. Barth's towards St. Maarten, where the hurricane was delivering its full fury. Between the water seeping in through the leaks and the water being tossed in from the sea, he knew the ship would go down soon. By now, they weren't far from St. Maarten, a mile at the most. The screams of the girls stopped, and he looked down into the cabin now nearly filled with water. The girls were still struggling, but with each scream, more water filled their lungs. Then they hung there, silently suspended in the water-filled hold, held in place and together by the chains he had put on them earlier. He didn't want to die with them, so he cut the ropes that held him to the steering column and jumped into the enraged seas. As he did, he saw in the swirling sea the face of the devil smiling and laughing at him; he knew that he'd be safe, and that he'd been praying to the wrong spirit. The last thing he remembered before waking up on the shore was being tossed back-and-forth in the angry waves, hearing the devil laughing at him.

He lifted his head and looked around. The skies were now pretty much calm. The fury had moved on. He looked out onto the sea, knowing the yacht was now resting at the bottom somewhere. There was debris everywhere. He spotted a small boat with a motor on it that had been thrown about twenty yards inland. It looked intact. He took the motor off and carried it to the shoreline, then dragged the boat to the water's edge, and reattached the motor. He searched the shoreline and found a five-gallon red plastic container of gasoline. He wanted to get out of there and get back on St. Barth's where he had connections and could establish an alibi if the ship and the girls were ever found. When he pulled the cord and the motor started, he smiled, remembering the devil's face and laughter he had seen and heard in the enraged waters just hours before. He chuckled to himself. "I've heard of a guardian angel, but I've got a guardian devil."

Once over on St. Barth's, José found a slightly damaged empty house, broke into it and decided he'd use it for rest and as his alibi, if anyone asked. He would say he broke into the house to seek shelter from the storm, and who would blame him? But as it turned out, there was so much destruction all around that no one ever asked or cared. In the medicine cabinet, he found what he needed to clean and bandage up the wound on his leg he had received on St. Maarten. Then he lay down and got some badly needed rest.

Over the next few days, he connected up with his contact who lived on St. Barth's, then he slowly made his way back to Trinidad, catching rides with people eager to help anyone who had encountered the wrath of Irma. He was most angry with himself for losing his pearl-handled revolver, a gift he had gotten for himself after his first successful slave run. He had no thoughts of the sixteen girls still entombed in that small cabin that lay at the bottom of the sea. He knew where to find more of them.

José had grown up in Comuna 13, the slums of Medellin, Colombia, during the heyday of drug lord Pablo Escobar. But his interests lay in things other than drugs; what excited him was flesh. He procured girls for the cartel's brothels, and he was good at his job. He found he could go into the poorest villages and purchase a sixteen-year-old girl for between five hundred and seven hundred dollars. By the time a girl was used up, she would likely have made the cartel around $25,000 to $30,000 from her misery. Their owners figured those numbers were a good return on investment. José developed a route of procurement throughout Columbia and in the countries that surrounded it.

After the death of Pablo Escobar in 1993, José became an independent contractor. For years, he took ten to sixteen girls every three months to his contacts in Puerto Rico. He would sometimes deliver cocaine as he went about procuring and delivering the young girls. He found that if he specialized in the very young ones, he could even make more money by selling to those who supplied the pedophiles in United States, Canada and sometimes Europe. He could immediately get $20,000 for a 10- to 12-year-old girl, and $25,000 for someone six to nine years of age. He guessed his customers resold the girls for double that amount. The youngest he ever sold to be resold to a pedophile was a four-year-old. He felt no guilt, just excitement about the $28,000 price he got for her.

The youngest he ever had for himself was a six-year-old. He found that was a bit too young for him – he liked them between ten and twelve, depending on their body type. He was always happy when a good friend and slaver from Africa showed up; sometimes he brought José a few girls in exchange for cocaine.

He developed his business to where groups often waited for him on the beaches with young girls, he would buy for around $2000 apiece. It was much safer for him when they came to him, as he didn't have to worry about bandits in the jungle. It also saved him from going into the villages and dealing with the parents; he always hated their sad goodbyes, though they also excited him a little. He would take the girls that cried the most for his own pleasures.

He was proud to be a modern-day slave trader. He was totally delighted when, on one recent voyage, he delivered thirty-two girls to his contact in Puerto Rico. That's why he always kept extra chains tucked away in compartments, for he truly never did know how many young girls might be waiting on the beach when he motored in.

He'd always liked virgins; it was his perversion. With his concentration on the younger girls now, he always had a steady supply of virgins for himself. He and his crew would always take one or two girls on each trip and use them for their own pleasure. José, being the boss, was always the first to take them. He loved the tears and screams of his virgin victims, and how they would finally melt into whimpering sobs as they finally succumbed to their fate. To distinguish the girls, he and the crew had used, he would make them wear a little necklace with some cute name on it so he could tell quickly who he had used and distinguish them from those that might still be virgins. Each year he would buy a box of these necklaces, a hundred to a box. Each year it would be a different name. The first year he came up with this system was the year of *Kitty;* and after that so many others: *Barbie, Sonya, Nancy, Trixie,* and so on. The year of Irma was the year of *Tammy.*

He didn't care he couldn't get top dollar for the girls they used; to him, it was worth the loss of revenue, it was one of the perks of his business. Anyway, José had enough money put away that he could have stopped years ago, but he loved what he did, and he loved its perks. He felt he was the luckiest man alive. He was truly evil, and the devil loved him; José was one of his favorite sons.

There was a growing need for the young and the innocent, so José had recruited a couple of guys into the business. He got a twenty percent cut from their revenue. José hunted and bought girls from the Amazon north; his two apprentices took the territory south of the Amazon all the way down the coast of Brazil, Uruguay, and Argentina. Though they bought plenty of girls, for them, it was less lucrative because of the greater time and expense involved in returning to Puerto Rico where José's connections waited to purchase the girls. His apprentices also knew that someday he'd retire, and they would take over his business. They were already getting hungry.

It had taken him a little while after Irma, but he was back in business with two new yachts. The bigger one could easily hold twenty girls; the other was somewhat smaller. Pressure from the cartel was growing; they needed help moving more cocaine, and with his connections in Puerto Rico, José was highly sought after. He had special compartments built into the bottom of his boats where he could carry 200 kg of cocaine per trip. Things looked better than ever. He was happy that first voyage after Irma, and he was hungry to feed his perversion. He and his crew had celebrated being back in business by taking an extra girl for their own use.

Trinidad was where he owned Clifftop Villa, where he had lived for fifteen years. He had purchased the villa for three million dollars cash. He liked Trinidad, for it was centrally located on his routes and gave him a false sense of dignity and prestige. It also gave him some distance from Columbia and the cartels, which were potentially a threat and could easily swallow him up.

José was furious when he heard about what had happened down in St. Maarten. He was especially mad about Sanctuary. "How dare they put them in graves! I wanted them lost forever on the bottom of the sea until the animals were done with them. They were whores – little beginning whores – but they were still whores!" He would rant at his crew. Through one of José's connections in Columbia, he hired an assassin from a gang from Domenica. José was totally incensed when the assassination failed. He was angry at the disrespectful message about his business nailed on the tree. Nobody was going to tell him what to do! He tried to hire more assassins, but after what had happened on St. Maarten, the price skyrocketed for anyone willing to take the risk of trying to assassinate Cédric. José was also cheap. He figured he'd wait a year or two until the price came down. But to him, Cédric was marked for death.

José was also deluded. He didn't fully realize that his "apprentices" now saw themselves as his competitors. They were the ones who leaked that José piloted the sunken slave ship; they hoped the information would find its way to the members of Sanctuary. As proof, they let it be known that José had left his pearl-handled revolver, his pride and joy, on the slave ship. Eventually, this information made its way throughout the circle of flesh dealers, where Ms. Dominique Bute overheard it and eventually provided it to Cédric.

Chapter 14

Things were about to change now that they had the name of the man who had owned the pearl-handled revolver. Every ounce of their energy went toward learning about him and his operation to prepare for the pursuit to come. Cédric was ready. He had enjoyed the quieter time with his family and his girls. Two wonderful events had taken place during these quieter times, and his spirit was refreshed.

The first involved Juliana. She had continued to draw pictures daily; most were still angry, but some allowed a peek at a heart softening. She now drew pictures of her sisters. She had warmed up considerably to Marie. She had even drawn a beautifully detailed picture of Marie, which Cédric had framed and proudly hung in their living room. But Juliana still had very little to do with Cédric, and still hadn't spoken a word to anyone.

One day when Cédric was working in the yard cleaning up his equipment after a salvaging job, Juliana challenged him. She was playing a few feet away. Only the two of them were at home at the time. He saw Juliana look at him, then pick up a rock and throw it through the window of the house. Then she turned and stared at him intensely. He walked over to where she was standing, and she quickly picked up another rock and faced him. For a moment, they stood there facing off with each other. Then Cédric slowly bent down, picked up a rock, and cautiously stood up, never taking his eyes off her. She stood there at the ready, when suddenly, Cédric turned and threw his rock through another window of the house. Juliana looked at him as if he was crazy. Cédric was remembering all the teachings of Marilyn. She had often told him and Marie that someday Juliana would test them— that she would put them in a double bind and watch how they would respond, so she could see if they really loved her.

Cédric looked at Juliana, "Come on, it's your turn. We still got more windows." Juliana, who in her surprise had dropped her rock, picked up another stone and threw it through another window. This time she smiled at Cédric. He picked up another rock and crashed it through another window. Soon, there weren't any more windows in the house. Then Cédric got an idea. Juliana could tell he was very excited.

"Honey, quick, come with me!" He ran down the hill to where the car was. When he was about halfway down the hill, he stopped; Juliana was at the top watching him. "Come on, honey! This is going to be great fun! Come on!" There was high excitement in his voice.

Suddenly, she ran down the hill and joined him, not knowing what he would do, but trusting him. They drove for a while, and he kept telling her how much fun they would have. Finally, he pulled into a parking lot of one of the large hotel complexes destroyed by Irma but not yet torn down. On the side facing the sea, all of the windows had been blown out and part of the structure had collapsed, but on the other side, there were dozens of windows, some broken but many not.

They got out of the car. Cédric reached out his hand, and Juliana grabbed it for the first time ever. They ran over close to the building. Cédric picked up a stone and threw it through one of the windows, laughing. "Your turn, honey, your turn!"

Juliana picked up a rock and took out another window. They kept throwing stones, hearing the crash of glass, and at times laughing when they missed. Cédric, in his excitement, picked up a stone and was going to throw it through a window when suddenly, he heard Juliana say, "No! It's not your turn, it's mine!"

He turned to her, "What did you say?"

"It's not your turn. It's my turn!" Those were the first words she had spoken in many, many months.

Cédric ran to her and hugged her as he tearfully told her, "I love you. I love you so much."

She whispered, "I love you, too. And Mommy. But I hate him," and Cédric knew she meant her stepfather. "Can we throw some more stones?"

For the next 15 minutes, Cédric fed Juliana stones, and she threw them until all the windows she could reach with her throws were knocked out. The whole time Juliana kept talking with Cédric, the two of them deciding which window to knock out next or what stone to use.

When there were no more windows – at least that they could reach – Cédric turned to her, "Honey, how about I make you a slingshot and we can come back tomorrow and go for those higher windows?"

"Really? That would be great! We could bring my sisters."

Then Cédric looked at her a bit sheepishly, "You know we're in big trouble."

"You mean the windows at home?"

"Yep, big trouble!"

"I'll tell Mom I was the one to throw the first stone."

"But I want to tell her I threw the second one. It was a good throw. Deal?"

"Deal!"

"Here's an idea. How about we stop down at Ace on the way home get a bunch of glass and putty, and I'll teach you how to fix broken windows? We'll do it together."

Juliana smiled.

As they drove to the hardware store and Cédric collected the supplies, Juliana talked on about everything. She talked about what she saw in the hardware store. She talked about how much she liked her sisters. And about how she especially liked Marie's macaroni and cheese and lemon poppy seed bread. "Mom's really a good cook."

"You'll have to tell Mom; she'd love to hear that."

They pulled the car into the parking area and started up the hill. Standing at the top, with hands on her hips and an angry look on her face, was Marie.

Cédric looked at Juliana. "I told you. It sure looks like we're in big trouble."

Juliana yelled out, "I threw the first stone, it's my fault! But Dad threw some, too."

Cédric laughed, "I didn't think you'd throw me under the bus so quick."

Marie stood dumbfounded, her mouth open. Now it was she who couldn't say anything. She looked at Cédric, and he winked at her.

Juliana grabbed and held Cédric's pants leg since his hands were full of glass for the repairs. "How much trouble do you think we're in?"

Cédric chuckled. "A lot, honey, but you use your words and explain everything we've done today to Mom. That will help, and I think she'll let us off the hook. But we're still going to have to fix the windows."

Marie had still not said a word when they got up to where she stood. Juliana sensed she had better talk fast, so she explained to Marie about how she had been angry earlier, and that she threw a rock and broke a window. Then how her Dad did the same. "Then we kept going until we broke all the windows! Then he took me to this old building, and we spent the afternoon throwing rocks and breaking windows! It was great! He's going to make me a slingshot so we can get the rest of the windows tomorrow."

Cédric added, "After we fix the house."

Juliana looked at Marie. "I'm sorry, Mom. It must be a big mess inside the house. But I'll help."

Marie, tears running down her cheeks, got down on her knees and hugged Juliana. "I'm not sorry, honey. I'm not sorry at all. But it is really a mess inside, and I am going to need your help. Your sisters are wondering what happened. Why don't you go tell them?"

Marie and Cédric stood, arms around each other, listening to Juliana tell her sisters the story of her day. The whole family spent the rest of the evening cleaning up the mess, repairing windows, eating macaroni and cheese and listening to Juliana chattering about everything. Daniella and Monique peppered her with questions; there were so many things they wanted to know about her.

The next afternoon, they all got in the car and went back to the shattered hotel. Cédric had made slingshots for each girl, and they spent the afternoon taking out the rest of the windows. When the job was finished, Cédric and Marie stood the girls in front of the car. "No more window-breaking at home! Deal?"

The girls looked at each other laughing and smiling, then all together agreed. "Deal!"

Cédric set up a shooting range on the back of their property where the girls could practice with their slingshots, knocking over cans and bottles. Sometimes Juliana would spend hours perfecting her skills. One day she and Marilyn went out back to the shooting range with the big cardboard drawing of Juliana's father, and Juliana spent a good part of the afternoon screaming at it, crying, and shooting holes in it with her slingshot. Finally, she fell to the ground, totally exhausted to where after a few minutes, she had fallen asleep in Marilyn's lap.

The second event came about a month later. Marie received a phone call. "Marie, this is Karen, Daniel's cousin. He told me to call you. I work at the airport. Just a little while ago, a WinAir plane landed. The flight attendant came looking for me and pulled me aside – we're lifelong friends. She said there was a little girl on the plane, and when Ariel – that's my friend – asked her where she was going, the girl smiled happily and said, 'I'm going to a place called Sanctuary on St. Maarten. My mother put me on the plane and told me when I got to St. Maarten, I should ask to be taken to a place called Sanctuary.' Ariel knows about Sanctuary; hell, by now, everybody in the Caribbean has heard about it. But she also knew that if she took her into the building and the customs officials, she would be put into the system and probably never make it to Sanctuary. We need your help."

Thinking quickly, Marie asked, "How long can you keep the girl out of sight?"

"Marie, if you folks can take her, we will find a way to keep her out of sight as long as you need," Karen responded.

"Give me three hours, then walk down the fence line with her to where the Red Cross building sits across the road. We will meet you there."

Marie quickly enlisted John, and within two and half hours, they had parked John's car on the side of Airport Road across the street from the Red Cross building. They stood at the fence, watching the planes land and take off, something that was not uncommon. What nobody could see, because Marie was blocking it, was that John was using a small bolt cutter to cut the links up and down the fence.

At the prescribed time, Karen came walking down the fence line with the beautiful little girl. When they got to where the two were standing, Marie smiled at her. "You want to go to Sanctuary? Just run through the hole in the fence when we pull it back. Hurry, okay?" The girl smiled and nodded. Marie and John pulled on the fence, the girl hurried through the opening, and the three of them ran and practically dove into the car. Karen casually walked back to the airport's cluster of buildings as John drove away with Marie and the child sat in the backseat.

"Sweetie, where are you from?"

"I'm not going to tell you until I'm in Sanctuary. My mother told me not to tell anyone about anything until I was in Sanctuary – and this is a Chevy, not Sanctuary." Marie sighed, chuckled and put her arm around the excited girl. In the rearview mirror, she could see John smiling.

Arriving, John parked the car at the bottom of the hill and said goodbye to Marie and the girl, as he had to get back to his work. They got out and walked uphill toward the mystery girl's destination. Daniella, Monique and Juliana came running down the hill toward them, waving. Catching her breath, Juliana asked, "Who is this, Mommy? Do we have a new sister?"

"Honey, I don't know her name yet. She said she's not going to tell me until she gets to Sanctuary. But I do think you have another sister."

"I'll know Sanctuary when I see it," the girl said. She pulled out a piece of paper. "My mother drew this. She saw it in the paper." The picture was of the gate and the sign that Thomas had made with his cutting torch.

The girls jumped up and down. "You're almost there! Then we can know who you are." After about another 50 feet, the young traveler looked up and saw in front of her what her mother had drawn. She stopped walking. She looked at the drawing, then at the gate. Then she sobbed, "I'm safe now, my mother said once I got the SANCTUARY, I'd be safe! I'd have a new home. That no one would ever do those things again to me that he did." She looked up at Marie. "Is this really SANCTUARY?"

"Yes, honey, it is. Your journey is over, you're safe now. This will be your home as long as you want it. And these are your sisters: Daniella, Monique and Juliana. And what's your name?"

"My name is Mirabella, my mother told me it means beautiful."

"Your mother is right, you are beautiful. Girls, why don't you take your sister Mirabella and show her SANCTUARY? It's probably been a long journey for her. I'll go get us some lemonade." The three girls grabbed for Mirabella's hands and walked her up to the graveyard. They went inside, talking and playing among the graves that always seemed to bring peace to its' visitors.

Marie wanted to find out all about Mirabella, but she patiently sat at the table with the lemonade, waiting until the girls came. She knew that was most important.

Eventually, the four girls came to the table. "Sis, you've got to try some of my Mom's lemonade – it's the best!" Juliana bragged.

Mirabella looked all around. "I do like it here. It's like my mom told me it would be. Can I really stay?"

"As long as you want honey, as long as you want. Now, you've got to tell us about you and how you ended up on that plane."

Mirabella told her story of how her father had used her sexually – "done naughty things to me down below" – and how her mother had found out and confronted him. "My mother yelled and screamed at him and called him all types of horrible names. But then he picked up a stick, a big stick, and started beating her with it. After a while, she didn't move. Then I crawled on top of her and stayed there; at first, I was afraid she was dead, but she was still breathing.

I was so scared and sad. Eventually, my mother AnnaMarie – that's her name, AnnaMarie – woke up. After that, he still did those things to me. Usually, she tried to protect me, and then he'd beat her, then he would do those things to me in front of her. I hated watching her cry. Pretty soon after that, she started telling me about Sanctuary and how she was going to send me there because she needed to do some things and she didn't want me around." Mirabelle whispered, "I think she's going to hurt him really bad. I saw her sharpening the big kitchen knife." She made it clear to me that once I made it to Sanctuary, I needed to stay there because there would be nothing more for me back home."

"Where is that honey, where's your home?" Marie asked.

"A small village in Venezuela not too far from the ocean. It's called Masita."

Mirabella reached into her little knapsack and pulled out a folded piece of paper. She unfolded it. "This is my mother, AnnaMarie. I already miss her so much! Do I have to let her go?"

"Oh no, sweetie, no. Here, wait a second." Marie went into the house and came back with a picture frame, took it apart and put the picture of Mirabella's mother in it. "Here, you put this next to your bed, and you talk to her each night and tell her that you're safe and tell her what you did during the day. No, never forget her. You'll need to love her even more because this is what she wanted for you. Will you tell us all about her?" For the next half hour, Mirabella told them all everything about her mother and very little about her father – just that he was a bad man.

Daniella spoke up. "You're going to have to tell my father all about her and show him the picture. I know he'll want to see her and hear all about her." Then the other girls talked about what they remembered about their mothers. There were lots of smiles and tears.

One morning shortly after Mirabella's arrival, Marie, Cédric and the girls woke up to the sounds of trucks and people. A knock on the door turned out to be Rachelle, Thomas's wife, and Pastor Eboune. Still rubbing the sleep out of her eyes, Marie opened the door. "Rachelle, what's going on?" Rachelle, whose father had been a prominent reverend on the island, had helped her develop a deep faith. She had deep connections with all the various faith communities on the island.

Rachelle smiled at Marie. "You and the girls better get busy making some extra batches of your lemon poppy seed bread!

We've got some folks who are going to be around here for the next few days."

"I don't understand."

"With all your new daughters (my new nieces), and if we welcome more daughters and nieces, you folks already need more space, and will probably need even more. We're here to build onto your house. You surely need more rooms and a bigger kitchen. And people from many of the churches on the island want to help. We've got a couple of architect's plans, put together by that really good Dutch architect in Philipsburg, Ruben en Verkeer. He donated them. Pastor Eboune and I would like to come in and show you, Cédric and the girls. If you approve of one, we'll start construction today. The designs are beautiful."

"Oh, sweet Rachelle, this is so nice, but we can't afford it."

"Yes, you can! It's already paid for. Plus, the man who owns the property next to you donated two lots of his land. He doesn't have any children, and he figures you'll put it to good use. Everybody from all the churches on the island wants to donate their time with the construction. Also, churches throughout the island – even one on Saba – have been taking up a special collection at their services for a while now; that was Pastor Eboune's idea." Then she leaned over and whispered in Marie's ear, "And that little white guy Mr. Sam give us a bunch of money. He said it was from a gang down in Dominique that had given him a lot of money when he visited them. Money is no excuse. So, if you don't mind, we'll come in and go over the plans."

After a bit, Marie pulled Rachelle aside. "There's no money donated from Ms. Dominique Bute, is there?"

"Not a guilder. She really hates you, especially after you spit in her face and she and her whores had to run for their safety," Rachelle whispered.

"Not my finest day."

"Nope." Being a deeply spiritual woman, Rachelle, like Daniella, had given Marie the "all God's children" lecture. But **surprisingly**, she had no problem with killing the pedophiles or those who sold children. Something about the wrath of God.

Within an hour, Marie, Cédric and the girls had picked out the design they liked most, and bulldozers were flattening out the area west of their house and of SANCTUARY. There would even be a little hut built about 50 feet behind the house dedicated for Marilyn to do therapy with the girls, for she was now spending lots of time working with them on transforming their suffering into growth.

Two days into the construction, Juliana approached Pastor Eboune, who she had quite an affection for from their visits to church each Sunday. She had told Cédric, "He is a really good man. I like his stories from the Bible, and he wears such pretty robes."

Now she addressed him. "Pastor Eboune, these are for you and the church. I hope you like them." Inside a good-sized package were four drawings illustrating in great detail four stories from the Bible. He was **particularly** taken by the last one; it showed Jesus suffering on the cross between the two criminals with the dark skies swirling above Him, and Mary on her knees, praying for her Son. Underneath she had written, *Father, forgive them for they know not what they do.* "I'm sorry, Pastor Eboune, I wanted to draw more, and maybe I will later. But for now, I've got to start drawing more pictures for our new home. With all the new rooms, we're going to need a lot of pictures. It's so nice what you and the others are doing." Juliana's recent drawings were mostly scenes of life around the island: the markets, men fishing, the tourists with their cameras getting off the cruise ships, men playing dominoes, people singing at church, and many pictures of her sisters. She was drawing pictures of life.

Within a month, the construction was finished, the rooms were fully furnished, and Juliana's pictures were being hung throughout the house.

Chapter 15

Everyone set about learning everything they could about José Zavaia. They were gathering small bits of information; it was as if they'd been given a giant jigsaw puzzle, and now it was time to pour it out of the box onto the table and put it together.

They learned that he now owned two yachts, *"FRESH MORNINGS"* and *"MORNING DEW."* José worked one of the yachts and his cousin and now partner, Roberto Rodriguez, worked the other. They usually had a crew of three on each boat. Cédric would find out later that the three who had been on the boat during Irma had been lost almost immediately after the anchor broke loose, tossed into the sea. The girls would have been thrown overboard too, if they hadn't been chained in. It was only by a miracle – an evil miracle – that Zavaia had hung on and eventually made it to land.

They set about asking questions of everyone they could who lived over near Babit Point, the section of shoreline nearest to where Cédric found the wreck, to find out if anyone had seen José Zavaia make it to shore. They ran into an old fisherman who saw a man steal his boat and motor after the storm. The fisherman lived up the hill a bit. He happened to look out and saw his boat had been moved onto the shoreline and a man was dragging the motor towards it. He hurried down to stop the theft, but because of all the debris thrown about by the violent storm, he wasn't able to get there until the man was motoring away. He watched until the man was out of sight. He was sure that the thief had used the boat to go to St. Barth's. In fact, a couple of weeks after Irma, the fisherman had gone to St. Barth's and had retrieved his boat helped by the authorities.

They thought it was worth checking out, so John and Daniel were sent over to St. Barth's along with Alma, who had grown up over there. As luck would have it, Alma was a childhood friend of the police officer who had helped the old fisherman get his boat back. "You need to talk with Darryl Harrison. He's a petty thief and a smalltime smuggler. He's the man who had the boat. He reported he found it abandoned on the shoreline, so he just kept it as his own."

"Do you have any idea where we might find him?"

"He lives somewhere over near Pointe Milou on the north side of the island. I think his ex-wife still works at the Hotel Oskar; it's up and running – it wasn't beat up too bad by Irma. We located him through her last time. There's no love lost between the two of them."

A cousin of Alma's who owned a taxi business, Daniel DePree, said he'd be glad to chauffeur them around for as long as they needed. He was proud of what his cousin was doing on Saint Martin, and glad to help. When they got to the Hotel Oskar, they had no trouble locating Sophia Harrison. She was one of the head chefs at the hotel.

"Sophia, we'd like to talk to you about your husband if you wouldn't mind."

"Ex-husband! I got rid of that fool four years ago. Is this about that fishing boat I already helped the authorities get it back?"

"Yes, it's about that, but we also want to know everything we can about what Darryl was involved in. Have you ever heard him mention the name José Zavaia?"

"Hell, yes, he's one of the reasons why we got divorced."

Right then, Alma's cousin Daniel DePree threw in. "They're from Saint Martin; they're part of Sanctuary."

Sophia's eyes perked up. She stuck out her hand. "My God, I'm glad to meet you! Everybody's talking about the good work you're doing! It's an honor to meet people from Sanctuary."

Alma smiled as she thought to herself, *I guess we really are making a difference.*

Sophia suggested, "I get off work in an hour. How about I set a table up over in the corner for us and I'll fix you the best lobster dinner you've ever had? We'll finish it off with my award-winning chocolate mousse – I just made it this afternoon. It's always better to talk over good food."

They were all hungry, so they quickly agreed to her generous offer. She brought them over some Heinekens and appetizers while they waited for her. An hour later, Sophia and two waiters piled the table up with lobsters and all the fixings of a banquet. They were all enthusiastically smiling. "Everybody's so excited and proud to have people from Sanctuary here at our restaurant. You have no idea what an honor this is," Sophia emphasized. Their eyes widened as they surveyed the table laden with a five-star meal.

During their delicious supper, they learned that Sophia had divorced her husband because he was whoring around, and one of the persons he whored around with was none other than José Zavaia. "I came home one night after work, and the two of them were going to town with one of the ladies from the hotel here. I kicked his ass out that night, and I gave her a black eye."

"Do you know anything about what your ex up to now?" John asked.

"He's dealing cocaine and marijuana to some of the celebrities that have villas on the island; he's always dropping names. Also, he's been selling some of the things that looters stole after Irma. He buys them pretty cheap, then takes some over to other islands and sells them to the retail stores for double what he pays. When he loads up his boat, he can make a few thousand. In fact, he's on one of those runs now. Should be back from it tomorrow or the next day. I keep pretty good track of him because he still owes me money."

"We're wanting to talk with him about his operations and his connections with José."

"When he comes back from one of his trips, he always stops at the little island called La Tortue, where he stores stuff – mostly his cocaine – in a small cave. He doesn't think I know about it, but I do."

After the meal, they asked Alma's cousin David if they could have some time alone with Sophia. He totally understood; he grabbed his chocolate mousse and coffee and moved to a table on the other side of the restaurant, which was pretty much deserted by now. As they sat around eating the best chocolate mousse any of them had ever tasted, Daniel asked, "How much does your ex owe you?"

"Eighteen hundred dollars. Why?"

Daniel reached into his wallet and gave her two thousand. "Consider his debt paid. If he's involved in what we think he is, you won't see him again. Please don't tell anyone about our visit. We don't want him to know that we're looking into him. And if you could ask your coworkers to keep our visit quiet, at least for a week or two?" She understood what Daniel was telling her, and she nodded.

Sophia smiled. "Good riddance! Especially if he's involved with what you and I think he is, again – good riddance!"

They made small talk and laughed as they took turns telling island jokes for another 15 minutes or so. As they prepared to leave, John said again to Sofia, "Please. You must keep our visit secret."

"You have my word and my ancestors' word on that."

Daniel then added, "In about a week, why don't you go over to that cave Darryl has on La Tortue. Anything you find there is yours to keep or sell. And if you ever learn information that you think we need to know, come over to Sanctuary. There will always be someone there you can leave the information with; you are part of us and what we're doing now."

Sophia was very proud to hear that. "Then let me tell you one thing more. There's an actor over here – he was famous in his time, but now he only does B and C movies. I've heard he is a friend of Roman Polanski, and I know that José regularly brings him young girls from time to time." She wrote down his name and address on a piece of paper. "He's on the island now. He'll probably have some helpful information for you about José." More pieces of the puzzle were coming together. Daniel was excited. To have this lead on a pedophile who had actually purchased young innocents from José would be big for them.

As they walked out of the restaurant, who was waiting there for them but Sam Dresser! Daniel smiled. "I wondered when you were going to show up again."

They were all happy to see Sam, but they didn't introduce him to Alma's cousin. Instead, she told DePree that she, John, Daniel and the new guy were going to walk for a bit. She asked if he'd wait back in the restaurant and have some more chocolate mousse and coffee. He got the message right away. He knew it was some important Sanctuary talk above his pay grade, so he headed back into the restaurant, eager for another bowl of Sophia's masterpiece.

They walked and talked, filling Sam in with all the information they had learned that night. As they were getting back to the Hotel Oskar, Daniel addressed John and Alma. "Why don't you two go back to St. Maarten? Sam and I need to have some conversations with the actor and with Darryl Harrison that you two don't need to be part of. In fact, I prefer that you're not part of them."

John started to object, so Alma grabbed her husband's arm and said as sweetly as she could, "John, please listen to your friend; he cares about you. We've all got different things we need to do and are good at. You need to let Daniel do the sad things that God has given him the burden of doing. There's a different Daniel – a darker Daniel – that he's going to have to let out. He doesn't want you to see him; he doesn't want his best and longest friend to meet that Daniel. Please, John, let him protect you and your friendship and let him do what he must in private."

"But he may need help! He doesn't know what he'll run into," John weakly answered back, knowing he would not win this argument.

Compassionately, Sam stepped in. "That's why I'm here, John. I'll take good care of your friend. He'll be back in a couple of days. I guarantee you that."

Daniel kissed Alma on the forehead. "Thank you, you said it well."

John and Alma walked back to where Alma's cousin was enjoying another bowl of chocolate mousse. John looked over his shoulder, but Daniel and Sam had already disappeared into the night.

David asked where Daniel was. "He's got things to do with his friend," John answered. "Can you give us a ride back to the harbor? I think we can catch the last ferry back to Saint Martin."

Chapter 16

It was around 1:30 in the morning when Daniel and Sam cut the alarm lines in a way that would not alert the security company about the visitors now inside Harry Crane's villa. They wore masks in case anyone else was there; they only wanted Harry Crane.

As they made their way through the house, they passed posters from the movies he had been part of, the good ones and the ugly ones. They quietly searched the house, finding it empty until they reached the master bedroom, where a young black housekeeper was in bed with the actor. They were quite startled when two men in masks held them down, putting gloved hands over their mouths.

Sam was holding Crane, and Daniel said to the young woman, "I want you to come with me into the other room. We want to talk with Harry, not with you. In the morning, when you wake up, we want you to leave as if things are normal. You know nothing of what happened here tonight. If you talk to anyone about us, we will be back for you.

I will take a picture of you before we leave, so we can find you if we need to. Do you understand?"

The young woman nodded vigorously with fright in her eyes, indicating that she understood. "I'm going to take my hand off your mouth now, and you and I are going into the other room. You're not going to scream, are you?" The woman shook her head, indicating she'd cause no trouble.

Daniel took his hand off her mouth, and the only noise she made was her heavy breathing out of the terror she was feeling. Daniel walked her into the other room, laid her on the sofa and took out a syringe of medications. It would put her asleep for the next eight hours. Sam had mixed up a few of these on his boat. Once she was asleep, Daniel took off his mask and walked in the bedroom where Harry Crane was now tied to a chair.

The 53-year-old has-been actor's eyes, wide with fear, shifted back and forth between them. "What is it that you want? Why are you here? Why don't you have your mask on?" he asked, staring at Daniel.

Sam looked at Daniel and took his mask off, too. "I guess I won't need mine either. These damn things are so hot."

"What do you two want? Are you going to kill me?"

Daniel responded, "That truly depends totally on you. We're going to hurt you, but whether you live or die is up to you. It all depends on how much information you give us."

Sam looked at him. "The first bit of information I want to know is this: what is the combination to your safe?"

"I don't have a safe."

"Bad start! You mean you don't have a safe that's behind that picture over on that wall? That's strange. I'm sure I saw one there. I'm sure you won't be needing this then." Sam reached in the man's pajama bottoms, grabbed hold of his member and pulled it out while unsheathing his Bowie knife.

Crane shouted out, "25-6-45!"

Sam walked over, took the picture off the wall, spun the cylinders and the safe's door opened. Inside were two Rolex watches and $223,000 in cash.

Daniel hadn't expected this; he watched Sam and said, "We're not here to rob him."

"My friend, you've got so much to learn. This is tax – perversion tax. We need money to finance what we do. This perversion tax pays for it. It paid for my boat, and the additions to Cédric's and Marie's house were mostly paid by perversion tax. These pedophiles always have cash around; you don't buy little girls with a credit card."

"Why don't the guys they buy from just rob them then?"

"They wouldn't be in business very long if they got a reputation for killing their clients. Plus, they know they're going to get the money in the long run anyway. Mr. Crane here would be paying it to José Zavaia, but tonight he pays us." Daniel smiled. It made sense to him. His education was continuing.

Daniel zip-tied Crane's hands and linked about three of them on his feet so he could shuffle along; they wanted him walking on his own down to the boat.

When they were all in the boat, Sam looked straight into the eyes of the terrified man to make it crystal clear that he was speaking truth. "Again, Mr. Crane, your fate is up to you. We are taking you out to La Tortue to question you about your dealings with Darryl Harrison and José Zavaia. Tomorrow we're going to talking with Darryl Harrison, asking him many of the same questions. The person who answers them honestly and truthfully gets to live. The other dies."

Harry interrupted, "Ask me anything! I'll tell you whatever you want to know. I just don't want to die. I'm too young."

"All of these girls are also to young." Daniel said in a stern unforgiving way.

Harry was going to say something else, but Sam interrupted him: "Please, I wasn't finished. If what you tell us is true, then you'll watch as we torture and kill Darryl Harrison, so you know what we're capable of. If you tell us the detailed truth, you live, and all you've lost is your Rolexes and the money that was in your safe. You get to go back to making your shit movies. But truthfully, we should kill you because those shit movies you've been making this last decade are really bad – I've seen some of them. If you live, we don't want you coming down to the Caribbean anymore. There, I'm finished. Now, what do you have to say?"

"Whatever you want! I'll tell you whatever you want to know! Please, just don't kill me!" Crane screamed, his voice filled with panic; he was coming to understand the situation he was in more and more completely. It was clear he wasn't acting; he'd already wet himself.

"Who is José Zavaia?"

"He's the guy that Darryl deals with; you could say he's the guy Darryl works for. I mainly deal with Darryl, not José or his partner, a Rodriguez fellow. Sometimes Darryl joins up with José's crew to go pick up the girls. But I have met José Zavaia, I've partied with him. I don't want you thinking I don't know who he is, I'm not saying that at all." Harry understood that his value and his life was based on the information and it's accuracy that he could provide to these two men.

"Do you know where they get the girls from?"

"Most of them speak Spanish, so I believe they all come from South America – Venezuela, Columbia, and countries down in that area. Some they get from the Amazon rainforest; they hunt them down there. But mostly they buy the girls. Most of the girls don't know any English at all. But I'm not buying them to talk, you know that."

"Mr. Crane, we do know what you are. What we want to know about is how it works between you and them."

"Because I'm a good customer," (both Sam and Daniel were sickened by the words 'good customer'), "they drop off a girl about once every four months, and I keep her and use her until they return again. I give them the girl back, usually in very good condition. I'm not one of those guys who beats them. I know there are those types, but I'm a nice guy. Darryl can sell her to someone else as slightly used. I give them $15,000 and they give me a different girl and an ounce of cocaine." Crane's rationalizations made Daniel's guts tighten. He was going to let himself enjoy terminating this guy; he was going to be "nice" to him.

"Why the cocaine? Is that for you?"

"No, that's mostly for the girls. It helps the younger ones let go. It helps them feel good and they get into the sex more aggressively after the first couple of weeks."

"Are you buying virgins from them? I know that's a specialty of theirs. And remember, I'll be asking Darryl the same questions." Sam asked as he was sharpening his knife.

"I have in the past. When I was making better movies and had a lot more money, I would always buy virgins. Now I only treat myself to one about once a year. They cost a hefty price, $30,000. Please, I want to live! I'm telling you all the ugly truth. I'll help you in any way I can. José Zavaia, he carries cocaine in the bottom of his boats for the cartel. So does his partner. He's got a friend from Africa who brings him girls from Angola and the Congo; they trade them for cocaine." He was talking nonstop, giving up all the information he could. He gave up the name of the slaver from Africa, a guy named Akachi Botenda. Crane had met him once. The name of Botenda's sailing ship was *Nahuel*, the Tiger. Crane was desperately searching his memory, spitting out any information that might save his life.

Daniel, who was taking notes, had to ask Crane to slow down at times. Harry understood that his life depended on the usefulness of the information he gave up. Once they got to La Tortue, they went over all the information again more slowly.

"How old is your housekeeper we met tonight?"

"She's fourteen. She's been with me for three months."

"How would I know José Zavaia?"

"I can't remember which one, but on one of his arms, he has a tattoo of a naked lady under a palm tree."

"Now I'm going to ask you a question that I know Darryl will know. You guys always keep track of these things, and you better be honest, because if the number he gives me isn't the same, then you die instantly."

"What? What do you want to know?"

"What age was the youngest girl you ever bought?"

"Ten; she was ten – no, no, I was wrong – she was nine." Sam and Daniel cringed and died a little bit inside. After about four hours of going over all the questions several times they had all the useful information they would be getting from actor Harry Crane.

"Okay. We've got one more thing we want you to do for us. Come with us into this cave."

The three walked into a cave, of which there were many on the island. They purposely stayed away from the one where Darryl kept his second-hand loot and the cocaine he was accumulating. They knew that Sonya would be going to that cave in a week. And in case the insects and little animals hadn't cleaned up things by then, they didn't want her to find any evidence of what was going to transpire.

"What can I do for you? I'll do anything."

"Good. We're glad to hear that, because we need your help to send Darryl a message that he needs to take us seriously."

They suspended Harry Crane from the ceiling after Sam secured a bolt and hook in one of the cracks. They stripped him naked. Daniel looked him in the eyes as Sam was putting a gag in his mouth. "You're going to help us send a message to Mr. Harrison, and by the way, we lied! We're going to hurt you! We're going to hurt you really bad for the things you have done to those girls you bought. How dare you buy sex slaves and use them for your own sexual gratification. Do you know what the owners would do to their slaves in the old days when they had offended them? They whipped them. That's what we're going to do to you! We're going to whip you until our arms are tired, and I hope you know where we're going to concentrate the whipping. But don't worry; we'll do it in a *'nice'* way."

Sam and Daniel both took bullwhips out of their duffels. The first lashes fell on his genitals. He squirmed all over, trying to lessen or protect himself from the lashes that bit into his flesh. After they were done with the organ he had used to hurt so many young girls, they continued whipping, crisscrossing his entire body until he was dead. Then they went into the ocean and washed off the blood and flesh, cleansing themselves of Harry Crane. They wanted to be ready for the arrival of Darryl Harrison.

Chapter 17

Back on St. Maarten, someone stopped their car on the road in front of *El Capitan*, lit a rag hanging out of a bottle of oil and gasoline, and threw it over the wall into the courtyard. Flames erupted through the yard. Alfred and the ladies ran out into the courtyard and, using anything they could grab, worked at killing the fire as their customers scurried into their cars, some of them singed from the flames, and hurried off. On the outside of the wall was spray-painted the word "Sanctuary." As Alfred and the ladies swatted out the last of the flames, Ms. Dominique Bute stood leaning against the door, watching.

The next day the flag was flying high at *El Capitan*. Cédric took a walk and retrieved the message under the stone. It read:

> There are those on the island that hate
> the fact that prostitution is legal. They
> are trying to feed off what you're doing
> and use it for their cause. Last night was

their way of getting attention, trying to use your good name and reputation to strike against us. They put my ladies' lives in danger. They will be destructive to what we're trying to do regarding child slavery and child sex trade. It's different than prostitution. You can't let them be combined. I need your help.

Cédric knew that what Dominique was saying was true; the group would need to talk.

Cédric made calls to all the members of Sanctuary, asking them to come to the house for barbecue that night; that they needed to talk. This was the day that Alma, John and Daniel were on their mission in St. Barth's.

As they sat around eating, Cédric tossed the latest addition of *The Daily Herald* onto the table. On the front page was a picture of the burnt courtyard of *El Capitan* and the wall with the word Sanctuary spray-painted on it. "This is what we need to talk about."

Marie angrily threw out, "So what? Somebody's trying to chase the whores out of town and using our name to do it. It's okay with me! You know how I feel about them."

Margaret spoke up. "But that's not the issue. I personally don't like prostitution either. But whoever did this is trying to take the work we're doing and use it for their cause."

"If it brings an end to prostitution, then what's wrong with that?" Marie added, with a bit more determination in her voice.

"Marie, it won't bring an end to prostitution, it will just put it back on the street corners in Phillipsburg, and here on the French side of Saint Martin, our problem will get worse, too. Right now, people don't risk getting arrested and their names put in the newspaper when they can just drive a few extra miles and go to the legal brothels on the Dutch side. We all know the Dutch regulate it tightly."

"But it is still prostitution," Marie said, staring at Margaret.

"The oldest profession in the world," Margaret shot back.

Rachelle, the one who held the most moral high ground within the group because of her religious background and the way she conducted herself, spoke. "Marie and Margaret, you know I'm with both of you on the issue of prostitution. But we need to put our feelings and egos aside for the cause. I am personally enraged – and you know I don't get that way often – that prostitution opponents are trying to steal our name, earned by *our* hard work on *our* cause, and tie it to the issue of prostitution. We have only one issue, and it is about, *and only about*, children being sold into sexual slavery. We can't lose our focus. Our message has to be simple and clear, with one clear goal, with one clear purpose in our name, "Sanctuary." What would have happened to Monique, Juliana, Mirabella if there wasn't Sanctuary? We can't solve all the world's problems. We mustn't lose our focus. Prostitution is a separate thing. The women at *El Capitan* are all of age. The women who work there make their living using their bodies, something none of us approve of. Perhaps it will be an issue that some choose to tackle someday. But meanwhile, we can't let the anti-prostitution demonstrators steal our name, our cause, our dream."

Thomas enjoyed listening to his wife. She had a very good way of presenting her thoughts in a clear, concise way.

Marie hated that she knew that Rachelle was spot on. "I think I still have some resentments left over from Carnival."

Rachelle looked at her, sympathetically. "I would, too."

Marie added, "So what are we going to do? I agree we have to find a way to keep the dream of Sanctuary pure. We owe it to my daughters and your nieces, all of them. But I have to say," looking directly at Rachelle, "I hate the fact that you're right."

Rachelle said, "To me it's clear what we have to do. Cédric should hold a press conference in front of *El Capitan* and make it clear that Sanctuary had nothing to do with this." She looked at Marie as she added, "And, because of your history with Ms. Dominique Bute, it would be best if you were standing next to him."

"My God, I hate how smart you are! Couldn't you be stupid for once?" Marie said, smiling at Rachelle.

"We will all be with you in spirit, sweetie, especially your girls." Rachel said, never forgetting the cause.

The rest of the evening, the group – particularly the ladies – worked out what Cédric would say at the press conference. It was an important step; this would be the first public statement ever given by the group.

The next day, Cédric stood in front of the gate to *El Capitan* with the cameraman and reporter in focusing on him. Marie stood next to him, and the rest of the group was hard at work scrubbing the word Sanctuary off the wall.

"I have a brief statement. I am speaking for those of us who started Sanctuary, carry its message, and do its work. We have no position on prostitution or on sex workers. Those of you who are using our name regarding the issue of prostitution, *stop*. We are from the French side where prostitution is not legal, but here on the Dutch side, it is legal. It is well-regulated. These women are over 21, they choose to be sex workers, they drive to work and drive home from work. The sixteen young girls –our daughters – who we carried from the bottom of the sea *had no choice*. Slaves don't have choice; sex workers in legal brothels do. We are angered that you have tried to bring us into your political fight. We will not be part of it. Our war is with those slave traders who buy, steal and sell innocent children to provide victims to pedophiles; and with the perverted pedophiles who feed off destroying the innocence of the young. Leave us to our work. That's all I have to say."

The reporter quickly turned to Marie. "Marie, what do you think about what your husband is saying?"

Images of her daughters and of that first day when she stared into Tammy's eyes for the first time at the bottom of the sea raced through her head. She knew she would be speaking for them. She spoke clearly and concisely. "My husband speaks our words. He's better at speaking than I, but we sat with the members of Sanctuary and we all wrote these words together. Many of the words he speaks are mine. His message is my message; we are of one voice."

"But what about that day at Carnival – what you did and said?" The reporter threw out, looking for a reaction and hoping to throw her off guard.

"What I did that day at Carnival was childish and immature. I was angry, and I let my anger speak, but not my true feelings. If Ms. Dominique Bute is listening," the cameraman panned over to Dominique as she stood in her doorway watching, smoking a cigarette. "let me use this time to publicly apologize to her. As my daughter reminded me, we are all God's children and deserve to be treated with respect and dignity. What I did that day at Carnival had no dignity and throwing a firebomb into this courtyard and spray-painting the name of our cause on that wall has no dignity, either. We are done here."

The reporter tried to ask more questions as they always do, but Cédric and Marie were finished talking. They joined the others to help scrub the wall clean. Ms. Dominique Bute walked back into the brothel.

The next day, the flag was flying high at *El Capitan*. Cédric went to the rock. Underneath it was a message:

> Perfect. What you and Marie said, and what you all did – it was absolutely perfect. Thank you! God, how I wish I could have met the others and Marie in another world. How I wish she had been my mother. She honored us all yesterday, especially your daughters. I can see why you love her. I wish I could have been her friend. I think we would

have gotten along well, but we never
know where fate will take us.

Cédric had always destroyed the messages until now, but this one he would save and give to Marie someday.

Chapter 18

Before dawn, Sam moved and moored his boat about 2 miles away and then swam back, so there would be no suspicious boats around their cave site. He'd left a few supplies with Daniel, mainly maps, so Darryl could show them precisely everything he knew about José's operations and ports of call. If what Harry Crane had told them was true – and both felt sure it was – Darryl Harrison had sailed with José Zavaia as he bought and sold girls, so he would know the routes and the pick-up points where the girls had been bought. The maps would be invaluable.

Around noon Sam and Daniel spotted the 19-foot catboat sailing towards them as they hid near Harrison's stash cave on La Tortue. Daniel felt excitement, knowing he would finally stand face-to-face with one of the traffickers they had been chasing.

Now they watched as Darryl, suspecting nothing, entered his cave and packed away another quarter pound of cocaine into his weatherproof storage box. There was not much else in the cave:

a half a dozen microwaves, and about a dozen high-end blenders and Keurig coffee makers, all still in the original boxes and wrapped with layers of plastic to keep them looking fresh.

When Darryl turned around, he was surprised by Daniel and Sam standing there with Sam's gun pointed at Darryl's gut. Daniel patted Darryl down, found no weapons, and handcuffed him.

"Who the fuck are you guys? Take what you want and leave, but know I will find you later."

Standing squarely in from of him, Daniel burned his gaze into their captive, with the eyes of the devil that lived inside of him. "We don't give a damn about your little trinkets and baubles or your cocaine. We're here for information."

With fire in his eyes and stupidity in his voice, Darryl shot back, "I'm not in the information business."

"You might want to rethink that. We've got something we want you to see before we start our conversation."

They walked Darryl over to the cave where Harry Crane was still hanging. They had purposely not whipped his face, so he would still be recognizable. Once Darryl turned the corner and saw what was hanging in the center of the cave – even though he was a hard man who had seen much – he immediately shrunk back and threw up.

"Harry wasn't truthful with us last night. We hope you'll do better. Maybe you're in a better mood to give us information after viewing our work," Sam said. "It was very interesting; once our whips had stripped away the flesh on his chest, you could actually see his heart beating inside his rib cage. He didn't give up his life easily."

Darryl threw up again.

"We are going to kill you, just so you know that. But the choice of how you die is up to you. We want information about José Zavaia and his operation – detailed information. If you give it to us, you will die from a simple bullet to the brain; it will be quick and painless, we promise you that. Otherwise, what we did to your friend will seem like a picnic compared to what we do with you."

They set a chair directly in front of Harry Crane and tied Darryl to it. He was inches away from the body.

"We'll give you a few minutes to contemplate your decision. We're going to have lunch. We'd offer you some, but it seems like you have an upset tummy at the moment."

"You bastards! Bastards!"

"You sit here and contemplate your friend and work on your attitude – or not."

When Daniel and Sam finally got back to him, Harrison's attitude had changed.

"Promise that you will kill me quickly if I cooperate; I don't want to die like Harry did."

"We promise, Darryl. We promise. We didn't like having to do that to him, but we needed to give you a message of how seriously we want your cooperation. We told you that we're going to kill you, because we know that after seeing what we did to Harry, you wouldn't believe us if we told you we just wanted to talk. Truth be told, if you can help us catch José and help to shut down his operation, there's a small chance you might live. We could use a man of your talents as an informer if any other child sex slave networks get set up. But you need to tell us everything, in detail. We don't care how ugly the details – we want to know everything. And as you can see, we're not squeamish. We are members of Sanctuary."

When he heard the word Sanctuary, Darryl's eyes widened; he had heard they were honorable men, so maybe there was a chance. Darryl smelled a small fragrance of hope in the air because he so desperately wanted some. But in reality, there was no hope.

Daniel was surprised how much both Harry and Darryl seemed to believe in the word *promise*. Harry and Darryl would never keep promises; why would they think Sam and Daniel would? He found it interesting how these desperate men hung on, hoping and believing in one word.

"What is it you want to know?"

"Everything. Starting with, what does José Zavaia look like?"

"He is six foot tall. He's proud that he's the tallest in his family."

"Are they in the business?"

"No. Most of them are dead from the drug wars. But he has a cousin, Roberto Rodriguez, his partner since Irma – the only person he really trusts in the world.

"José has jet black hair which he parts on the right side. He keeps it slicked down; he really likes that greasy look; sometimes he uses the grease in his hair as a lubricant if the young ones are really tight. He's a real sick bastard, the sickest I've ever met. He makes the devil look like a choir boy. He's the worst I've ever seen, and I've met a lot of these creeps." Talking as if he wasn't one of them.

"He's got a tattoo on his right arm of a nude woman lying under a palm tree. He's got a little limp since Irma; he had a chunk of wood shoved into his left leg from when he was being tossed on to the shores of St. Maarten. I helped him clean it out once he made it over to St. Barth's from St. Maarten after Irma. There's a good scar from it. He never tucks his shirt in; he's got a bit of a paunch. He loves his black beans and rice, which he mixes with sweet potatoes. He was always cooking up something as we traveled up the coast. Sometimes we would stop, and I dove for fresh conch that he would cook up and throw in his stew, which actually wasn't that bad. That was basically all we and the girls would eat, unless we caught a fish or two, or I found some lobster. He's a big eater, and he fed the girls well. He always wanted them in good shape when he sold them."

"What if a girl got sick?" Daniel asked. Darryl looked at him like he was crazy.

"He would throw her overboard. You have to realize there's always more just up the coast; there's an endless market and an endless supply. We were providing what was needed as fast as we could provide it. That's why he got a second boat – the guys in Puerto Rico needed more. They now have factories that make IDs, always indicating that the girls are older than they actually are, and the documents are good, really good. They could easily ship fourteen- or fifteen-year-olds to a pimp in the states with all the documentation that they were eighteen. Just explain they had just been malnourished and underfed when they were young; when actually, the girl might only be thirteen, fourteen or fifteen or younger. The girls didn't speak enough English to say different. And all of them learn to be quiet and do as they were told. It's just the way it is.

"José grew up in Comuna 13, a bad, bad slum in Medellin. 'The meaner you were, the better you did' is how he talked about his growing up. He could've easily got into selling and dealing drugs, but he loved the young girls, having power over them. He loves seeing fear and terror in their eyes and watching it shift into despair, suffering and hopelessness as he destroys something precious in them. He is the worst of the worst. He told me he killed his first person when he was eight. He hates Columbia and Colombians. I think it's because he had three brothers who were killed in the drug wars. That's why he lives in Trinidad."

"But he sells their cocaine?"

"Actually, he doesn't really sell it; he *transports* it to Puerto Rico to their folks there. He says it's like having an extra-high-paying passenger on board. If the product gets there safe, he gets $200 a kilo, so with 200 kilos, that's $40,000."

"What's his route?" Sam pushed.

"He usually starts just over the border of French Guinea in Brazil. He's got contacts that hunt and buy what he calls 'jungle girls.' In some areas, it's very easy to steal them; you know, machine guns against bows and arrows. The men make more profits if they don't have to buy them. José always enjoys it when he gets a young "jungle girl" just starting to bud. He's always pushing these contacts to go deeper into the jungle; he believes that the deeper they go, the fresher the girls will be.

"There's a beach area on the west end of Cadela Norte Brasileria where he meets up with hunters. It's about twenty-five miles before the border of French Guiana. The hunters can access the mouth of the Amazon and travel the river hunting for slaves. But more and more, they are buying them from their parents; José likes his 'jungle girls' and he'll pay extra for them. There're some villages where for a fifty-pound sack of beans and two sharp brand-new machetes, you're guaranteed a young girl just entering puberty, and for a 100-pound sack of beans, you can have the most beautiful one in the village.

"It's become part of how they survive. Many of these villages have adjusted to donating between four and six children a year. In French Guinea, they mainly buy the girls. They tell the parents that their girls are being sent to families who want and can't have children, mainly in America. They often bring pictures of nice places in America to show them where their daughters will be going. The parents love the pictures of the Midwest, where there's plenty of food, and it's so green, and the cows fascinate them. These hunters are quite good salesmen. They're always very polite, and there's nothing that hints about the girls being used sexually. That never happens until we get them down to the beach. Then we might gang rape one or two of them; it would give us instant control over the entire group."

"Were you ever part of that?"

"Yes, José saw it as part of the job, a perk. But he always takes their virginity; it's part of his perversion. He loves to hear their screams and cries. He isn't a small man. He gives each of the ones that get raped little necklaces with a name. The year of

Irma it was 'Tammy', this year it's 'Ginger.' It helps in Puerto Rico, sorting the virgins from those that have already been used. That transfer always needs to be quick.

"He has rendezvous beaches in French Guiana, Surinam – a favorite of his, always a guaranteed three or four girls because of the poverty – Guyana, Venezuela, and Colombia, where he meets up with hunters and purchases girls or even sometimes joins a hunt. After Columbia, he heads up to Puerto Rico to unload his merchandise. Sometimes the boat is full after just one or two stops, so let's say after Guyana, if he has a full load, he quick heads over to Columbia to pick up the cocaine and get to Puerto Rico as quick as he can to unload his merchandise. He transfers his payments to his accounts in the Grand Caymans, minus twenty-five percent he keeps in cash for purchasing. Then he heads back to Trinidad and gets ready to make 'the circle' again, turning around and heading out again as quick as he can. That's where the fun is for him. He loves the wheeling and dealing, pointing out a flaw on a girl and getting her for $50 less. And of course, he loves what he does to them each night."

"What if it looked like trouble?" Sam asked.

"I've seen him march the girls onto the deck and shove one over. They were all chained together, so they fell over like dominoes and sunk straight to the bottom. But that's rare; I think that's the only time he actually did that. He has lots of people paid off to make sure it doesn't happen. He also has a deal with the Colombians: each trip that he gets their cargo to Puerto Rico safe, he gets a little more payment for the next trip. His boats are set up so that if they suspect trouble, the compartment holding the cocaine can be opened just by pushing a button, and the cocaine will drop to the bottom of the ocean in a secured case with location trackers that they can activate. So, if it isn't too deep, the Colombians can have someone retrieve it later. They assume they'll lose three out of a dozen trips, but José's percentages of success are very good. That's why everybody puts up with him and his perversions.

"When he scouts for pickups, he cruises about a mile offshore. If there's a fire on the beach, it means there is merchandise for him to pick up. They devised a set of signals, so José signals them what he is interested in as far as ages and numbers of girls. Usually, he stops, but if they only have one girl for him, he might pass on by. Then probably his partner Roberto, who is usually a week behind him, would most likely stop because by then they usually had more girls for sale. Roberto usually stops, even if it's for a single girl. José won't.

"For years, José trafficked about 100-120 girls a year; but now with Roberto, they've increased it to 200-plus, and with the cocaine, they are doing quite well. He's been training some other guys, too, and they go south on the coast buying and picking up girls all the way down to the tip of South America. Less profit, since it costs more to transport them back to Puerto Rico, but it is still good money, and they have to give a cut of it to José. Lately, they're starting to trade with the Russians. The Russians like the darker-skinned girls, and José's guys like the light-skinned girls with big breasts that the Russians always have for trade. But they're not as young and that's Jose's specialty.

"I suppose you guys also want to know about the ships on the west coast of South America? Those guys send most of their girls over to Asia."

Neither Sam nor Daniel had ever heard of this, but Daniel said, "Of course. We were going to get to asking about that. Go on."

"There's a huge market over there. The husband gets a young girl, and the wife doesn't have to be bothered by her husband, or she gets to join in. Plus, they get a maid to keep the house clean and do their bidding. I know they're providing at least 1,000 to 2,000 girls a year to Japan and the new wealthy people in China. I was thinking of getting my own ship and going over to that side of SA (South America) and building my own business. But I guess it's going to be a little late for that now."

Daniel pumped more hope into the air. "I don't know. You're being very helpful. You actually have more information than we thought you did. There may be some reasons to keep you alive if you can convince us of your value."

"Oh, I'll guarantee you I've got exact pick-up locations, names, and even villages where they've taken girls from. I've kept diaries with dates, times, and details in case something like this happened. I was probably on about a third of his trips as a crew member."

"Once we read them, we'll decide. If they have the information you say they do, we might have to renegotiate how long you stay on earth," said Daniel.

Daniel and Sam knew they had hit the information mother lode. Daniel leaned into Sam. "I'm going to call Gloria and let her know it will be a couple of extra days. We need to get every drop of information we can from Mr. Harrison. Then I'm going to skin him alive."

Sam whispered back, "Tell Gloria to have Cédric start gathering men that he trusts. We've got a hell of a lot of work to do. There's a lot of men who deserve to die."

For three days, they questioned Darryl Harrison, writing down and recording everything they could. Names, points on the map where the beaches were, what the size of the fire on the beach meant, signals the boats sent to identify themselves and assure those on the beach all was on the up and up. The boats even had signals for what "merchandise" they wanted. Harrison also told what he knew about the trade on the other side of SA. He brought out the journals he had buried in another cave, and the three men spent hours going over all the information.

Once they had all the information they could glean from Darryl, they took him into the cave where Harry was still hanging. "Darryl, cut Harry down and drag him out of the cave. You've been very helpful; you'll die a quick death." Darryl shook as he cut Harry down and dragged him out of the cave. Then he marched back into the cave and accepted the handcuffs that were re-fastened around his wrists. Sam and Daniel suspended Darryl in Harry's place.

"Darryl, how could you ever do what you did to those girls? You don't need to answer; but I want you to think of each one of them and their suffering as you suffer. We lied to you about killing you quickly; your death will be slow and painful. I even wish we had more time. I wish we could make it last for a week, a month, a year – just as the suffering of the girls you sold goes on and on." Then Daniel took out his fillet knife and began to skin Darryl alive as Sam brought salty seawater to throw on the fresh cuts. It took Darryl twelve hours to die – twelve excruciating hours.

Then they cut him down. Daniel tied ropes to the ankles of both bodies and bagged the rest of the bloody mess as Sam swam back to his boat to retrieve it. He didn't take the 19-foot catboat; they would leave that to Sophia. Besides, he needed a good workout to release his tension, so the two-mile swim was just perfect. Daniel wrote a note for Sophia and put it on the catboat. "Sophia, this boat is now yours, along with everything in the cave with the big red X spray-painted on it. Sell it or use it. Thank you!"

When Sam returned with his boat, they loaded up their maps and notes, made sure they cleaned up and had all their gear, and set out. They just cruised, going nowhere as they dragged the men behind, trolling until they found a school of sharks. Once the feeding frenzy was over, they cut the ropes and headed back to St. Maarten. Sam dropped Daniel off with two knapsacks of detailed information, maps and $200,000 in euros and US currency. Then Sam motored off into the shadows, waiting for the next time he would be needed, which he knew would be soon.

Chapter 19

After the news conference, and when the wall was scrubbed clean of their name, the group picked up a couple of trays of chicken and ribs for an early supper. Margaret had stayed back with the girls and was ready with a pan of rice and peas warming in the oven, and beers and lemonade in the cooler.

The group was especially happy and animated. Everybody agreed that the news conference had gone well, especially the way Marie had handled the reporter. They were satisfied with their first press conference, and they had new leads to follow. Cédric and the others were cautiously optimistic and excited that things were getting ready to move forward. The group had finally met someone who actually knew José Zavaia: Sophia Harrison. And it was obvious that John and Alma, fresh from their boat trip to visit with Sophia over on St. Barth's, were bursting with good news.

Over supper, John and Alma were eager to report everything that had taken place on St. Barth's. They delayed a bit, however, until Juliana, who was off to the side drawing a picture she called *"Jesus Healing the Leper,"* which she wanted to give to Pastor Eboune this coming Sunday. She liked drawing pictures for the church. Finally, Juliana finished her picture and after the adults expressed their admiration for her work, they shooed her outside to join the other children in the yard.

Alma told the group she believed they had a very strong ally in Sophia Harrison. She told the story of their welcome from Sophia and everything that had transpired, including Sam's appearance, and Sam and Daniel's decision to follow up the new lead and look up Harry Crane. John added some details, describing the lobster and chocolate mousse dinner Sophia had fed them, but he seemed relieved to let Alma tell the story.

The truth was, John felt guilty that he hadn't fought harder to go with Daniel. He was ashamed that when Sam showed up, he felt relief, knowing he wouldn't have to go with Daniel to interview Harry Crane. Yet he knew that Daniel and Sam were better able to complete that work without him.

Though Daniel and John were best friends, they both knew they had one big difference in their personalities. John had known, ever since their childhood, that a distorted rage lived within Daniel. He really didn't want to see or experience Daniel's darker side; it scared him. Once, when they were in middle school, a bully was having fun showing off to his friends by humiliating Daniel and John. That day, John was introduced to Daniel's darker side in action. John was scared, but Daniel showed no fright. When the bully turned to laugh with his friends, Daniel picked up a two-by-four and smashed it across the bully's face. As he fell, Daniel jumped on top of him and began methodically hitting the young man's face. Daniel seemed to go into some strange trance. There was a crazed, devilish smile on

Daniel's face. He kept up the hitting until John and two others pulled Daniel off the nearly unconscious bully. Everyone present knew Daniel wouldn't have stopped if he hadn't been pulled off.

The next day, Daniel had said to John, "Thank you for getting me off him. I would've killed him. I was out of control. John there is something bad inside me. Pray for me, my friend." John never responded, but he knew what Daniel was saying was true, and he always included Daniel in his prayers. After that day, the bully stopped his bullying, and always gave Daniel a wide berth.

As the rest of the group speculated over the supper table, they knew from Gloria's account of Daniel's brief phone call that Sam and Daniel were likely still over on La Tortue extracting and recording information from Jose's celebrity customer and one of his actual crew. They knew that when the men returned and shared what they had learned, this would be the turning point. Finally, they had momentum; they would be ready to start the hunt in earnest.

Until now, they had just a name, a mission, and a few new well-loved daughters. But now, the ghost figure of the avenger was taking shape. Cédric was especially happy to hear about the support from Sophia, and the way people responded so positively to hearing they were from Saint Martin and part of Sanctuary. He was glad the movement was being noticed, and that most the people on the islands seemed to approve. His dream was to have chapters of Sanctuary on all the islands in the Caribbean. It was looking like one could be established soon on St. Barth's. A nice place to start.

Two days later, a young man came walking up the hill. "I'd like to speak to somebody connected with the Sanctuary movement. My name is Oscar. I'm from St. Barth's. Sophia sent me." He told Marie he would like to hear the story of Cédric finding the slave ship.

Marie walked the young man to and into the graveyard. As they walked around, he touched the chains that doomed the girls. As Marie began the story, she was surprised how much of it the young man already knew. He could have told it as well as her. Marie learned that 21-year-old Oscar was Sophia's cousin. "I'm so proud that my cousin is helping Sanctuary, and when she picked me to deliver this package… well, you have no idea how excited I was," he stated. "I want you to know there's many of us that totally support you. I am a descendent of Marie-Francoise, the last slave on St. Barthelemy. She was granted her freedom on October 8, 1847, along with seven other slaves."

Marie offered Oscar some lemonade and lemon poppy seed bread, and they sat down to talk. Marie opened the envelope and found inside it a picture and a note from Sophia.

> I was at a little neighborhood bar yesterday, The Shangri-La. Behind the bar was a picture of my ex-husband Darryl with another man. The man sitting next to him is José Zavaia. It was probably taken after they had dropped off a young girl to that actor Harry. I hope it's helpful. At least you now know what the devil looks like. Any of you are always welcome at my home. For our ancestors, for our children.
> Your friend and ally,
> Sophia

"Oh, sweet Oscar, what a wonderful gift! You must stay for supper and meet the rest of us," Marie said as she reached across the table and squeezed his hand.

"You're so excited. What is it?" Oscar asked.

"Your cousin is providing us with a vital piece of information we didn't have before. It's a picture of the slaver who, in all likelihood, piloted the slave ship that carried my daughters to their death. We now have a picture of the devil." She handed the photo to Oscar, José's image already etched in her mind forever.

Oscar stared at it, trying to remember whether he'd ever seen the man. Nothing came to mind. The two went together down to the PhotoMax store and had twenty-five copies made of the picture. They now had a photo they could show people as they sought to gather information about the man. On the way back to Sanctuary, Marie and Oscar stopped by the old fisherman's house, and he confirmed that it was the man in the photo who had taken his boat the day after Hurricane Irma.

That night at supper, photos were handed out to everyone. There was a strange few moments of silence as they all sat staring at the picture of José Zavaia. They had all expected him to look like a monster; but in reality, he looked like somebody you might pass by in a restaurant thinking nothing of him except maybe that he used a little bit too much grease in his hair.

Oscar sat proudly. Clearly the information he brought over was extremely important.

Cédric put his copy of the photo on the table. Looking at Oscar, he asked, "Young man, tell us what the locals of St.

Barth's are saying about Sanctuary. Are we making a difference?"

Oscar was nervous. Here he was speaking with members of Sanctuary, and now the founder was asking for his input. He took a sip of lemonade, for his mouth was instantly dry. "Mr. Cédric…." The group laughed.

"Cédric, Oscar, please, just Cédric."

"Cédric, it's strange, but all of this has awoken something ancient – an ancient resilience almost unknown until now – inside the hearts of us locals. Being a descendent of a slave now means something to be proud of, and it's as if the ancestors are offering us a challenge. I swear that the singing at Sunday and Wednesday church – though it's always been good – is louder and more soulful than I've ever heard it before.

"Last week I found a picture of Marie-Francoise in my old history book. She was the last slave emancipated on St. Barth's. As I was telling Marie, I am descended from her. I framed the picture and put it on the wall. There's lots of talk not just of Sanctuary but of our past, of our ancestors. I saw how beautiful the flowers on the graves in SANCTUARY, but you should know that recently our graveyards have more flowers in them, too. Our ancients are speaking to us. Many, especially the old ones, speak of a feeling that the spirits of our ancestors – of our history – are awake and walking the island. It as if our ancient past and our present lives are standing together, gazing at each other as equals. We're not only talking about the suffering that our relatives must have gone through; we're also talking about how our heritage is one of taking suffering and transforming it into dignity, spirituality and community. It's almost as if we can hear our ancestors demanding that we do something. That's why I was so excited when Sophia asked me to bring you this envelope. I was doing something, and it felt good." Cédric and the others knew **exactly** what Oscar was talking about; the same type of thing was happening on Saint Martin.

"Oscar, we're going to need good men. The time is coming to take the fight to the slavers. Do you believe there are any young men like yourself who would be willing to go with us? We're starting to put a list together of those who might be willing to fight for the cause."

"Paper, please." Alma gave him a sheet of paper, and Oscar wrote. "Cédric, here's a list of eight. My name's on top. They are my dearest friends. I know they would be honored to help in any way, to do what the cause asks of them. They're from my childhood soccer team. All eight are good men. Hell, there will probably be a lot more. Do you want me to ask around and recruit for you? I'd be glad to do this!"

"Talk with your friends, but talk with them individually, so there's no group pressure. This is an important personal decision, and there's no shame if a person says 'No.' Then if they are willing, have them call us. One of us with military training may come over to start training you, depending on the numbers, or we may have you come stay here. We haven't decided yet. We want to have a core militia of around seventy. But please, talk about it and emphasize the dangers. These are not nice people we are dealing with; nothing is sacred to them except money and their own survival. If you come with us, you'll be putting your life on the line; some of us will die. It would be naïve for any of us to think otherwise. When an animal gets cornered, that's when it's most dangerous. Sacrifices must be made and paid most often with blood.

Chapter 20

The next day, Cédric went to the fruit stand with a rotten pineapple. Inside it was a note and the picture.

> "Is this the man? Do you recognize him? We been told it's José Zavaia."

Three days later, the flag was flying high at *El Capitan*. Cédric went for a walk and came back with a note from Dominique:

> Dear friend,
> I'm sorry. I should've replied to you sooner, but when I saw the picture I was sent back to that night on the beach. I've been in bed the last two days shaking, with Alfred in the room with me offering protection. Yes, it is him. Let me say it, "This is the man

who raped me, who stole my innocence, who started me on my trek through hell. I had hoped to never see his face again, unless I was standing over his dead body with a knife in my hand. Yes, it's him. Hunt him, kill him, a thousand times a thousand. Send him to hell."

Cédric noticed that the paper was spotted, most likely from Dominique's tears falling as she wrote the note. Her wounds had been torn open again, her child's heart was bleeding again.

Cédric's insides ached. He wanted to go to *El Capitan* and comfort Dominique. He knew he had no idea of the suffering she was reliving. He hated feeling powerless. He was glad that Alfred was there for her; he knew that Alfred could comfort her. He so wished that Dominique's daughters could know about their mother; they would be so proud. Instead, all he could do was secretly promise her vengeance would be served.

Cédric felt so powerless. He needed something to do, so he went back into SANCTUARY and knelt next to the grave of Tammy. He whispered Dominique's story to her. "Your sister in misery is helping us. She will help us get justice. Help us, please! Be with us and guide us. We need you and your sisters to talk with God, ask him to help us be true to our resolve and what lies ahead. It is your turn to carry us. I don't even really know you, and yet I miss you so much. How I long to meet you someday, my dear daughter. But for now, please be with your sister in misery, Dominique, if you can. Bring her comfort, watch over her. In God's name, I pray."

Cédric kept talking to Tammy as he went about the graveyard picking at the weeds that were ever present. Daniella came up to him. "Dad, is there anything I can do? I can tell from the way you're wandering around the graves that you're deeply troubled. You've been talking to her again, haven't you?"

"Yes, sweetie, I have."

"You can talk to me, you know."

"I know, sweetie, I know. This may not make sense to you, but sometimes I find comfort and a kind of peace just sitting with your dead sisters."

"I get the same comfort, Dad, and I've never met any of them, either. You might think I'm crazy, but sometimes they whisper and talk with me. Sometimes we laugh together, sometimes we cry together."

"What do they say?"

"You may not want to hear it, Dad, but they tell me their stories. They tell me how they were taken from their homes, sold by parents who didn't really care. I know what happened that night on the beach with the one you call Tammy; she's told me what they did to her." Cédric sat in horror.

"Oh, my God! Honey, I'm sorry that I brought so much pain to our home."

"Don't be. I love my sisters. So, what if we do cry together sometimes? They listen to me and offer me comfort, too. You know I'm afraid. I know you're going to be hunting and finding the men who did this to them. That means you'll be in great

152

danger. It means I could lose you. They promise me they will watch after you. Tammy was so happy it was you who carried her up from the ship. She told me how you stroked her hair and kissed the top of her head like you do mine when you put me to bed. After that, she wasn't scared anymore. None of them are scared anymore, you need to know that. These are things we sisters talk about."

Cédric sat stunned. His daughter really was talking with the girls. "How long have you been talking with them?"

"Since the first night. Remember how I went out there and just sat for a long time? We've been talking ever since then. You know how some nights, even when the winds are still, the shackles clatter? That means they want me to come visit with them."

"Do you know their names?"

Daniella laughed. "We play games. One of them is that they're not going to tell me their names until he's gone, and until a girl named 'Kitty' joins them."

A chill ran up and down Cédric's spine. He had never felt so cold in all his life, even though it was ninety degrees out. "Kitty? Who's this Kitty?"

Daniella smiled at him. "She's a sister — an older sister – to all of them. She's a friend of yours. They really like how much you care about her. She's helping you. They won't tell me her name, but I think I know who it is. I haven't mentioned this to anyone else, and I will keep your secret."

"Is Kitty going to die?"

Daniella's voice got quite sad. "I don't know. Daddy, I truly don't know, but I think so. I don't know if that's what they mean, or if they mean that she'll come to visit SANCTUARY. She's not been here yet, but you know that."

"Oh my God, honey, you're too young for all of this."

"No, Dad, they are the ones who were too young. But not to worry. You know how everybody feels peaceful when they come to SANCTUARY? It's because they bless everyone who walks through the gates, especially the little children whose spirits they play with. They all feel peace now, some of them for the first time. And they offer that peace to all of good heart who come to the SANCTUARY. You need to remember that I'm their older sister just like I'm Juliana's, Monique's and Mirabella's. Dad, I really like being an older sister; it's a lot of responsibility, but it's really cool. Come on; let's go get something to eat. I'm hungry."

Daniella took Cédric's hand, for he was in shock, and led him outside of the graveyard.

"Oh, and don't tell Mom any of this. I'll tell her later, when she's ready, but right now it would scare her too much. She can be a little bit overprotective. We're both good at keeping secrets; this will be our secret. Okay? Dad, okay?"

Still in shock, Cédric agreed.

He stopped and looked down at his daughter. "Sweetie, before we go, please do something for me. Tell them I love them."

"They know Dad; they know." Daniella kept walking her father toward the house.

Chapter 21

A few days later, Daniel was back from La Tortue and St. Barth's. Everyone, especially John, was happy to see him. "Are you okay, my friend?" John asked.

Daniel had loved John throughout his childhood. John had always been there for Daniel, especially during the tough times, though he **didn't have any idea** or ask any questions about what was happening in Daniel's home life. It was John who was stood next to Daniel at Daniel's father's funeral after he had died of cancer. Daniel loved John even more after the incident with the bully. John had seen Daniel's darkness, what he was capable of, and still, he clung to Daniel as a best friend.

"I'm good, my brother, I'm good—we did what had to be done, and you won't believe all the information they gave us. The gentlemen sang like songbirds after a heavy rain when the sun and rainbows come back out." Daniel patted his friend on the side of his face the familiar way they always had done. "Come, let's get the others together so we can all go over the treasure trove of information we now have. We have so much to do, and I want to stop at *Carrefour* and get some things."

That night they all gathered, but instead of barbecued ribs, Daniel brought over ribeye steaks for everyone. "Compliments of that actor Harry Crane. He also has donated $195,000 to our war chest – perversion tax, as Sam calls it. Actually, it was $223,000; we gave $23,000 to his fifteen-year-old housekeeper to start her new life, and $5000 to Sophia for everything she did for us." Daniel didn't yet know that Sophia had provided a picture of José Zavaia. As he was putting the money in the center of the table, Rasmus tossed the picture of José Zavaia and Darryl Harrison on the table in front of Daniel. Daniel recognized Darryl, as he had skinned him alive not more than thirty-six hours ago. "Who is he?" he asked, pointing at the other man.

"José Zavaia," Margaret said. "He is the devil! Sophia sent a young man – Oscar – over with it the day after John and Alma got home."

"Has it been confirmed? I don't see any tattoo."

"It's been confirmed, totally confirmed. You can't see the tattoo because his arm is around that other fellow, but we know for sure that's José Zavaia." Cédric added, "Daniel, do you know where Sam is? He could be quite useful in helping us plan our strategies."

"He said he's gone to get a couple of his friends and some special equipment, and that he'll be back before he's needed. He has perfect confidence that we can plan what needs to be done better than he can."

The food was ready, and as they sat to eat the steaks and Margaret's special Jamaican rice and peas, all was quiet, a sign of how good the food was. They decided they would develop a list of tasks that needed to be done.

"Before we do that, let us celebrate Juliana's birthday. I've got cake and presents for her. We'll tell her they're from all of us."

Thomas spoke up. "How do you know it's her birthday?"

"I don't, but Pastor Eboune and Marylin think it would be a good idea if each of the girls has a birthday a couple of months apart from each other."

"That's not a good idea. That's a *great* idea!" Rachelle said. "Let me get my guitar from the car and I'll play when we sing *Happy Birthday*. She disappeared down the hill.

Fifteen minutes later, the girls had joined them, and they were all sitting around the table, Rachelle strumming on her guitar and everyone singing the Birthday Song. Juliana smiled, staring with delight at the cake and the candles. Daniella was yelling, "Blow out the candles!"

"Why? They're so pretty."

"That's what you do. You make a wish, and then you blow out the candles. And if you can blow all of them out in one breath, your wish will come true."

Margaret saw Juliana's confusion and rubbed her cheek, asking, "You've never had a birthday party before, have you?"

"No, but I like it."

"Okay, here's what we're going to do. We're going to sing Happy Birthday again, even though that means we have to listen to Rasmus sing again!" Everyone laughed except Rasmus, who pretended to pout. "Next, you're going to make a wish and blow out the candles. Then we're going to eat cake and ice cream. And *then*, you get presents!"

Juliana's eyes lit up. "Presents too?"

"Yes, presents! Even your sisters each get one."

They all sang, with Rasmus singing especially loud and off key. Then Juliana leaned in toward the candles with the wish, "I wish that my mother is safe." Finally, Juliana blew out her twelve candles. "How did you know it was my birthday?" She asked, looking at Marie.

"Mothers just know these things."

"Do you know when our birthdays are?" Monique and Mirabella excitedly asked.

"Absolutely, sweeties, absolutely! Monique, yours is two months after Daniella's, on September 20th. Mirabella, yours is December 17th." Marie got the calendar from the kitchen and showed them where she had written in each girl's birthday. To the girls, it was official when they saw their names followed with the word *birthday* on the calendar.

Juliana loved her sketchbook and new set of colored pencils; she had almost used up her old ones. She also got a pretty new church dress, as did each of the girls. "This Sunday, you'll need to stand up in church and thank the church ladies. They made your dresses." The girls nodded as they headed for one of the bedrooms to try them on.

It was around ten o'clock that night when the girls finally headed for bed. As Cédric bent down and kissed Daniella on the forehead, she smiled at him. "It was a nice party! I'm glad they all have birthdays now, but what about my other sisters up in SANCTUARY?"

"How about we make the day I found them their birthday – all of their birthdays? We could have a big party each year on October 6th. It was one month to the day after the hurricane that I found your sisters."

"I'd like that," Daniella responded. "I'm sure Juliana, Monique and Mirabella will like that, too."

Cédric started to leave when Daniella asked, "How about another kiss on my forehead – this one for Tammy?" Each night after that, Cédric planted seventeen kisses on her forehead.

The next day as the girls went off to school, the ten adults gathered with maps and a flipchart in front of them, and Daniel taught and showed them the information he had received from Harry Crane and Darryl Harrison.

Chapter 22

The group decided to put the $195,000 perversion tax from Crane into the safety deposit box at the bank. Everyone knew it would be needed later. They were all surprised at the support coming in from people. Churches from around the island that had donated money for the additions onto the house were still dropping off small donations and foodstuffs. Twenty-four donated chickens roamed the property. Most of the time, the donations were small enough they went into the petty cash cookie jar in the kitchen. Anyone could take from it when there was a need concerning Sanctuary.

They all felt a new level of tension in the air; the time was fast approaching for taking the fight to the traffickers. Detailed maps of the northern end of South America hung in the large room built as a playroom for the girls; now, it was serving as a strategy center. They also hung detailed navigational maps for that area and for the area around Puerto Rico.

Gloria and Margaret, both detail people, were going over all of it with a fine-tooth comb – every bit of the information gathered by Daniel and Sam's "interviews" with Harry Crane and Darryl Harrison. As information came together about a town or region, they peppered the map with Post-it notes.

John and Daniel, chosen because they both spoke near-perfect Spanish and were excellent sailors, set off in an easily borrowed sailboat. The owner told them, "Use it as long as you need it." Their journey was to study shorelines, investigate and become familiar with the routes the sex traffickers were using.

Rasmus accompanied them; he spoke a bit of Portuguese he had learned when he worked in a magnesium mine in Brazil for two years when he was in his teens. Because of this and his ability to fit in anywhere, he would be dropped off in areas where suspected trafficking took place. Rasmus would be their recon man, gathering information about the areas and people. Rasmus could fit in at a high-society meeting or at the grungiest alcoholic bar; he was a true chameleon.

They figured they would do their first reconnaissance in the area of Macapa, Brazil. Darryl had talked about this area as a place to get jungle girls. It was not far from the mouth of the Amazon, sitting at the edge of the jungle. This was a favorite area for José Zavaia. Next, they would sail northwards towards French Guiana, looking for the beaches where Zavaia traded money for young girls. Once they arrived at Macapa, they dropped Rasmus off at the northern edge of town, the one closest to the jungle, to see what he could find out.

That afternoon, Rasmus found a bar on the outskirts of the jungle frequented by miners, ranchers and loggers, all of whom are eyeing the lands of the indigenous people. To him, it seemed like the perfect place, so he hung out there. His hunch turned out to be right. After a couple of days, he fit in well, and he was hearing all the racist rhetoric the roughnecks were using about the indigenous natives who lived not far away in the jungle. The rich jungle: rich in gold, magnesium, iron and copper. The talk ran to mining, and to burning the jungle and clearing land to create fields great for cattle grazing.

One of the guys who frequented the bar, a man named Garcia Bolson, took a liking to Rasmus. He found Ramus's broken Portuguese funny; they would sit at the bar and laugh and talk for hours. After a couple of days, Rasmus figured it was time to test the waters, so one night he said to Garcia, "My friend, I'm in need of a woman. How about you? I've had a good month and have a little extra money, so if you know a good place, it'll be my treat. My Portuguese isn't good enough for me to find a brothel and get a crazy-good woman, so I'll want your help. I don't want to end up at some disease-riddled whorehouse with used-up women who just lie there. I want the young pretty ones, who know how to move." Rasmus made some movement with his hips and they both laughed.

Garcia smiled. "Oh, my friend, you're generous! It's been a while since I've had a woman. I know of several good places where the women are beautiful and know how to bring some excitement. Oh my god, they will pleasure you in ways that will make your head spin; both of them."

Rasmus slapped him on the back. "My friend, you know exactly the type of place I'm looking for. I must tell you I like them young."

"You dirty old man!" Garcia said, laughing. "I know just the place. They round up girls from the reservation and bring them to work at the brothel. We can get you a nice young girl there since you're a dirty old man. Or, if you're a really sick bastard, I can take you to a place where we can get you a young girl not more than a year or two off her mother's tit."

"No, no. I'm not a sick bastard, but really you know places like that?"

"Oh, hell yes! There are two brothels not far off, in the rain forest territories, who specialize in the very, very young – girls and boys. We have an old priest in our area who goes out there often. We also have tourists coming in from Europe and the US who like them right around five or six years old. In my last job, I delivered beer, and these places were on my route. There were three or four bars in the center of the village where the tourists make their deals with the pimps. Those tourists are so excited and nervous they drink a lot of beer while they hang around waiting for their turns. One day when I was making a delivery, I watched some fat old slob deal with one of the pimps, who signaled to a lady standing in front of a hut. She brought out a young native girl who couldn't have been more than five years old, dressed in a T-shirt with the word *Sexy* on it and a skirt so short you could tell she wasn't wearing panties. She rubbed the old man's leg. The fat old tourist handed the pimp money, then the little girl led the fat guy back into the little hut. They can buy them by the day or by the half-day. I'm glad you don't want to go there. We can go to a good place to get you a nice sixteen- or seventeen-year-old."

"Jesus Christ, I've heard of places like that, but I didn't really know they really existed. I've heard of places that even sell girls so you can have your own sex slave."

"This place I was telling you about would be one of them. I know they sell to traffickers who come by in boats every few months. The pimps who own the girls have guys who hunt up and down the Amazon looking for young and pretty ones. They either raid a village and take what they want or buy girls or a boy or two from poor parents, or from warriors who have raided other villages. They then bring them back here. Some they keep, so they always have fresh stock for the tourists. The rest they sell to the traffickers."

"My God, why don't the police stop them? Stupid question; I'm sure they pay off the police."

"Absolutely. They pay them well with money and girls. And if anyone crosses them, they're ruthless. I once had a friend who stood up to one of them who hit a woman in the face. They killed him, his wife, and took their three daughters and sold them to the traffickers. They are soulless creatures, but they are also some of the wealthiest men around here; these folks who come from America and Europe pay lots of money in hard currency or gold."

"It would be interesting to see one of those places."

"If you go out there, you better buy a girl and take her to one of the huts, or you might not be coming back. They don't trust strangers. The tourists are always accompanied by a local who vouches for them. Adao over there," Garcia pointed to a man drinking alone in the corner. "He's one of the locals who works with travel agents who set up these sex trips and takes these perverts out there. Everybody gets their cut. I was just out there delivering beer, so I was different, but if someone came asking about the girls but not willing to be with one, they would assume it's the police, and send the girls into the jungle until it would be safe to start up again. They're not dumb people, just soulless creatures."

Rasmus made a mental note about Adao and memorized his features, thinking he might be a good man for Daniel to interview to learn more about these travel agents and the whole set-up.

After using the outhouse, they headed out to the brothel. Rasmus picked out a **pretty** young seventeen-year-old who spoke Spanish. He followed her into the room, then he told her he wanted her to lie on the bed and make sounds as if they were having sex. He asked her not to tell anyone that they didn't have sex; he'd pay her extra under the table if she would do this. It was no problem for her – easy money. She rolled around on the bed making noises as if she was enjoying her client, and then Rasmus made noises that signaled he had finished.

He paid her fee to give to the madam, along with an extra $20 bill US currency, which made her eyes pop out. She put it in her panties to keep it secret and then kiddingly said, "You were really good. Come back anytime." They waited another 10 minutes, then walked out to the lobby, the girl with her arm around Rasmus, who looked **quite** satisfied. They walked to the bar and the girl handed over her earnings. Garcia was already done, sitting at a table drinking a beer, with the girl he had chosen sitting on his lap. Rasmus sat down and ordered a beer. The young girl he had been with sat on his lap and put her head on his shoulder. "You wore me out, you crazy man, you!"

Garcia laughed, "You two were going nuts in there!"

"Hey, like I said, it'd been a long time, and I wanted my money's worth! And you must admit, she's very pretty and sweet."

"That she is, my friend, that she is." Rasmus and Garcia sat talking while they drank their beers. Then they shared cheek kisses with the girls and headed out.

The next day, Rasmus was back on the boat with Daniel and John. They shared information and ideas for possible strategies, writing everything down. Then they called Cédric and John did most of the talking as they filled him in. They all decided that trio would sail north up the coast, taking the time to learn anything and everything that might be helpful.

As they reached the coast up towards French Guiana, they watched carefully and found a location that Darryl had described: a small beach area where bonfires had been held, with a hut off to the side. They marked this location on the map, then continued up to another area in French Guiana that Darryl had talked about, just north of Kourou.

They used the same plan as before. Rasmus left the boat and unobtrusively scoured the environment for anyone who seemed like they might have information. He had no luck this time, but they did find the beach with the small hut and area where a signal fire had been used. There were some bloody rags in the hut. They also noticed there were three areas surrounding the beach, back about 15 yards into the jungle, where the vegetation was trampled down and cigarette butts were strewn around. They assumed this was where the traffickers posted their security men.

They left French Guiana and headed up to Suriname to an area about a hundred miles south of Paramaribo and the same distance north of Mana, French Guiana. Darryl had always smiled when he talked about this area; it was always easy to purchase girls in Suriname because of the poverty.

Eventually, they came to a long beach area where they could see there had been a big bonfire, but there were also lots of people on the beach. It appeared to be market day. They anchored, and all three men got in the sailboat's dinghy to explore the place and restock needed supplies. Pulling up on the shore, they were quickly met by people selling all types of items from carvings to trinkets and weavings.

They found some folks who spoke English, not just the official Dutch language, and asked where they could get supplies. They were directed to a vendor who had the rice and peas they needed. As they stood there, a woman who looked to be around thirty-five walked up to them with her arm around a girl who looked to be twelve years old at most. The vendor shook his head, indicating she should move on. She addressed them in Dutch, which none knew, while pointing to the girl. The vendor explained, "She's wondering if you'd like to spend some time with her daughter."

John, Daniel and Rasmus said nothing. The woman pulled up her daughter's shirt, showing she had little buds for breasts, and they were bruised. The woman was frantically saying something else. The man said, "She's telling you she's becoming a woman, so you'll enjoy her very much."

Daniel's insides were going crazy, remembering his own abuse as a child, remembering his father giving him over to a friend. Daniel had an instant urge to cut the woman's throat, but instead, he said, "Will you sell her, so we can keep her on our boat?" John and Rasmus said nothing.

The woman looked surprised and then she smiled. Now speaking English, she asked, "How much will you give me for her?"

Daniel looked her in the eyes. "How much do you want for her?"

The woman studied him, trying to figure out how much she could get. "Nine hundred dollars."

Daniel waved her away and turned to walk away with their food purchase. "You insult me, old woman! You insult me!"

They had walked about fifty feet, the woman following and dragging her daughter along. Finally, she asked, "Okay, okay. How much will you give me for her?"

"Is she a virgin? She sure doesn't look to be."

"She's only been used a few times. Only a few times. She's still very fresh."

Daniel put a look of disgust on his face. "Four hundred dollars. Not a penny more." Daniel stared directly into the older woman's eyes, looking right through her; she could tell he meant business. "Look at us. We're three big men; in two weeks, she'll be no use to us anymore. You want us to pay nine hundred dollars for something used that will only last us two weeks. Do you think I'm a fool? Four hundred dollars. Not a penny more!"

He turned to walk away again. He wasn't even ten feet away when the mother, knowing he meant business, responded, "Okay, okay, you can have her for four hundred dollars! She's not that well-behaved; I'll be glad to get rid of her. You boys can have fun with her, then she can cook for you and keep your boat clean. That's a good deal!"

Daniel pulled out four hundred dollars and gave it to the woman, who then let go of her daughter's hand. Daniel reached out and grabbed it. The young girl offered no resistance; it was clear she had been through this before.

As they were walking away, Daniel turned around and yelled at the woman, "What's your daughter's name?"

The woman yelled out, "Esperanza! It means…"

Daniel yelled back to her, "I know what it means — HOPE."

John and Rasmus carried the supplies, and Daniel gently held the young girl's hand on the way back to the landing. They loaded up the dinghy and motored back to the sailboat. Sitting next to Esperanza, Daniel stared into her frightened, sad eyes and frantically kept saying out loud, "You're safe now. You're safe now! It's over." John and Rasmus both knew, from being present that night when Daniel had told his secret to the group, that Daniel was speaking not just to Esperanza, but also to himself. The young girl was changing Daniel; all of them knew it except Esperanza.

Once back on the boat and sailing away, Esperanza sat still, not even looking back at the island or out to sea. She sat quietly, her hands folded on her lap, looking at the boat's sail, waiting, assuming that soon she would be taken inside the boat and be made to do all those things her mother had let the men do to her in their home. Her mother's last words still rang in her ears, "Give them what they want; they'll treat you better." There was no *Goodbye*, no *I love you*, no *I'll miss you*, just a "Give them what they want" as she counted her money. Esperanza had no idea that she had been sold into freedom.

John moved closer to Daniel. "You saved one, my friend, you saved one! And we'll save many more. Good call, Daniel! I'm proud of you."

Turning to face John, Daniel was crying. "There's so many, John; there's so many. And that woman will probably go back to her village, get pregnant, have another little girl and be on the beach again in seven or eight years selling her. For God's sake! She sold her daughter to be a sex slave for four hundred dollars!"

John hugged his friend, "Yes. But today, there's one less slave because of you."

That night the men all slept on the deck, letting Esperanza sleep in the bed below deck. In the morning, Ramus fixed a big breakfast of fried pork, beans and eggs. The group made three more stops on the beaches of Suriname, gathering information that proved to be easy to obtain for a small price. They expected to find people selling children at each of the stops, but there was no trade happening. The group learned there were certain times of the month that people knew when the traffickers would be there, right around the times when there was a full moon and when there was a new moon. They were a week behind the traffickers. They figured that the mother they bought Esperanza from was just down on the beach getting supplies and saw the three strangers as an opportunity just to make some quick cash.

Esperanza became more comfortable as the days went by. She soon realized that the men did not want her in ways that other men had wanted her. She would often now sit next to Daniel as they ate meals, or at night when they would watch the skies, looking for shooting stars. As their exploratory voyage continued, the men delighted in teaching Esperanza some English. She already knew just a little from listening to her mother. They told her they'd be taking her to a place called Sanctuary where she would have sisters and would be safe. They all agreed that somehow Esperanza understood what they were saying, for the more they talked about Sanctuary, the more she smiled and came alive.

John, Ramus and Daniel were gone for a little over two months. As they returned to Saint Martin, they felt satisfied. They had everything they needed to make a real difference — *plus* a new sister for the girls, or a daughter for Daniel and Gloria.

Chapter 23

They were about three miles away from Saint Martin when Daniel tapped Esperanza's shoulder, lifted her up, stood her on the seat, stood behind her and pointed toward Saint Martin. "Home!"

Esperanza looked back at him with raised eyebrows. Daniel pointed again at Saint Martin, then tapped his chest. "Home!" She smiled.

She looked at the island, then she pointed at it, tapped her chest, and looked at Daniel questioning, "Esperanza's home?" Daniel nodded, smiling, letting her know this would now be her new home. She looked at Daniel with a mixture of hope and fear in her eyes and questioning in her voice. "With you?" Daniel nodded. Esperanza smiled, put her arm around him, and snuggled into Daniel, saying, "Good with you."

Daniel had talked with Gloria about it on the way home. If Esperanza wanted to live at Sanctuary with sisters, that would be her home; but if she wanted to live with them, they would raise her as their daughter. They were childless by choice, but the young girl had **already** worked her way into Daniel's heart, and he was sure that Gloria would love her too. Daniel had never wanted to be a father. He **was afraid of** his background, the darkness that lived inside; he was always afraid maybe he would be as horrible a father as his own father had been. All that melted away in Suriname when Esperanza grabbed his hand as they walked down the beach towards the dinghy and her new life.

As the sailboat pulled up to the dock, Cédric and Marie were there to greet them. Gloria was also there, her body shaking with nervousness and excitement – two sides of the same coin. A tear came to her eye when she saw Daniel. He looked eager to disembark with an excited Esperanza, wide-eyed, trying to take everything in while also calming herself by gripping Daniel's hand. Cédric and Marie stood back a bit as Daniel picked Esperanza up and placed her on the dock. Then he got off the boat, grabbed her hand, and walked up to Gloria. He bent over so he was eye level with Esperanza. "This is Gloria, my wife."

Gloria also got down, kneeling so she looked up into Esperanza's face. "Hi, honey," she said, with tears running down her cheeks. "You're so beautiful."

Esperanza looked back and forth at Daniel and Gloria. Then she pointed at Daniel, and then pointed at Gloria. In her own way, she was asking if they were together. Daniel nodded, letting her know that she understood correctly. She did this a couple of times. Each time Daniel smiled and nodded. Esperanza surprised them when she pointed at Daniel, then pointed at Gloria, and then pointed at herself. Both Daniel and Gloria nodded excitedly with joy shining in their faces. "Yes, honey, yes! Oh, God, yes!"

Gloria said through her tears of joy. Esperanza smiled. At that moment, a new family was born.

Daniel and Gloria stood up and each stretched out a hand, and Esperanza joined hands with them. John and Rasmus, who had been hanging back watching the meeting, climbed off the boat and shooed the trio down the dock to where Cédric and Marie waited. Hugs and greetings erupted, and Marie gave Esperanza a doll, explaining, "This is from my daughters. They can't wait to meet you!"

Marilyn had suggested this would be enough greetings for Esperanza's first day, not wanting to overwhelm her. Daniel, Gloria and their new daughter left to take Esperanza to see her new home. The three could have a couple of days together before meeting the rest of the group.

Throughout the week, John and Rasmus worked with Margaret, adding all the new information they had gathered on their trip to what they had already learned from the torturous but informative interviews Sam and Daniel had conducted. They now had somewhat detailed information on twelve beach sites where the exchange of children for money regularly took place.

They posted pictures they had gather on their surveillance trip so everyone who would be in on the assaults could become familiar with their targets. Cédric spent hours upon hours studying and planning. They would be chasing two boats. One was owned by José and captained by Roberto Rodriguez, and the group still did not have any photo or alternative way to identify Roberto. The second boat would be captained by José Zavaia himself, whose picture hung in the top left-hand corner on the large sheet of plywood that had stapled to it a large map showing the routes of the sex traffickers. When Cédric became tired, he just looked at the picture of José Zavaia, and his insides would stir with hate, giving him the energy to stay on task.

It was decided that they would intercept the boat *Morning Dew* – which, if all their intelligence was correct, would be manned by José Zavaia – right after it picked up the usual load of cocaine at a place in northern Venezuela, on the north end of a small peninsula. The Colombians always hooked up with José or Roberto on a beach halfway between Punto Fijo and Pueblo Nuevo, where the sex traffickers would pick up the cocaine to be delivered to Puerto Rico. They expected Zavaia would then follow a course between Aruba and Curacao; from there, they would have a straight shot up to the southern shores of Puerto Rico, where they planned to deliver the girls and the cocaine and collect their payment. The Sanctuary team planned to intercept *Morning Dew* in the straits between Aruba and Curacao. At about the same time, another team would be intercepting the boat *Fresh Mornings*, which would be about a week's distance behind them, still collecting girls from the beaches of Guiana.

Everyone agreed that it was a good plan — or at least the best one they had. Each team would comprise ten men and two boats. One would be a speedy cigarette boat, which could out-maneuver and intercept almost anything on the water. On that boat would be their best marksmen and snipers, seeking to move in quickly and take out the resistance there was sure to be. Now the group needed firepower. Cédric assumed that Sam Dresser was around somewhere. He put a sign up on the side of the house reading, "SD, we need to talk."

The next morning when Cédric woke up, grabbed his coffee and went outside, he noticed that the sign was gone. Up in SANCTUARY, sitting on the grave of the young girl they all knew as Tammy, sat Sam Dresser.

Sam greeted him with, "You got any coffee for me?" Cédric smiled, turned around, and went back into the house. Inside, he grabbed another cup of coffee for Sam and a loaf of Marie's lemon poppy seed bread. Then he headed up to SANCTUARY.

"Good to see you, Sam."

"Good to see you, Cédric." The two men sat chatting over their breakfast, filling each other in on what had happened since last they met. Sam already knew about Esperanza. "Daniel and Gloria look so happy with her." Sam stared out into the Caribbean as he mused in a contemplative voice, "Sometimes it takes a child's love to heal a childhood wound. A child's love is a powerful salve; look how much Daniella's abundant love has helped heal the wounds of her sisters. You can already see Daniel's heart starting to heal. He's in love with his new daughter, and she is with him. They complete each other."

Cédric knew **exactly** what Sam was talking about. He remembered back to the day he held Daniella for the first time. He remembered that instant connection of hearts that clicked in when she looked up at him. The anger he held toward his father was instantly transformed into sadness for him. Cédric knew that when this moment had come between them – this moment when hearts form a life-changing bond that also comes with responsibility – his father had become afraid and turned away. Whereas, Cédric had run into that moment with Daniella as fast and completely as he could.

Cédric came back to when he heard Sam saying, "That's why these soulless monsters go after children. They want to kill off their innocence, their boundless ability to love. They feed on their naive hearts and innocence creating pain and fear so much that to survive it changes to hate until eventually the child hates love as much as they do."

"Sam, you know this better than I, so let me ask you: after what Daniel's father did to him, how could Daniel still be such a good man?"

"His father did him a favor by dying when he did; another couple of years of Daniel's father and his friends feeding off his innocence, pissing on his soul, would have destroyed him completely. Yes, the only fatherly deed that Daniel's father ever did for him was dying when he did. It's going to be interesting to see how Esperanza's love will change him. You know how I always say Daniel's been bit by the devil? In the past, two things have been the salve placed on these wounds: First, the love you all have for him; and, more recently, his opportunities to inflict pain on these predators. But now, with Esperanza's innocent child's love being applied to his wounds, I don't know if he'll be able to do what he does to the predators. Or, maybe he'll be able to punish them even more fiercely, knowing they tried to ruin Esperanza and turn her into a soulless creature like her mother was. We are in for interesting days, my friend. But you wanted to see me. I'm sure it wasn't to talk about these things?"

"No, it wasn't. But thank you. It answers so many questions about my lifelong friend. And I'm sorry for what was done to you; you're been bit by the devil too. I've heard you say that. How did you not become a monster?"

"Prison and death. My uncle, who was sexually abusing me, would "babysit" me on Saturday nights when my parents would go out for date night. My mom got suspicious that something was wrong; she got one of those nanny cams, and he went to jail the next day. By the end of year, he was in prison and he was killed there. Most inmates in prisons hate pedophiles because most have children of their own. It's strange in a way, how they parent and love their children from a distance. They find a pedophile, make his life a living hell, and eventually kill him. And they do it every time. That was the case with my uncle. One morning the guard found him hanging upside down in his cell. That image still offers me comfort. I was lucky that my abuse only went on for about six months and not every day. It's rare — very rare — that a person can sustain years of sexual abuse and still keep their humanity alive. Plus, I had the love of my mother, sister and father and later the love of my SEAL brothers."

"I had one friend like that. She lived that hell for years but still ended up holding onto and believing in life. She's one of the most decent people I know." Cédric had immediately thought of Ms. Dominique Bute.

"She's a rare soul, my friend, a needle in a haystack. But enough of this crap. What is it we need to talk about?"

"I want you to look at our plans. Tell us if they make sense."

"They do! They're good plans. I would only make a few minor changes. I'd suggest coming in at night with no lights whatsoever, then blind them with floodlights as we pounce on them. This would give us a couple more seconds of surprise, and the lights would become targets, taking some of the fire intended for the men. But that option may not be available depending on their movements." Smiling, Sam added, "I've been coming down at night and looking your plans over, adding small pieces of information. It pleased me greatly when you folks realized that taking out both boats at exactly the same time is the only way this would truly be successful. I'm sure they're either in constant communication or have some way of notifying each other if there's danger. So, we do it simultaneously or we'll let one slip away. I knew you'd come up with a good plan; your military training shows."

Cédric felt huge relief hearing that Sam liked the plan. The group was right in the middle of discussions about daytime versus nighttime assault; plans would be drawn up for both.

The next issue was firepower. "Weapons. We're going to need weapons. I've seen the arsenal you have inside your boat."

Acting like a schoolgirl finally getting asked to the prom, Sam responded, "I thought you'd never ask."

Sam suggested to Cédric how he would arm each boat and every man who would be part of the assault. "I've got some really nice machine guns tucked away in the hills; Thomas can mount them on your boats. Plus, I've got a real treat for you: three of my SEAL buddies came down to help. So, there can be two of us on each team. You have no idea how excited we are, and how much we look forward to helping you destroy this nest of parasites."

Chapter 24

Later that morning, everybody arrived for a Sunday barbecue. Everyone was excited to meet Esperanza. Marilyn was there too, watching over Esperanza's adjustment. If things got too overwhelming for her, Daniel and Gloria would take her home. Marilyn also brought a colleague, Heidi, who spoke Esperanza's language and came along to translate the conversation and smooth Esperanza's introduction to the group.

Daniella, Juliana, Maribella and Monique were the self-designated greeting party. They were so excited! They waited at the bottom of the hill for Daniel, Gloria and Esperanza to drive up in Daniel's old tattered and rusty Ford truck. Esperanza was sitting in the middle, and the big smile on her face widened even more when she saw the girls. Gloria, helped by Heidi, had taken the time the day before to explain to Esperanza who the girls were, and that they could either be sisters or cousins, depending on where Esperanza wanted to live. To Esperanza, there was no question – they would be cousins.

Esperanza climbed out of the truck and ran over to the four girls lined up and waiting impatiently to be introduced. She excitedly bounced in front of them, exclaiming, "Cousins! Who's who?" The line caved in, and five girls immediately blended like ingredients coming together to make a delicious soup. The girls brought Esperanza up to meet the others. Esperanza kept one eye on Daniel and Gloria, checking out whether they were okay with her enjoying and caring about the others. Heidi, who was there to translate, was soon sitting on the bench with the other adults since the girls seemed to communicate happily without her. Every now and then, one of them came over to ask her how to pronounce a certain word or what something meant.

The four sisters took Esperanza into SANCTUARY and they guided her through the cemetery-shrine. They finally settled, as they often did, on top of Tammy's grave, having a conference of their own. The adults, though wondering what they were talking about, knew not to disturb them. After about an hour, Marie called to them that lunch was ready. They shared a few more words, then stood up and dusted off their bums, and joined the adults around a large table built to hold everyone.

As they all sat around eating barbecue, Daniel turned to Esperanza. "So, what do you think, sweetie? You can stay here and live with the girls if you'd like, or you can live with me and Gloria."

Esperanza, in her broken English, said, "You mean Mom. Sorry, you saved me! Now you're stuck with me!"

Daniel laughed and relaxed. "So that's how it works, huh? Maybe that's why Mom's still with me. I guess you could say she found me; I was so shy back then, she was the one who asked me out."

Daniel, whose hands were covered in barbecue sauce, leaned over and kissed the top of Esperanza's head. "The girls are going to be disappointed."

"No, they're not, Dad. I've already told them. They're totally okay with it, and what we've decided is I'll come over and spend a couple of days a week with them, if that's okay with you and Mom."

Daniel laughed, "You young ladies have got it all solved, don't you?"

Esperanza smiled. "No, Dad, the girls in SANCTUARY solved it for us. Daniella talks to them. I really like her. You know, she hasn't been abused like the rest of us have; maybe that's why they talk to her. I like her. She doesn't feel sorry for us. I like Juliana, too; she's tough like you, and she's also got a big heart just like you. Mirabella it is so sweet, she's a lot like Mom – very gentle and warm. Monique is the only one I worry about. They hurt her pretty bad; part of them is still up inside her. I hope that Marilyn lady can help her."

Daniel sat dumbfounded, totally surprised at how much the girls had already shared with each other. He guessed it was probably their way of seeing whether they would be accepted, telling the group: *Here is the worst part of me. Do you still care?*

After the meal, the girls ran off to play as the adults settled down to talk, going over the plan and putting together the two teams.

Almost daily, some young man or young woman and even some middle-aged men would show up, asking how they could help, asking if they could be part of the militia that Cédric was putting together. Margaret was to take down their information, especially what skills they had, and she started the vetting process for letting volunteers into the group. Oscar and four of his friends from St. Barth's had moved over to St. Maarten, a huge commitment to Sanctuary. John and one of Sam's SEAL friends were already training with them mentally and physically for the dangerous work ahead; everyone knew this would not be resolved without bloodshed.

One day, the flag was flying high over El Capitan, and when Cédric went to retrieve the note, he noticed that one of the young men from St. Barth's was in the area, so he waited until the coast was clear before retrieving the note. It said:

> One of your recruits works for José. I don't know who — I just know that there's a spy amongst you. They were bragging about it. Be careful. They know that you're up to something. They know you were checking on their routes. There's also a man on the island, André Barkus, who sells high-grade weapons. They've been talking to him. I think they've been buying special weapons from him. There's also talk of another possible attempt on your life. Things are heating up. Be careful, my friend.

Cédric wasn't surprised. There was a different feel in the air. Marie felt it too; she kept telling him lately to be careful. Later that day, he met up with Sam, Daniel, and Margaret. "I want to tell you some new information, but I don't want it getting out past the four of us because it could spook the person we're looking for. I've been told that we have a spy in our ranks – one of our new recruits. I've also been told that André Barkus, a man on the island who sells high-grade weapons, has been selling José some special equipment." Then he swallowed. "And there may be another attempt on my life soon."

"How reliable is your information?" Sam asked.

"Extremely. I'd bet my life on it!" Cédric responded.

"You may be, my friend. You may be," Sam casually emphasized the danger.

"Who could the guy be? I've really worked hard checking all the recruits out. Shit! Who?" Margaret was clearly in distress.

Daniel sat down on the bench, reflecting and weighing all the options. "Okay, so we don't know who the spy is, and we don't know who might be trying to assassinate you. The only tangible lead we have is André Barkus. We know who he is, and we know where to find him. That has to be a starting point. I suggest that Sam and I have a visit with Mr. Barkus, find out who he is selling to, what he has sold to them, what he knows about the spy, and who might be trying to assassinate Cédric. We have to start with what is in front of us." His logic was straightforward and simple.

Margaret was still in distress about the possible spy; that's where her mind was focused. To bring her attention back into the group, Cédric asked, "Margaret, what do you think of Daniel's plan?" He suspected she probably hadn't heard a word of it.

"Yeah, yeah, sounds good to me. But did you hear anything more about this spy? Who might it be? Do you know if he's from our island? Do you know if he could possibly be one of the recruits from St. Barth's or from Saba?"

Cédric smiled. He loved how she always looked for details; then, he remembered seeing the recruit from St. Barth's. "It probably doesn't mean anything, but the other day up on the point, I noticed one of the recruits from St. Barth's walking up at the top of Butte Hill. Probably out keeping in shape – it's a good hike up there – but he seemed a bit out of place. He's the one who's always wearing a New York Yankees T-shirt. He's a little shorter than the rest of them and looks like a runner – he's got that type of body." Margaret immediately knew who Cédric was talking about; she always thought the guy was kind of cute – always a warm smile and a twinkle in his eyes.

"Yeah, I remember him. One of the Yankee players has a villa on St. Barth's, and they got to be friends. Whenever he's down on the island, he gives Marcus – that's his name – a couple of T-shirts because Marcus loves baseball. Now that he knows one of the Yankee players, that's his new favorite team. He said the player even told him that someday he'll give him plane tickets and game tickets so he can see a baseball game live. Marcus seemed like a nice guy. I'll check him out again. Hell, I'm going to go over all of them. Who's to say we don't have two spies? If I let one get by, maybe I let two get by! Hell, maybe all of them are spies! Maybe I screwed up royally." Margaret was a bit mad at herself, wondering if she was mesmerized by his charm; she knew she could have checked him out better. She still hoped that it wasn't Marcus who was infiltrating the group; she wanted to keep her enjoyable fantasies about him.

"Margaret, don't be so hard on yourself," Daniel told her. "We will find out whoever it is, and maybe Mr. Barkus will help us."

"How can he help us?" Margaret asked.

"You didn't hear a thing we said, did you? Sam and I are going to have a talk with Mr. Barkus about him selling weapons, and to see if he knows anything about the other things. You didn't hear that, did you?"

Margaret shook her head. "Not a word of it! I'm just going crazy that we may have a spy or even an assassin in our group, and I may have let him in."

Chapter 25

André Barkus lived on the French side of the island between Grand Case and Friar's Bay. He lived in a small villa perched on an outcropping of volcanic rock that gave him a perfect view of the Caribbean. He had purchased it from his profits selling guns to the drug smugglers that operated throughout the Caribbean and northern South America.

André had acquired his love for guns from his two cousins. These cousins had lost their parents in a car accident when the boy, Alex, and his sister Emmanuelle were two and three years of age. Having no living relatives other than André's mother, who didn't want them – in fact, she didn't really care for André and his sister that much, as having children cramped her bar drinking and carousing lifestyle – they became orphans.

Alex and Emmanuelle were sent to a Lutheran orphanage on the island. Within a year, they were adopted out to a stern and stoic Norwegian couple outside Cambridge, a small Minnesota town.

The move was quite a culture shock for the children. Their new parents seemed motivated by their need for helpers to work the farm more than by a love of children. It wasn't an easy life for Emmanuelle and Alex. They worked hard and put in long hours. With little parental care, the only love they experienced was the brotherly and sisterly love they had for each other. Because they were the only blacks in a basically racist rural community, they were made fun of, teased and bullied, but both were quite resilient and quickly learned how to take care of themselves.

They learned to hunt at an early age. Their father taught them, taking them along as he hunted game for the family's table. By the time they were eight, they each owned a .22 caliber rifle for hunting rabbits and squirrels, and they provided most of the meat for the family. Together they spent many hours in the woods, soaking in the rhythms of nature. They took excellent care of their guns, these instruments that gave them fun, comfort, and a sense of power.

For their eleventh birthdays, they received used shotguns. That was a lucky break for them; their father had taken them along to a gun show, which was his other hobby besides hunting. He was always looking for bargains, and these events allowed him to be out of the house and away from his wife. At one of these gun shows, he found a couple of banged-up shotguns he paid next to nothing for because they needed a couple of parts. Alex actually pointed out to his father that another dealer had the needed parts. All told, they got the two shotguns for a little under $50. Those banged-up, unwrapped gifts they fixed themselves were their favorite gifts ever.

After that, Alex and Emmanuelle always went to the gun shows with their father, an interest that developed into an obsession with guns. The guns gave them a sense of power in the uncomfortable situation they lived in. And, they provided a way to connect with their father.

Connecting with their mother was hopeless. She was a closet racist, but at home, the closet was open; she always wondering where her "blacks" were, and regularly slapped them for the smallest of reasons. She loved exerting control over them. She was a mean, ugly, overweight "good Christian" woman who was angry at the world and took it out on Alex and Emmanuelle. Whom she saw as her property.

By the time they were twelve, Alex and Emmanuelle were excellent duck and geese hunters and very skilled in avoiding the state's Department of Natural Resources officers. They lived on a flight path for Canadian geese. There were plenty of deer to shine at night. They did well enough with their hunting that their father sold some of the extra meat, bringing in a little extra money for him to buy more guns.

Alex, who had a **particularly** keen eye for firearms, read everything he could about guns. He found the best bargains at the gun shows and pointed them out to his father, who usually bought Alex's finds and then resold them later at a good profit. The boy impressed people with his vast gun knowledge and his charismatic personality, becoming a pal to most of the gun dealers; sometimes, they even tapped him for his knowledge.

Emmanuelle developed the same love for guns as her brother. They became experts at reconditioning old guns and selling them for a good profit. It became the family's side business.

Alex stayed on the farm, but Emmanuelle left when she graduated high school. She moved to Minneapolis, looking to experience city life. She was tired of being the only black, tired of being an outsider; she longed for a community that would be a more comfortable fit. She got a job at a department store and rented a small room up in the North Side neighborhood. She met a boy who was part of a gang with connections to Chicago, *The Vice Lords,* and soon they were boyfriend-girlfriend. Soon, she threw herself into the gang lifestyle and the sense of community she found there.

Her boyfriend, Robert, quickly realized that Emmanuelle was starved for affection and longed to fit in. Early in their relationship, he tested her to see what she would do for him. Once at a gang party, he got her to give him a blowjob in front of everyone. She secretly loved the cheers of the group when she was done. She felt like it gave her some status in the group. Afterward, she proudly snuggled up to him on the couch. Robert wanted her to be a pass-around girl, but she drew a firm line; she had too much self-respect for that. But she didn't mind putting on a show with him at the gang parties like some of the other girls did with their boyfriends. She knew she was quite pretty, and she found out she was a bit of an exhibitionist. She, like some of the other girls, was using her body to gain some acceptance and what seemed like respect within the gang.

Then one day, she found another, better way to earn respect that raised her status to near-equal with the guys in the *Vice Lords.* A few of the men were sitting around cleaning and breaking down kilos of Mexican Tijuana Gold. Their guns lay on the table. Feeling fidgety, Emmanuelle picked up one of the Glock 19s. She broke it down and put it back together in a matter of seconds. Everyone stared at her. She was more comfortable with firearms than any of them. As they questioned her, they were impressed with how much she knew about guns. That she could get firearms for them at a reasonable price through her brother brought grins from them all. Within a matter of weeks, she earned a valuable place of respect within the group. Within a year, Alex had moved down to the Cities. Emmanuelle and he had a very good business providing firearms to the Minneapolis gang and its Chicago affiliate. All the contacts Alex had made throughout the years at the gun shows were really paying off.

By the time Alex was twenty-three and Emmanuelle twenty-two, they had plenty of money in their pockets. They made a trip back to St. Maarten to see the island of their birth and look for any relatives they might have there. That's how they met up with André Barkus. There was an instant connection, and soon André was as fascinated by guns as they were. Hanging around with them, it wasn't long before he knew almost as much about guns as they did.

André regularly visited his cousins in Minneapolis, and they made the rounds of all of the important gun shows in the Midwest. Each time, André returned home with a suitcase full of handguns. He sold guns to all the petty criminals on the island and then branched out to some of the other islands. He was making a pretty good living and developing quite a reputation.

About a year before Irma hit the island, Alex had connected with a crooked supply sergeant out of Fort Bragg in Alabama, which enabled him to purchase a whole new class of weapons – ones he had dreamed of. André went to stay with his cousins when the island anticipated Irma's possible landfall, during the trip he fired his first grenade launcher. After Irma, André became the main weapons dealer to the drug runners throughout the Caribbean.

But no matter how clever André was, he was **totally** surprised when he walked into his house one night. Within seconds he was unconscious on the floor, and when he woke up, he was on Sam's boat out somewhere in the Caribbean. He recognized Daniel, but he had no idea who Sam was. "André, sorry to have to do this, but we need to know about all your connections to the sex traffickers run by José Zavaia and what weapons they've been buying from you."

André smirked. "Can't tell you that, Daniel; it wouldn't be good for business. Who's your friend?"

"I'll let him introduce himself," Daniel responded.

Sam took out one of those long Bic lighters used to start grills. He burned off André's eyebrows. "You don't need to know my name. All you need to know is that I'm part devil, and I love doing his work. I'm sure when I go to hell, I'll get to torture a lot more guys like you, but for now, I'm going to enjoy torturing you unless you give us all the information we need."

André spat out, "Fuck you." Within seconds, a hammer slammed down on André's baby finger. His hand was tied to a block of wood, fingers spread wide. Vulnerable.

"I was trained by a Russian friend. He taught me how to break every bone in a person's body while keeping them alive to feel it. There are 206 bones in the human body. I just broke two of yours, and I've got 204 more to go unless you start talking."

André was tough; only when all the bones in his right hand were broken, and Sam released that hand and **began to tie** his left hand to the block of wood, did André cave. Through his tears, he whimpered, "Okay! Okay! What is it you want to know?"

"When did you start selling guns to José Zavaia? And what type of guns are you selling him?"

"I haven't sold him any guns." Sam started to raise his arm, firmly grasping the hammer. André, his body already shaking and sweating, spoke quickly. "Wait! Wait, I wasn't done. I haven't sold him any guns – he has enough of his own. He wanted grenade launchers, and I sold him 40mm M203s. He wants those for his boats. He said somebody's after them, trying to pirate his boats. I'm assuming that's you?" Sam rested the hammer by his side and André relaxed.

"How many did you sell him?"

"Four. Two for each boat, plus a hell of a lot of ammunition. He wanted some to practice with, and plenty to use if someone came after him and his cargo. He wanted a lot of ammunition for his automatic weapons and the machine guns, too. He has one on each boat. I've been on his boats with him and Roberto."

"Has he bought any sniper rifles?"

"No, why?"

"You don't need to know."

Sam wanted to know because it would be to their advantage if they could stay at a safe distance, using their sniper skills to take out anyone shooting heavy weapons. He had often overpowered more heavily armed men by just sitting out of their range, picking them off while they fired their weapons that fell short. People often underestimated the lethality of a well-trained long-distance sniper. He anticipated they would be firing from a moving boat, which presented a special challenge, but Sam and his friends had **already** been practicing. The maximum range of the 40 mm grenade launcher was approximately 400 meters. Sam's sniper rifle, an SSG 69 bolt-action, was perfect for him. He particularly loved the feel of the stock; he could cradle it securely even from a moving boat. The only thing he didn't like about it was its five-round capacity, so he used a 10-round magazine and always carried an extra one. The rifle had an effective range of 800 meters; he was always deadly under 600 meters – and he wasn't even the best sniper within his group of friends.

By the time they were halfway through his left hand, it was clear that André knew nothing about who the possible assassin might be. He did know that José Zavaia was feeling **pretty** smug.

Daniel took down all the information about André's cousins **in case they** came looking for revenge. André's stash of weapons was in two storage lockers: one on Saba and the other one on Anguilla.

"Have you ever sampled any of José's cargo?" Daniel asked.

"Not much. On a couple of occasions to help earn his trust. Little girls are not my thing."

That was the wrong answer for Daniel. The thought of the men who had crawled all over his sweet Esperanza created an ever-growing rage inside him. He borrowed the hammer from Sam and used it to finish André, taking his time. Then they tied weights on his body and tossed it into the Caribbean.

Within two days, André's house had been searched and his money confiscated to pay his perversion tax. The weapons from his storage lockers on Saba and Anguilla had been buried in invented gravesites on St. Maarten.

Sanctuary bought two cigarette boats fast enough to intercept the modern-day slave ships. They considered whether they might sell José and Roberto's boats if they didn't have to sink them – possibly to the cartels. Everything was set to put their plans in motion.

Chapter 26

Margaret was obsessed with reviewing everything she had on every volunteer in her effort to determine the identity of the spy. She had combed through all her material twice, and still, nothing seemed to catch her eye. Then one day, she received a call to come over to Cédric and Marie's. Sitting at the coffee table was Sophia from St. Barth's.

Marie addressed both women. First, she said, "Margaret, I think you're going to want to hear this." Then, to Sophia, "Tell Margaret what you've just told us."

Sophia looked at Margaret. She had only met her once before and had sized her up as a very strong, confident woman. But today, she looked crazed and **totally** stressed out. She suspected that Margaret's apparent stress was connected to the news she was here to deliver.

"A friend of mine gave me some information that I thought would be important for the members of Sanctuary to know, so I decided to come over to Saint Martin and deliver it myself. I knew where John and Alma lived, so that's where I went. They got very excited when I showed them the picture and told them the information. They brought me here to talk with Cédric, and he said we needed to tell you right away. So that's why Marie called you to come over. I have information about another pedophile. I don't get what's so important. To me, he's just another one of those creeps who rapes little girls – another famous one, but still a kiddie creep."

"I'm in the dark, here. What's so important that I need to be here? I'm working on some very important things and my time is very valuable," Margaret said, looking at the others scornfully. "So please get on with it."

"One of my friends is a housekeeper for the rich and famous, as we call them. She was cleaning one of the villas on St. Barth's when she found a dresser that had a false bottom. She found it purely by accident; she moved a heavy vase to dust, and under it was a button. She pushed it and a panel on the bottom of the dresser opened. Inside it were photos of the owner of the house and José Zavaia and a nude little girl. She took pictures of all the photos with her phone and brought them to me, because she knew that I was connected with Sanctuary." Sophia was very proud when she said that, proud that people were seeing her as part of Sanctuary. She handed Margaret the phone and let her scroll through the pictures.

The pictures turned her stomach and almost made her want to throw up, but then Margaret saw what she was supposed to see. The man holding the girl on his lap was wearing the New York Yankees cap. She looked at Cédric and Marie, and then at Sophia.

She asked, "Is that the Yankees player that we've heard lives over on St. Barth's?"

Sophia smiled. "Yes, it is! Nobody on St. Barth's had any idea that he was a kiddie creep until my friend found these pictures."

Margaret asked, "Who knows about this?"

Sophia responded, "Just me and the housekeeper. I swore her to secrecy, and she is a woman who can keep a secret. That's why she works for the rich and famous. But this is different. She's very sympathetic to what you're doing." Then Sophia restated it, saying proudly, "What we're doing."

"Damn! Damn! Damn!" Nothing had been let on to Sophia about the possible spy in their midst, or how Sophia may have solved their problem. This new information was the best lead – and a damn good one – about who the spy might be. Everything pointed toward Marcus.

"What? Is it important? I mean, besides that the man is a creep?" Sophia asked, staring at all of them.

"Of course. It's very important. You've helped us find another one of them – and most importantly, another one with connections to José Zavaia. He's another Harry Crane, just better at keeping his secret. The only problem is that most of us are Yankee fans and this is terribly disappointing. The group knows this is my favorite player. Damn! Damn! Damn!" Margaret quickly came up with the lie, trying to provide a plausible explanation to Sophia to explain what all the fuss was about. Sophia seemed to buy it. But Margaret was immediately thinking of Marcus.

"I get it; I've always been a Yankees fan, too, and I was quite disappointed in this pervert. I'll have to start following the Minnesota Twins, their archrival, instead," Sophia threw in.

"Well, let's not get carried away. He's just one player; we shouldn't give up on the whole team. But you need to understand, Sophia: this connection to José Zavaia maybe a missing piece of the puzzle we've been looking for. You and your housekeeper friend are a godsend! There's no other way to put it – a blessing from above."

Cédric spoke up, looking at Sophia, "Can you stay for supper?"

"No, darn! I wish I could, but I've got to get back and cook at the restaurant, so I've got to catch the ferry back. But thank you; it would be an honor and a great pleasure to have supper with all of you. Maybe someday I can come over and cook a meal for you all."

"Only if you make that chocolate mousse – they all wouldn't stop raving about! How about if I give you a ride over in my boat? It'll be a bit rougher, but it will get you there quicker, and it would give me a little more time with you. I'd like to know you better; you are a very big help to Sanctuary. You have no idea how important you've been. You may have saved someone's life, and at the very least, you'll be protecting a bunch of girls from this pedophile."

The life she may have saved was Cédric's, and he knew it. More and more, the group had been thinking that the spy was also probably the assassin; it would make good sense.

Before they left, Sophia looked at the group, particularly John and Alma. "Please thank Daniel and that other guy. When I went back to La Tortue, I found the cave and my ex-husband's stash of goods, cocaine and the boat – all of which I've sold. They have helped me out considerably. Who'd knew I'd ever benefit so much from my ex-husband's…" Sophia stopped herself. She'd been going to say, "death," but then she changed it, "Who knew I'd ever benefit so much from my ex-husband's decision to move away…"

"Okay! Well, I'm going to ride with you and Cédric," John said. With the threat against Cédric's life, he wasn't allowed to go anywhere without somebody else who was armed.

"Great! I get to have an exciting boat ride with two handsome men! The ladies at the restaurant will be so jealous when they see me pull up to our dock in a boat with you two," Sophia said jokingly. Then the trio left to get her back to St. Barth's and her kitchen, cooking her fantastic meals for the guests at the resort.

Margaret was secretly disappointed in herself. She felt she been taken in by his sweet smile and twinkling eyes. She knew now she should've investigated Marcus much more.

As soon as the three were out of sight, Margaret turned to the rest of them. "Where's Marcus? Does anybody know where Marcus is? I think the rest of them are safe, but we need to watch out for all of those guys that came over from St. Barth's. Where are Daniel and Sam? We may have some more work for them."

Alma was already off to the side, dialing Daniel's phone. Shortly she called over to the group. "Daniel and Sam are over at Marks Place having ribs."

Calling over to Alma, Margaret said, "Tell them to meet back here around 8 o'clock tonight. Cédric and John should be back by then and we can all talk about what's next."

They decided to search very discreetly for Marcus, careful to avoid raising any suspicion or concern in him.

Later that day, someone reported they had seen Marcus walking the trail near Butte Hill.

Margaret made sure to find and "accidentally" run into Oscar, the young man who brought his friends over from St. Barth's. "Hey, Mr. Oscar! How are you this fine day?"

"It's Margaret, isn't it?" asking, though he already knew the answer.

"Yes, it is. How is everything going for you and your friends from St. Barth's? Are you enjoying our island? We don't have all the celebrities like you guys do, but we're still a damn good island," she said in her friendliest voice.

"Everything's fine with us. We enjoy the training; in fact, I just got done for today." The group of recruits had been receiving daily military training, getting them ready for the battle that lay ahead.

"Oscar, if you've got some free time, would you like to go to CostULess with me? I've got some shopping to do, and I could use some help with those big bags of rice." In reality, Margaret needed no help – she had been slinging around 50-pound bags of rice ever since she was a teenager. But she wanted some time with Oscar, who she trusted, to ask questions about his friends, and engaging his heroic tendencies seemed like a good way to start their conversation.

Margaret flashed on the young girl she had carried up to Sanctuary during the middle of the night over a year ago. She had brushed her long black hair before the journey up the hill. That heavy load still weighed down her heart. She said a quick prayer, as she always did, whenever she remembered the little angel's sleeping face.

"Absolutely! I'd be glad to help." The invitation pleased Oscar. Spending some time with Margaret would be nice; he'd always respected how smart she was and how she carried herself. She had a regal quality about her.

The pair set about the afternoon task of getting supplies, chatting throughout their afternoon errand.

"Oscar, maybe you could teach me about the other folks from St. Barth's? I don't really know much about them, except that they're friends of yours, so they'll probably be good members of the cause. It would be helpful for me to know about their skills."

Oscar laughed. "Yeah, we've all known each other since we were kids, except for Marcus, who came over to the island from Puerto Rico when we were about twelve. He joined our soccer team. He was a damn good forward."

"Marcus, now which one is he?" Margaret casually asked.

"He's the smallest of us St. Barth's guys. He's got black curly hair and he's always wearing a New York Yankees shirt."

"Yes, yes, I know who you're talking about now. I'm a Yankees fan myself, but to wear only Yankees shirts, what's that about?" she asked, smiling.

"Marcus met a Yankee player who owns a villa over in St. Barth's and they've become pretty good friends. Every time the guy comes down from the States, he gives Marcus a new shirt; some of them are even game worn. Now Marcus is the guy's biggest fan."

"Who's the player?"

"Salvador Mendez – he's one of the few guys hitting over 300. Do you know him?"

"Oh my God, yes! How could you not? He's Hall of Fame material. Marcus is friends with him? Wow! Wow, that's crazy special! I'd probably be wearing Mendez's shirts too, if I was his friend. Hell, I'd go shirtless for him – he's cute!" That stopped Oscar for a couple of seconds; he thought Margaret was quite beautiful, and the thought of her shirtless threw him into pleasurable thoughts and images for a couple of seconds.

"How long ago did the friendship start?" She asked it again, "Oscar, how long ago did their friendship start?" That pulled Oscar back into the moment.

"Oh, excuse me. Hmm, maybe about three years ago? Marcus's aunt started working for Mr. Mendez – cleaning, looking after the villa and running errands for him. One day Marcus was helping his aunt, and that's how he met 'Sal,' as Marcus calls him. They hit it off right away." To Oscar, they were having a casual conversation; but Margaret was listening to each word intensely, seeking clues to determine whether Marcus was the spy, assassin or both.

"Does Marcus have a girlfriend?" Margaret kept pressing, trying to get as much information as possible.

"He does, and he's crazy about her. But she's probably not the best material for a girlfriend. I'm sure that's partly why he came over to St. Maarten – because she's here. He's a firm believer in Sanctuary and what it stands for, but his girlfriend, well, she's not. She's afraid Marcus is going to get hurt or killed. Cherie moved over to St. Maarten about a year ago. He knew her from Puerto Rico; they actually grew up together, on the same block, but sad to say now she works over at El Capitan."

"What does she do there; does she clean or cook?" Oscar wasn't responding positively to either of Margaret's guesses; then it dawned on her. "She's a prostitute?"

"Yes, sad to say, but yes; she's a prostitute there." Oscar saw Margaret's disappointment, so he added – as if it made a difference – "She makes real good money." That didn't seem to impress Margaret, so he just went on, "She's very pretty and has, well (hesitating a bit) big …"

Margaret, having adjusted to the reality of what Oscar was talking about, finished the sentence for him, "Boobs."

"Yeah, not overly big, but big. Marcus and her call them her moneymakers." Margaret nodded to let Oscar know she understood. "The money thing is really important to both of them. They both grew up very poor, and they want to be rich someday. Marcus is a hard worker. That's why I was surprised when he was willing to give up his good-paying job over on St. Barth's and come over here with us to help with Sanctuary. But I think the largest part of why he's here is because she's over here."

Margaret was still thinking about her being a prostitute. "But the idea of her with all those men – doesn't that affect him?" Margaret was **truly** trying to understand the concept.

"Well, they both have this attitude that 'a person's got to do what a person's got to do' – use the talents they've been given – and, like I said, they both want to be rich."

"Does Marcus have any way of making money while he's staying here?"

"He picks up odd jobs whenever he can, like the rest of us. He's doing some work for a tire company fixing flats."

"Have you met his girlfriend, the prostitute?"

"Yes, she's a little too showy for me. But Cherie – that's her real name, at the club she goes by 'Lily' – is really nice. I think she's good for Marcus. She keeps him focused and out of trouble. He was leaning that way, but since he hooked up with her, he has been on the straight and narrow." Oscar **chuckled a bit.**

"What's so funny?" Margaret asked.

"I was thinking about something Marcus said the other day. He finds it funny how most of the girls down at El Capitan go by names of flowers, you know, like Rose, Daisy, Sunflower and his girlfriend Lily. And then Marcus said, "There's not much dew left on their flowers.""

Margaret chuckled, and in keeping with the spirit of the moment, added, "Yeah, I bet not, working at a whorehouse. But I'm sure their petals are getting watered a lot." Oscar chuckled.

Margaret was forcing herself to stay as casual as possible, but inside she was furious, mainly at herself. "How the hell could I have missed all of this?" she fumed. Then she remembered how she'd heard Marilyn talk about how cunning and manipulative psychopaths can be. Margaret also realized that she was asking all the wrong questions in her interviewing process. She was basically gathering factual histories; she needed questions that would dig down deeper. Marilyn would tell her to stop beating herself up; that interviewing people to see if they would be good and loyal to the mission of Sanctuary was not something she'd ever done before. It dawned on her to talk about what really mattered.

"Oscar, let me ask you a very serious question about Marcus and the others: do you think he –they – have it, when the fighting begins, to do the hard things? Do you think you all of you would be able to take a life?"

"That's a good question – it's the one we are all asking ourselves. I think most of us see violence, even killing, as something we must be ready to do. I think we all want to be ready when the time comes, because we know this is a war for what is right. Marcus is different; I have no doubt that of all of us from St. Barth's, Marcus will be the one who can most easily go into battle. Behind his pretty smile, there's a part of him that is stone cold. Once, I watched Marcus pull a knife, hold it to a guy's throat, and twist it until a little trickle of blood ran down the man's neck. It happened on a night when I was out to supper with them, and one of Lily's customers from El Capitan recognized her. As he walked by, he made the mistake of saying, 'I suppose whores have to eat, too.' Marcus stood up, calmly walked up to the man, and within a second, Marcus's knife was up twisting into the man's throat. He made the guy apologize to Lily, and also made the man pay for our supper. You could tell the guy was terrified; he had sweat pouring down his face; his knees were shaking. I think what scared the guy the most was Marcus's calmness, and a cold intensity in his eyes that replaced his usual twinkle; his eyes looked like death. That look in his eyes let everybody, especially that guy, know Marcus would've easily shoved the knife through the man's throat if the man wasn't willing to back down. Hell, I was afraid. I thought for sure the guy would wet himself as he stood there sheepishly apologizing to Lily. After Marcus sat down at the table, I said to him, 'Jesus Christ, man! I've never seen you like that!'

"That's when Lily told me about how in the Puerto Rico neighborhood where they grew up, you need to be fearless because any sign of weakness or fear leaves you vulnerable to the next level of predator. Then Marcus said, 'Our neighborhood was called…' (he pointed at Lily, and they said together in threatening voices), 'The Valley of Death.' They both laughed, but then they both said how glad they were to be away from there.

"All I can say is, I'm very glad Marcus is on our side."

By now, Margaret wasn't so sure Marcus *was* on their side. Margaret felt sad, especially for Oscar; he truly did not know that his supposed friend would most likely kill him in a heartbeat. Margaret understood they had a psychopath amongst them. Margaret knew that Sam and Daniel would need to have a talk with Marcus. A new question now lurking in Margaret's head: *Was Marcus just a spy, or was he also there to assassinate Cédric?* It was clear he had the skills to kill, and from everything Oscar had said, he probably had already used them.

Chapter 27

José's yacht sat a little over twelve miles off of Puerto Rico in international waters after delivering 22 young girls and 200 kilos of cocaine to his contacts. He was waiting for Roberto, who was on his way to Puerto Rico with a full load. Roberto had nineteen girls chained in the hull of his boat, and 175 kilos of cocaine; that was the maximum his yacht could hold. They were having an **extremely** good season. Times had been tough down in the areas where they acquired their young flesh because of an enduring drought.

José believed in climate change. He saw the weather patterns changing, but he was glad, for it was making his job much easier. Almost always now, when their boats landed on the beaches, there were many families waiting for them on the beach with a daughter or two or to be sold. For them, it would mean one or two fewer mouths to feed and money in the pocket. José would always sell it to the parents as a win-win, assuring them that their daughters would go to nice homes in America or Europe where they would not have to endure such hardships.

It had been three days since he dropped off his own cargo. It would be another two days before he would connect up with Roberto. Then they would make their way back to Trinidad to strategize and test out their new weapons. He had kept a young one to help pass the time – a black-haired girl with big almond-colored eyes no more than twelve years old. He had enjoyed entertaining himself with her as long as she fought him, but he had eventually tired of her as he always did – they only struggle for so long. So, he had shackled 50 pounds of weights to her feet and dropped her overboard that morning. Now he was lying back sipping on a cold bottle of Corona, thinking about the dilemma that Sanctuary presented for him.

Whenever he thought about Sanctuary, the 6-inch scar on his leg would hurt. It was his reminder of that morning after Irma when he was tossed ashore on St. Maarten, landing on a splintered 2 x 4 that had also washed up on the shore. He rubbed it, smiling as he pictured the laughing face of the devil he had seen in the swirling waters of the hurricane. He was sure that his guardian devil would watch out for him, but also believed that it demanded regular sacrifices. To him, that's what the terrified young girl he had dropped in the water that morning was – a sacrifice to his protector.

He was eager to get home. He knew that the 40mm grenade launchers, the machine guns, and the extra ammunition were already on Trinidad, delivered by André about a week ago. José had no idea that André was probably giving up information about him and his new weapons at that exact moment he sat there sipping his beer.

He was eager to try out the grenade launchers; he had never used one before. He fantasized about watching a cigarette boat speeding towards him, then exploding like he'd seen in the movies. He pictured himself standing on his yacht, weapon in his hand, laughing his own devil laugh at Sanctuary's folly in trying to take from him what wasn't theirs to take. Nobody steals from José; he was not just fighting for his livelihood, but for his reputation.

He knew the Colombians were watching how he dealt with this situation. If he could render Sanctuary obsolete, he would have a new level of status and prestige, bringing more lucrative opportunities his way. All that stood in his way was this pesky group of do-gooders — Sanctuary, as they called themselves.

The first thing he planned to do, once he rid himself of the son-of-a-bitch called Cédric and his friends was to go to Saint Martin. He would find SANCTUARY, reclaim the girls he still saw as his property, and return them to the sea. Then he would bulldoze their pathetic little graveyard. The thought of it turned his stomach and enraged him. He'd show them! If Sanctuary could make a statement, so could he. He would take Cédric's daughter, use her for his own pleasures, then deliver the girl and her mother to the sleaziest brothel he could find in the Caribbean or Mexico. Nobody's going to mess with what he had spent a lifetime building.

The next two days were relaxing for José. He felt a smile come to his face when he saw his cousin's yacht on the horizon. He took out his binoculars and focused on the boat, and there was Roberto, standing on the deck using his own binoculars to make sure that everything looked safe with his cousin. They waved to each other, giving the thumbs down sign – their own little way of letting each other know things were okay. If someone were controlling them, maybe with a gun trained on them from inside the cabin, they could give a signal that had one meaning to the enemy and the opposite to their partner. Thumbs up meant danger; thumbs down meant safety. Both hands up in the air meant *get the hell out of here as quick as you can, dump the cargo, extreme danger* – most likely Coast Guard.

Roberto pulled up next to José. They tied their boats together and Roberto climbed into José's yacht. José handed his cousin a cold Heineken and they sat down to fill each other in about how their dealings had gone. Roberto had been feeling ill most of his trip, so he had not indulged with any of the girls, which meant there were five extra virgins delivered to their Puerto Rican connection. That meant an extra $30,000 in profit. José told his cousin to keep the extra cash. "You weren't feeling good, so use the money to party later. You deserve it."

Then he changed the subject. "I heard from Hector; the machine guns and grenade launchers have arrived safely. I'm anxious to see how they work."

"Maybe we should go out and find some retired couple who sold their home and all their possessions to buy their dream ship and sail the Caribbean. We'll turn their lifelong dream into a nightmare!" Roberto said, sending José into a fit of laughter. "What are you laughing so hard about? It's not that funny!"

"I get this image of some old fat American in his Speedo hanging onto a life preserver, swimming around in the wreckage of his boat and thinking to himself, 'What the fuck just happened?'"

Roberto joined in the laughter, flapping his arms around and adding, "And his little trophy wife with big boobs in her tiny bikini swimming around looking for something to hang on to, thinking to herself, 'I should've stayed home and screwed the gardener.' By now, they were both howling to the point that they were bent over, their stomachs hurting from laughing so hard.

Then all of a sudden, José turned serious. "I've been thinking of trying the grenade launchers and machine guns out on Juan's yacht. He should be in the area when we get back to Trinidad. That sonofabitch is getting too big for his britches. After his last route, he wanted to give me fifteen percent instead of keeping our deal for twenty. We need to set an example before the others start believing they can do better with the Russians. They'll thank me later. Them fucking Russians are ruthless! I know they're offering our guys better prices, just to get closer to us and take over what we spend a lifetime building. I hate those fucking Russians."

Roberto smiled. "Damn, that's perfect! We'll get some live practice under real circumstances and we'll get the other ones back in line. Taking Juan out will scare the shit out of the rest of them; he's the only one with balls anyway. We'll set it up to work well for years to come. I can see you now, spending your days sipping wine and enjoying your little delights, a life of pleasure." He didn't ask where José's newest girl was; he shared José's habits and tossed a few girls over the rails himself. Instead, he continued, "You're smart, my cousin, you're smart. But I'd still like to take out one of those tourists!" They went back to laughing and exchanging images of tourists trying to survive.

José told Roberto that he'd recruited the extra men they needed. Each boat would now have two more men, for a crew of five men total. They would travel in pairs; one boat would be armed with a grenade launcher and the other boat would be armed with a mounted machine gun. They would still work their routes, but they would be expecting an **ambush at some time**. Each group would be armed well enough to take on any ship with the speed to intercept, even a heavily armed Coast Guard ship. José wanted this solved. José was actually looking forward to the fight – he was **absolutely** sure he would be victorious. Things had always gone his way – and besides, he had a devil for a guardian angel.

Chapter 28

Cédric's heart was heavy. He was taking more long walks in the hills of the island, for as they got closer and closer to a deadly confrontation with José Zavaia, the danger he was bringing to his family and friends was becoming a heavier and heavier burden. He knew that what they were doing was right, but he also cursed the day he swam into the hull of that ship. He was having self-doubts: had his bravado and ego put those he loved in danger that all of them would regret? He knew those he was up against had no conscience, just a love of money and of all things dark. Why couldn't he just go back to diving in the sea he loved so much – coming home to Marie's welcoming smile and Daniella's big hugs, evenings of drinking beer and joking with his friends, some of whom may now lose their lives because of a decision he made. Maybe he wasn't the man for the job. He prayed more, but no answers were coming. He felt so alone with the burden he carried. He walked next to the old slave walls built by his ancestors touching them, hoping, seeking guidance from them, but all was quiet. Then one night, he received the help he so desired.

The morning had started with a steady nurturing rain that lasted until early afternoon. By two o'clock, the sun was high and shining, making the island beautiful. By three o'clock, because it was butterfly migration season, the hills around him were covered with small white butterflies dancing in the air. He saw more hummingbirds feeding on the hibiscus flowers than he'd ever seen before. Life was all around, singing loudly and clearly to him. And in the middle of all of it was SANCTUARY, filled with white butterflies blessing the graves of his daughters.

Around six o'clock, Marie called him for supper, and they sat down with the girls to a meal of goat stew and Marie's homemade lemon poppy seed bread, which she was now teaching her girls to make. As the sun went down and the crickets began singing, Cédric felt more at peace than he had in a long time. That night he fell asleep in Marie's arms.

It was around two o'clock in the morning when he woke up to the sound of pleasant conversation and the clanking of the shackles that hung on the fence of SANCTUARY. Never before had he heard the chains unless the wind was strong, but there was no wind tonight. He got up and followed the voices. He walked out of the house and up toward SANCTUARY, for that's where they were coming from. He was stunned when he saw Tammy sitting on the lap of an old black man who somehow seemed familiar to him. They were talking and laughing, then they lifted their gazes and looked at Cédric. The haunting look was gone from Tammy's face; there was only a big smile. She pointed at Cédric and told her elderly friend, "That's him! That's him! That's the nice man who brought me here. He brought me and my sisters from that cold dark place in the sea up to this sunny home on this beautiful hill."

The old man told her, "That's my great, great, great-grandson. He has a good heart, but he's afraid right now."

With the curiosity of a child, she asked, "Why? Why is he afraid?"

The old man smiled, laughed, and kissed her on the forehead. "You ask so many questions, young one. You're curious like he is; I like that about you." They both looked straight at Cédric. "He's afraid because he believes he's alone. He's afraid because he's been given the burden of doing the right thing." Cédric noticed that both had the same red marks on their wrists where shackles had stolen their freedom.

Tammy responded sadly, "He shouldn't feel alone. We're all with him." She got up and walked out of SANCTUARY to grab Cédric's hand, smiling up at him. He couldn't feel flesh, but he could feel love grabbing his hand and bringing him towards SANCTUARY. As they walked towards SANCTUARY, the spirits of the other girls appeared, all smiling. Tammy brought Cédric face to face with the elderly man.

The old spirit reached out and patted the side of Cédric's face, smiling at him. "I'm proud of you, grandson. We all are. What you're doing is good." At that, the old man motioned towards the hills. Cédric looked toward where he motioned, and the hills were covered with the spirits of the slaves who'd tilled and suffered on this island throughout the centuries. "As you've walked the walls, touching the stones that each of us here has carried, you woke us. We are here now to carry you. During our days, the only freedom we found was in the freedom of how we carried ourselves; now, let us carry you. It was our dignity, our ability to transform our suffering into a deeper faith that eventually allowed us to find peace and true freedom. You were born free, but when you found your daughters at the bottom of the sea, shackles were placed on you – shackles as strong as any that bound us. Wear them proudly, as we have work to do. Come, sit with me and watch."

They sat on a tombstone, and Cédric marveled at the ghost of his ancient ancestor comforting him. One spirit came down from the hillside, put a harmonica to his mouth, and played the sweetest music he'd ever heard. His sixteen smiling daughters danced among the tombstones, and the spirits of those on the hill clapped and danced along. For the first time in a very long while, Cédric didn't feel alone, didn't feel burdened.

In the morning, Marie walked out to find Cédric sleeping on top of Tammy's grave. He had such a big smile on his face she walked back into the house relieved and started making breakfast, knowing the smell of bacon would wake him up.

True to form, Cédric awoke when the smell of bacon filled his nostrils. He walked into the house to find it alive with the activity of Marie and the girls busily putting together the morning meal. The fresh homemade jams were on the table, as well as Marie's poppy seed bread. Marie was stirring up a large bowl of pancake batter, and Mirabella was standing next to her, throwing blueberries into the mixture. Juliana, the first to see Cédric, announced, "Dad's up." The girls each greeted him with a hug and a kiss, and he did the same with Marie.

Daniella said to her dad, "I'm so glad you got to meet the girls last night. They like you; they like you so much!" By now, they were all used to Daniella's talking about the girls, sharing with them the conversations she had with them. Marie smiled at Cédric.

He responded, looking at Marie, "There was an old man there, too – my great, great, great grandfather."

Daniella spoke up. "You mean Isaac. He used to fix wagons in the old days. He was called a blacksmith. He lets me call him Grandpa. Grandpa Isaac and I sometimes go walking in the hills." None of this surprised Cédric or Marie. They had always known there was something special about Daniella; they'd always sensed she lived between the two worlds. Even as a baby lying in her crib, she seemed to talk to things they could not see.

Marie, half-joking and half not, said, "So, now everybody around here except me is seeing and talking with spirits? Well, that kind of sucks!"

Juliana spoke for herself, Monique, Mirabella and Esperanza when she offered, "We don't see them. Just Daniella. We think it's because of the things that were done to us; were those things done to you?"

Her innocent daughters were asking about things she had never talked about with anyone, even Cédric. There was an awkward quiet in the room; would she be as vulnerable with them as they had been with her? She swallowed, feeling a tear welling up in her eyes. Their bravery was challenging her to finally share her own burden and she plunged ahead. "Yes, maybe that's why. There was a boy I cared a lot about – my first love – and I thought he cared a lot about me. One night he took me to what I thought was a party, but it turned out there were no other girls there except me." Looking at her daughters, tears now running down her cheeks, she continued, "Well, you know what that was like."

Juliana came over to Marie, put her arms around her and squeezed. "It's okay, Mommy. Like Marilyn tells us, it had nothing to do with us. It was all about them."

Mirabella spoke up. "Maybe you need to talk with Auntie Marilyn?" (That's what all the girls were calling her now, and she enjoyed it as much as they did.) "She's really good to talk to about those things."

Marie looked over at Cédric and saw tears running down his cheeks, but there was also a look of relief. They both had known there was an unspoken issue from Marie's past that someday needed to see the sunlight, and today, the sun was shining bright. He watched as their little broken angels were unknowingly helping to heal the part of their mother's heart that, before today, had been untouchable. Cédric enfolded her in a hug and the girls joined in. Marie cried uncontrollably as her family surrounded her, packing unconditional love into the wound she had let no one else touch before this morning. This was the reason she had gone into the military; she had wanted to learn how to defend herself so she would never have to experience that type of pain and fear ever again. She must have cried uncontrollably for fifteen minutes; every time one of her daughters reassured her that everything would be okay, more tears were released.

When the tears subsided, she felt exhausted from carrying her secret, heavy load alone for so many years. She felt tiredness that radiated out from her bones to the tips of her fingers. She could hardly stand.

Cédric could see the exhaustion encompassing and consuming his wife. "Honey, why don't you go lie down with the girls? You need to sleep. We'll eat when you get up. For now, you need to sleep."

Marie nodded, and the girls walked her to the bedroom. Soon they all were fast asleep, cuddled up in the middle of the bed like a lioness with her cubs. He stood in the doorway, gazing at them, so proud of their bravery.

He put away the food, nibbling on it as he did. He then walked out the door and looked up at SANCTUARY. Tammy was standing at its gate, smiling and waving at him. A new day had begun.

Chapter 29

Cédric was coming back from a long day in the harbor where he had been a part of a small crew working to retrieve the wreckage of yachts that still dotted the harbor of Oyster Pond since Irma. It had been a long week, but a good week. His legs felt tired as he started up the hill towards his house. He liked the feeling of exhaustion from a hard day's work and looked forward to relaxing with his girls and Marie. He knew that by the time he reached the top of the hill, **one of the girls** would be waiting for him with a Heineken chilled nearly to the point of freezing.

But suddenly, something went whizzing by his head and he looked up. There was Mirabella, standing with her slingshot and a look of fear on her face. She reached down, picking up another pebble, when he heard a moan. He looked behind him, and there was Marcus lying on the ground, a trickle of blood coming from a wound on the side of his head opened up by Marabella's shot. He was just about ready to yell at her when he saw a shiny flicker of the knife blade still in Marcus's hand. He hadn't even sensed

Marcus's presence. Mirabella was running down the hill, her slingshot now pulled back, her focus trained on Marcus. Any movement by Marcus would have brought a second – and most likely more deadly – projectile into his temple. Cédric reached down and grabbed the knife still clenched in Marcus's hand as he lay there, stunned. He threw it into the brush.

In moments, Mirabella had descended the steep hill and was standing next to Cédric. "Should I give him another one, Dad? He was going to hurt you!"

"If he moves, yes! By the way, great shot! You saved my life, sweet child, you saved my life." There was another moan from Marcus, and Mirabella pulled back on her slingshot. Cédric looked around and saw some wire lying on the ground. He quickly retrieved it and put it to use, binding Marcus's hands behind his back.

Higher up the hill, he could hear Daniella yelling, "Trouble! Dad's in trouble!" A few heartbeats later, Marie, the rest of the girls, and John came running down the hill. Cédric was tying Marcus's feet together with another strand of wire when they arrived, wondering what was going on.

Mirabella looked at Marie, saying, "He had a knife and was coming at Dad."

"A knife?" John asked.

Cédric answered, "Yeah, it's over there in the brush. I threw it there as soon as I got it out of his hand. I didn't know how much fight he had left in him." John searched through the brush and soon came back with an 8-inch fillet knife as sharp as any razor he had ever used to shave.

Cédric looked at Mirabella. She still had the slingshot in its ready position, clenching the stone between her thumb and index finger, the rubber from the innertube he had made the slingshot with still drawn taut. He smiled at her. "You can stand down, my little soldier, it's okay. I'm safe now, thanks to you." Everyone looked at her. Cédric smiled as he explained, "Our little soldier here took him down from the top of the hill when he was running full speed toward me. I never even heard him until I heard him moaning and his body hitting the ground; I just heard the whizzing of the stone going past my head."

Everyone stared at Mirabella in amazement, but she hardly noticed. She was still stiff and on guard from all the adrenaline pumping through her veins. "Are you sure you're okay, Dad? Are you sure?"

"Yes, my little soldier, but only because of you." The calmness, compassion and gratitude in his voice allowed Mirabella to relax. She dropped her slingshot, ran to him, and threw her arms around his neck. Tears of relief now flowed down her cheeks.

"He was going to hurt you! I can't lose you! I can't lose you!"

Framing her face in his hands, Cédric said, "You're not going to lose me, honey! You're never going to lose me. Sorry, you're stuck with me for life!" He picked her up, and they all started up towards the house, John basically dragging Marcus along, as he was still stunned from the blow.

Cédric looked at Marie with an expression of deadly seriousness. "Call Daniel and Sam. Tell them we have what they are looking for."

Once up at the top of the hill, John propped Marcus up against a tree and the rest of them sat around the picnic table, not knowing what to do. None had ever been in this circumstance before. None had ever sat around a picnic table staring at an assassin just taken down by a little girl and her slingshot. Juliana suggested to Marie with the innocence of youth, "Mom, can we have some chips and salsa and some lemonade? I'll help."

"That's a great idea, honey. I talked with Daniel and Sam, and they're on their way, but they're on the other side of the island, so it will take a little while." She and Juliana scurried into the kitchen and soon returned with a big bowl of salty lime tortilla chips and another one of salsa – her own special blend of tomatoes, corn, onions, spices and herbs and plenty of peppers.

Marcus sat under the tree, watching the group munching on chips and salsa and drinking lemonade, knowing he had messed up big time. He knew his hours were numbered. His mind was busy with trying to figure out a way to survive, but he wasn't finding any options.

After about half an hour, Daniel, Gloria and Sam came walking up the hill. Sam walked over and instinctively checked the wires to see if they were still secure. He added a pair of handcuffs, just to make sure. John showed them the knife, as the girls told them the story of how their sister had taken down Marcus.

Sam rubbed Mirabella's head, messing up her hair. "A real David and Goliath story. You're going to have to draw a picture of this one."

Picking up the slingshot resting on the table next to Mirabella, Daniel asked, "So this is your weapon of choice, young lady! And you took him down from the top of the hill?"

She nodded. "Yes, from the top of the hill."

Daniel laughed. "Impressive! Really impressive! Remind me never to get on your bad side."

She smiled, enjoying the attention. She'd always liked both of them; but she especially enjoyed the strange little white guy who popped up every now and then; she felt safe around him.

After a while, Cédric sat down in front of Marcus. "Why? That's all I want to know – why."

"It's simple, Cédric, very simple. I like you and respect you, but one hundred thousand dollars is a lot of money. Me and my girlfriend Marie could've started over in New York. It was only about the money. I truly believe in what you're doing, but you'll never stop the trade; good intentions rarely win out over greed and evil doings. But, this time, I hope I chose the wrong side. You can tell Sam and Daniel that there will be no resistance from me; I'll tell them all I know about José and Mr. Mendez. All I ask is that they make it quick."

Cédric thanked him for his honesty. "I'll make a recommendation, but I never tell my guys how to do their work."

The group set about consuming eight slabs of ribs that had been slowly cooking all day. Cédric even allowed Marcus to have his hands cuffed in front of him so he could enjoy some ribs. Sam complained about that. "I think it's just a waste of good ribs," an opinion he repeated each time Marcus asked for more.

When night came, John helped Sam and Daniel get Marcus down the hill and into the trunk of his car. Then the trio drove to where Sam's sailing vessel was anchored offshore. John stayed on the shore and watched the small dingy motor its way out to the boat and sail away with Marcus. John got comfortable lounging on the hood, enjoying the warmth the car engine had created. He settled in to wait for them to return. It was over two hours later when Daniel returned in the dingy. Landing on shore, Daniel just reported, "Sam's going to stay on his boat. Thanks for waiting, my friend." The two old friends talked as they drove home; Daniel telling John that the only real new information they got from Marcus concerned Mr. Mendez, the New York Yankee. The details Marcus provided painted Mendez as a real bad player.

The next morning, Cédric stopped at the fruit stand, complaining about the pineapple he held in his hand, telling the vendor that the fruit was bad at its core. The woman appropriately apologized, smiling the whole time. Later, Ms. Dominique Bute read Cédric's note.

> The spy and the assassin were one and the same. Marcus, a man from St. Barth's. He has a girlfriend who works for you, who goes by the work name Lily. He said it was all about the money – José offered him one hundred thousand dollars. I don't know what you want to do with this Lily. I miss you. Please be safe.

Two days later, the flag at El Capitan was flying high. Cédric went for a walk.

Under the boulder was a small note:

> I'm glad you're safe, my friend. Not
> to worry about the Lily. It's been
> plucked and is no longer part of the
> garden. I have no more news except
> everybody is quite tense and on alert.
> Be safe until we meet again. I heard
> what the little one did. That little girl
> is quite something. It's amazing what
> wounds love can heal.

Cédric thought how true that last sentence was; he was quite amazed at how well each of his broken little angels were doing. But he also knew they had spirits looking out for them, especially around Sanctuary.

Chapter 30

José waited impatiently for his regular communication from Marcus; the more time passed, the more strongly he assumed that the spy had been found out. He had gotten no real useful information from Marcus except that all the training they were doing was practice in how to intercept and take over a yacht. There had been no training concerning a land assault, so he felt safer in his home. He was angry, and his anger grew each day he didn't hear from Marcus; no news most likely meant that Cédric was still alive. *That sonofabitch must have his own guardian angel,* he thought. It occurred to him for a second that maybe he and Cédric were just pawns in a high-level chess match between two deities. José didn't like that thought; he didn't like the thought of being anybody's pawn. He preferred the image of having a protective devil watching out for him and working for him; that image sat much better with his narcissism.

The time was nearing; one more day until he and his crew were due to set off on the route with another boat following. He was ready. The test assault had gone well. They had targeted Juan, José's disloyal apprentice-gone-competitor-in-training. They had shot a couple of rifle rounds into his yacht so he would sense the danger and know that the assault was for real. Then José himself took aim with the grenade launcher. He missed with the first two shots; he didn't quite have the timing down, as both boats crashed up and down on waves to different rhythms. But his third shot landed directly on the deck of Juan's yacht.

José watched as two men were blown five feet into the air and overboard from the blast. He laughed hysterically as he watched the yacht, its motor still running, circle round and round without its pilot. His second in command then laid a roll of machine-gun fire just below the, waterline ripping into the fiberglass of the hull. The circles got smaller and smaller as it took on water, and it finally sunk, becoming another wreck in the Caribbean. They watched for a few minutes for any survivors, but none surfaced.

José felt a thrill at the kick of the grenade launcher against his shoulder. He could feel its destructive power. Then, the climax of the huge explosion. It was the perfect weapon. His immediate thought was that he should have gotten a few of these years ago and done a bit of pirating. He had planned to leave one survivor to spread the message nobody homes in on what is José's. But José's men would get the message out. His only real concern was whether there be any push-back from the Russians, who he knew were trying to make inroads into his business through the likes of Juan and the others now getting into this extremely profitable enterprise.

José had had a special rack built on each boat next to the pilot's seat so the grenade launcher and extra shells would be immediately available in case of any attack.

The next morning, he and his crew set out to collect his lucrative merchandise. Roberto's contingent would follow a week behind him. José believed if there were an attack, it would be on this trip or the next one; everything pointed in that direction. That's why he had spent the money for the extra boat that would carry five more men and a mounted machine gun. José was sure if they wanted to stop his slave trade and rescue his cargo, they too would want the confrontation to be sooner rather than later.

It took three days to get to their first rendezvous point, where they filled up with gas. His hunters were waiting with three young jungle girls for him. Two were probably fourteen or fifteen years old. The third one was younger, with her breasts just budding. She would be his tonight. They were still in their native dress, with grass and leaf skirts protecting their privates and colorful bird feathers adorning their hair and skirts. The hunters were especially happy because they knew the girls – especially the young one – were José's favorite type. They expected top dollar for these prizes and they got it.

The three girls were still terrified from the ordeal that they'd been through over the past couple of days. It started when they had been casually walking down a dense trail with their father. Two men sprang on them from behind some trees and shot the girls' father dead before he even took his bow off his shoulder. The girls screamed. The oldest tried to run, but, being disorientated from all the commotion and nearly insane from what she had witnessed, she ran directly into one of the hunters, who hit her on the side of the head with his pistol, knocking her out. The two younger girls froze. The hunters tied the girls together and marched them back to the river, where the third member of their party and a motorized canoe were waiting. It was a three-day journey back down the river and over to the beach where they would meet up with José. They fed the girls well; they wanted them looking good, not malnourished. They took turns dragging the oldest-looking girl into their tent, as they figured the depreciation for wear and tear would affect her price the least. The two other sisters watched in horror, fearing they would be next.

They lit signal fires to indicate they had merchandise. José arrived, and the exchange went off as usual. The hunters were very pleased with the prices they got, and José was excited when he saw the youngest girl. It had been a long time since he had one so young and fresh.

José was very pleased that night, for the young one did not give up her prize too quickly – she fought hard, even biting him to where she drew blood on his arm right above his tattoo of the naked lady under the palm tree. But as always, he eventually won out and then turned her over to his crew, who had been watching and waiting until the boss finished with her and placed the little necklace that said Ginger around her neck. Then was José's turn to take the watch as his crew spent the rest of the night with her. In the morning, the three girls were carried to the boat, the older sisters nursing the younger one as well as they could. She was nearly in a catatonic state when the shackles were put around her wrists and ankles. José's yacht sailed out of the harbor and towards the next rendezvous point, about two hundred miles north up the coast and into French Guiana.

When José and his crew arrived at the second rendezvous, he could see with his binoculars that six adults waited, each with a child or two to be sold. Nothing looked suspicious or out of the norm. He knew he likely would not be attacked at a rendezvous spot, since the jungle surrounding them would give his crew too many ways to get away. But still, José left one of the crew on the ship with the grenade launcher. The entire beach was within its range, so if anything happened, the grenade launcher could pepper the beach with shells. The second boat with the mounted machine gun was about a quarter mile back and would quickly join the fight.

José mentally dismissed the two older girls right away, since they looked to be around 18 years of age. They were not to his taste, but he was sure they would be sold to another boat in the near future, for they were of average looks and Mexican brothels always needed new faces. Times must have been tough in this region, for all the girls were skinny compared to their parents. During tough times, families who were going to sell a child often gave them little to eat, reasoning it did not make sense to waste good food on them. But José had a way of looking past that and seeing the potential of a young girl. It would be his job to fatten them up and get them ready for market. He always wanted them looking their best when it was time for him to parade them in front of his buyers.

José had brought some food supplies from the boat, and the women fixed up a big afternoon meal for everyone, including the children – probably their first real meal in a while. After the meal, José sat with the parents while the children walked and played on the beach. He showed them his laminated pictures of America, with happy white parents standing with their mixed-race children, all with big, happy smiles. He loved taking out the pictures of endless cornfields in the Midwest; there would always be instant chatter, smiles, and happiness. Depending on his mood and whether he had time, he would take out pictures of farms and cities covered in snow, and this always caused quite a reaction. Often people didn't understand what snow was. It always brought more questions than answers; it looked like sand, but how could sand fall from the sky? Frozen water didn't make sense, but they always thought it beautiful. His big finale was showing them pictures of herds of fat cows grazing in the fields. To them, cows meant wealth; a field full of cows meant extreme wealth and would help them mentally justify the selling of their daughters and sons. It reassured them that the children were going to a good home.

José's buyers had put in an order for two boys, ages seven or eight if he could find some in good health. There was one boy for sale on the beach who fit this description perfectly. He had a scar on his leg about 3 inches long that José would later use to bargain down his price when it came to negotiate the terms at the end of the day. In the end, José's crew motored out four young girls and the boy, who was bought at a good price, to the yacht. José thought to himself that the boat was filling up nicely. By the end of his route, he'd probably need the extra chains he kept under the seat on the deck.

There would be no beach party for the crew this night because José had not bought all the children, and parents still hopeful of selling their offspring still camped out on the beach, waiting for the next ship to come by. Normally when the beach party wasn't an option for the crew, José put a mat on the deck of the yacht and the rapes took place there. He never wanted to be denied his sick pleasures. But tonight, the radar showed what looked like a good-sized rainstorm heading their way, so they put off their fun and headed up the coast to a bay about 15 miles north that offered good protection for José and his escort boat to ride out the rainstorm.

They got both boats got anchored and everything secured just as the heaviest of the rain started. José got about fixing up a big batch of his stew, with the crying and whimpering of the young ones in chains as his background music. All ate well, except for the girl that José and his crew had raped the night before. She was still nearly catatonic and wanting no food; it looked like her spirit had been broken. José had seen this happen before. If, in two or three days, she hadn't snapped out of it, he would put weights on her ankles and throw her overboard so her space could be filled. He lost a child or two every now and then; it was part of the cost of doing business. But he would save the necklace to give to another young innocent.

Chapter 31

The most difficult part of the assault would be taking out the men manning the machine guns and grenade launchers in boats traveling at 50 to 60 miles per hour, likely in choppy waters. The whole plan was based on the snipers succeeding with this task. Thomas worked with Sam and his SEAL buddies to design, configure, build and install gun mounts on their boats to steady their aim under these conditions. Thomas had used shock absorbers from old Yamaha motorcycles as part of the mounts. They would absorb some of the pounding of the boat as it raced across the wave tops. Sam and his buddies were impressed with the design Thomas came up with. They were sure that the mounts would greatly increase the chances that their sniper shots would find their mark.

Once the mounts were affixed, the snipers took the boats out practicing for hours on end. A very brave man with a smaller boat loaded with a high-performance motor provided the moving targets by attaching rows of pineapples to the bow of his boat, then speeding around 500 to 600 meters away from Sam and his sniper buddies, who were also in speeding boats. This was their best idea for simulating the chaotic real-life situation they would encounter. The snipers needed to get used to the up-and-down motions of both boats and learn to mentally calibrate these motions into their shots. Most likely, their reasoning went, any man shooting a machine gun or grenade launcher at them would be standing in the front of a boat, thus pineapples about the size of a man's head were placed there. Oscar, the volunteer recruiter from St. Barth's, volunteered to drive the boat with the pineapple targets. Everyone knew he was doing it to make up for bringing Marcus into the workings of Sanctuary, something he felt horrible about. Soon, flying pieces of pineapple were feeding the fish. That's not to say there weren't a few holes in the boat Oscar drove. They all laughed when Oscar pulled his boat on to shore with his face and clothes covered in pineapple.

Their whole plan rested on the snipers taking out the heavy weapons. The machine guns would be taken out first, for their range was much farther than the 40mm grenade launchers and they posed the first level of threat. Sam and his SEAL buddies knew that the plan hinged on them and the accuracy of the first few – maybe first two – shots. The lives of their friends not only depended on their accuracy, but they all knew that within the yachts were hulls full of young girls and boys whose lives depended on them. They did not want to sink those boats. But if José decided to sink his own boat out of desperation and rage, diving gear was at the ready. Being skilled divers, they would try to rescue the children before the sea could claim them. Cédric and the others wanted no more graves in SANCTUARY if at all possible.

Meanwhile, tips were coming in, and the mission expanded. The group now aimed to take out all the sex trafficking operations they knew about in the Caribbean in one operation. Margaret and Gloria worked every possible source and connection they had throughout the Caribbean, and Daniel and Sam provided information from the interviews they had conducted. They identified four prime groups of sex traffickers, all smaller players than José and Roberto: two out of Trinidad – both former apprentices of José; another former associate working out of Martinique; and a freelancer working out of Turks and Caicos.

The plan came together. As the main forces of Sanctuary were attacking José and Roberto, smaller subunits would simultaneously attack the ships or homes of these four other groups. Timing would be important because once the main assault started, word of it would quickly spread within the community of sex traffickers throughout the Caribbean by phone and radio. Then the cockroaches would be scattering in all directions. Sam kidded, "It's going to be just like in the Godfather when all the other Dons were taken out simultaneously. Then we name you 'Don Cédric.'"

Cédric, Ramus, Gloria, Alma, and Sam and his SEAL friends spent their evenings going over charts, maps and every piece of logistical information they had, and were constantly collecting more. Thomas and John were collecting and organizing all the equipment they needed for each of the assault teams, who were beginning their own practice drills.

Marie and the other wives would stay on St. Maarten in case something horrible happened and the whole operation was unsuccessful. In that awful scenario, they would carry on the work to protect and raise the girls with Marilyn's and hopefully, the community's help.

At the same time all this would be going down, a SEAL friend of Sam Dresser's would visit Mr. Salvador Mendez of the New York Yankees, wherever he was – whether in New York or on the road for an "away" game. It was decided that Mr. Mendez would have an accident over and over again with a baseball bat, and photos of him with José and the young 10- and 12-year-old girls would be laid across his body. Police and the newspapers would receive tips about where to find his body because members of Sanctuary did not want Mendez's publicist or agent finding him so some spin could be done on his death to preserve his reputation and their streams of money from his merchandise contracts. He would be exposed for what he was—a pedophile.

The only flaw they could see in the plan was that José Ravaia would most likely be killed by a sniper's bullet; they all expected that, because of his narcissistic personality and inflated ego, he would either man one of the machine guns or grenade launchers. If this was true, he would have to be taken out quickly, experiencing too easy a death. If he could be taken alive –which all prayed for – they would stake him out on the St. Maarten garbage piles at the dump. Small cuts on his genitals should ensure that the smell of blood would attract the resident rats to feast on him until he was no more. The women of Sanctuary had decided this fate, should he be taken alive.

Three days before they were to set out on the synchronized assault, Cédric went to the fruit stand complaining about a rotten pineapple. The woman was very apologetic, and as always, took the old rotten fruit, giving him a fresh one. Later, Ms. Dominique Bute read the message transported in the spoiled pineapple:

Dearest Friend and Ally,

In three days' time, we embark on our mission to hunt and destroy the network and kill the man who stole your innocence. Pray for us! Please pray for us! Your prayers, especially, will help carry me and give me the courage to do what I must. I hope our ancestors will guide us and watch over us.

I ask a favor of you. I've decided that around my neck, I will wear "Tammy's" necklace, for I have no more innocence left in me, either. Please honor me by allowing me to wear the "Kitty" necklace you gave to me. I have added a couple of extra links to both so they will be next to my heart, as will pictures of my wife, my children, and my daughters who rest in SANCTUARY.

I hope if we're successful, we can soon meet again and tell the story of how you are the bravest amongst us.

With sincere love,
C.

The flag flew high the next day at El Capitan. Cédric hiked to the rock, contemplating everything that had brought him to this moment in his life. Reaching the boulder, he reached under it and took out Dominique's reply:

Dear Sweet Man,

I went to church today and lit a candle for all of you – but especially you. I will do that every day until you return. It is not you who is honored, but me. Yes, of course, wear "Kitty" next to your heart. I know Tammy already lives in there. I have only loved and allowed two men into my heart: one is my dear friend and protector Albert; the other is you. Be safe. I want to meet you again, this time as an honorable woman, not a whore.

Dear friend, I have no more words. I am tired, so very tired. I have a request. I don't know why I ask this of you, but if something happens to me, promise to go to France and see my daughters and tell them my true story as I told it to you. Let them know who their mother really was; children should know this. And most of all, tell them how much I love them.

May the ancient ones walk with you. Be safe.

Love,
DB

The night before the mission was to commence, the members of Sanctuary gathered. Pastor Eboune blessed the boats and the men, and the barbeque served that night was barely touched as everyone seemed to withdraw into their own thoughts in readiness for the battle. As the evening's gathering ended, Cédric walked up into SANCTUARY. He knelt at Tammy's grave, folded his hands, and prayed. He prayed that he could honor the task given him. He prayed that what they were doing would bring meaning for all those whose lives have been treated as if they were meaningless. He prayed that his ancestors who roamed the islands would watch over his family if something happened to him.

When Cédric finished praying, he opened his eyes. Kneeling next to him on his right, hands folded in prayer, was his great, great, great grandfather, and on the other side was sweet young Tammy. She knelt also, praying. He looked around. All his daughters of SANCTUARY were kneeling in front of their own graves, hands folded, praying. Looking around, he saw throughout the hills his slave ancestors also kneeling and praying. And then in an instant, in a soft breeze, they were all gone; but he knew they were not.

The next morning was cloudy and rainy when six groups of men and boats headed in different directions out into the Caribbean. They set out to be in position three days from that morning. The command would come over their specified radio frequency, and all assaults would be carried out simultaneously. It was time.

Chapter 32

José, his crew, and the boat following them had enjoyed a successful trip. They had only lost one this trip: the young jungle girl who José and his crew had brutally assaulted on their first night with "cargo" had been thrown overboard somewhere near Venezuela. The hull of his boat carried twenty-three young girls and two slight boys – all frightened, longing for their families, missing their homes, afraid of their future, and especially frightened of the men imprisoning them. Five young girls, none over eleven years old, wore necklaces bearing the name *Ginger* around their necks.

José was feeling a bit relieved; he thought for sure he would have been attacked by now. If those Sanctuary people knew as much as he thought they did, he reasoned that they surely would have attacked earlier to spare some of the young ones the fates they faced with him. *Maybe,* he thought, *they're not as brave as I've heard. Maybe they're more talk, rumor and myth than action.* But he knew they had killed. He decided he would not let his guard down.

He stopped at the secure beach in Columbia to pick up the cocaine as he had **many times** before. The cartel representative who was there to meet him asked if José would **be willing to** take an extra 200 kg up to Puerto Rico. A plane was ready to take off for the US the moment José docked there. Demand had been high of late, creating a shortage which they wanted to fill quickly. If José agreed, Roberto would also take more cocaine when he came seven days from now. The pay was right, and he was feeling safe, smug and arrogant, believing his guardian devil was doing a good job protecting him. José agreed. *Why not?* he thought, *I got all this extra protection, might as well make some extra money to pay for it.* The only problem was the space where he usually stored the cocaine would not hold that much, so he would have to keep the container down below with the children, but he figured it was worth the risk – good economics.

José sat in the Captain's chair as they headed back out to sea. He was feeling proud of everything he had put together during his life: he was proud to be a respected smuggler, slave trader and pedophile. He was thinking how some people were only good at one thing, but he was good at three. About two hours out to sea, he was lulled by the calm weather – a gentle breeze that kept the waves rhythmic, blue skies with the white puffy clouds that always reminded him of cotton candy and how, when he was in his late teens, he would lure little girls living in the ghetto with cotton candy to get them in his van. During this time, he developed his taste for young virgin girls. He was in **the middle** of these pleasant memories when out of the corner of his eye, he saw a fast-moving boat off to his right. That wasn't uncommon; **in fact,** on this trip alone, he had seen at least a dozen boats. But he needed to pay attention to it. The crew on both boats knew the procedure; they would get to their stations and take the safeties off the guns.

Cédric gave the signal to all six teams spread across the Caribbean. It began.

José heard a loud crack, looked over and saw the head of the man tending the machine gun explode. José pushed the throttle to full speed, flying over the waves, almost airborne trying to get away, but yachts don't travel as fast as cigarette boats. He was counting on his firepower to win this battle. His guard boat was keeping up, bouncing off wave after wave. Another man pushed his dead crewmate over the side of the boat and took his place at the machine gun, knowing it was their only hope. Soon he had met the same fate, except for him the blast and bouncing on the boat immediately threw him overboard. The sea streaked with red in their wake. José signaled for his second-in-command to come take over the controls. He grabbed a grenade launcher, armed it and shot off a round; it fell about 20 yards in front of the boat picking off his soldiers.

Sam loaded another shell in the chamber, this time taking aim directly at the machine gun. A second later, sparks were flying as the round found its mark. The machine gun would not bother them anymore. Cédric kept his eyes on the man with the grenade launcher, who was reloading and sending off another round. This one landed only ten yards from the boat, so Sam yelled to John, the pilot, "Too close for comfort!! Back off a bit! This contraptionThomas built is working perfectly so we don't need to be so close!"

Cédric yelled to Sam, "It's him, Sam! It's José! God be with your aim! Please see if you can just wound him!" Sam knew as well as anyone what type of evil José was but, he also knew his training: all shots were kill shots; it was always too dangerous to leave an adversary wounded. They circled around as José's boat swerved back and forth to become a more difficult target. As John circled the boat, another grenade landed 30 yards away.

Sam yelled out, "That's perfect, John! Stay this distance away and he can fire at us all day long and never hit us. I'll be done here soon." Sam was adjusting his sights for the new distance.

José saw what the problem was and shouted at his pilot, "Charge them! Go directly at them! We're too far away! We can't outrun them even with our extra motor." The pilot turned the yacht and pushed the throttle down, knowing that moments were important. José grinned and yelled, "Perfect! Faster if you can!"

Sam saw what was happening. He shouldered his rifle, taking it out of the mount. He saw José raise the now reloaded grenade launcher to his shoulder, and through his scope, he saw the sick smile on the slaver's face – right in his crosshairs. He squeezed off a round and just as the bullet was fired, the boat hit a wave, taking Sam's round off its projected course. The bullet hit the grenade launcher and ricocheted into José's shoulder. They all watched José spin around, the grenade launcher falling into the ocean as José fell out of their line of sight; they couldn't tell whether he was alive or dead. The two boats raced towards each other, and at the last moment, José's pilot turned away to avoid the collision. As he did, Cédric put a round in his shoulder, and the rest of the men exchanged gunfire in a heated firefight. John took a bullet, as did Cédric, but no others were hurt. As John fell to the ground, Cédric, though wounded, took control of the boat. The two boats turned around to charge each other again. Then suddenly, as they raced towards each other, the other boat lost power; its motor had been turned off. Two men appeared on deck with their hands raised high. Cédric pulled the boat up alongside the bobbing craft, raised his 9 mm and shot them both dead. "Only one prisoner, if he is still alive."

Sam covered any movement on the slaver's yacht as his Seal buddy quickly attended to Cédric's and John's wounds. Cédric's was through the fleshy part of his thigh, an inch away from his femoral artery. Had the artery been hit, he would have bled out before the gun battle was over. John was not so lucky – he had taken a round in the stomach. Cédric asked how his friend was, and the man called Gus didn't have the heart to tell Cédric there was no chance of saving his friend. "It's not good, Cédric," he reported, "but maybe we can patch him up and get him back home where a real doc can look after him."

Sanctuary's other cigarette boat chase down Jose's second boat and the snipers quickly made it useless because it was full of dead bodies.

Cédric was anxious. Sam quickly tied their cigarette boat and the yacht together, and cautiously he and Cedric climbed onto José's yacht. José was lying on the deck with a large wound in his shoulder. A smaller piece of shrapnel had taken out one of his eyes, but he was alive. Burning with rage, Cédric looked into Sam's eyes and snarled, "Make sure the son of a bitch doesn't die!"

As the intensity of the moment passed its peak, they heard the cries of the children below. Cédric climbed down into the hull of the yacht and what he found broke his heart once more. There were 25 children, all looking terrified. Their wrists and ankles were bloody from their shackles tearing their flesh as they were tossed about during the battle. They would have scars to remember the day they were set free. Cédric started with the closest child, unchaining each one, kissing foreheads and

247

hugging them. "You're free," he soothed them. "You're free. They'll never hurt you again." The children slowly climbed up on deck into the sunlight. As soon as the children were settled, he jumped back onto his boat to see how bad John's wounds were, he could tell John would not make it.

His heart had never known suffering as he was feeling right then. These children were alive, their fright was real, their brokenness – the hell they had been through – etched on their young faces. They were free but at a cost. He just wanted to get his friend home so he could die in his wife's arms. Cédric now knew personally for the first time in his life the true suffering that his ancestors had gone through; freedom came at a price. He could hear their cries of sadness and anguish in his mind or were they his?

The battle was over.

Cédric quickly got on the radio to see how the other attack teams were faring. In all told, three members of Sanctuary were dead. This was not counting John, who still had breath. Oscar from St. Barth's was the first of Sanctuary to die as he charged into the home of the trafficker living on Martinique. Ramus and three others had wounds, but it was believed that all would recover.

Forty-eight children were liberated that day.

Daniel, in the control center, had been listening to everything being said on the radios. In only a matter of seconds he and Alma were on a cigarette boat speeding to meet the boat where his friend lay dying. Again, the spirits of their ancestors offered John their comfort, singing softly and praying with him. He was praying to see his wife again.

Alma and Daniel arrived in time so John could die cradled in the arms of his dear wife and his best and oldest friend. But he knew it was time to go when Tammy and his mother stood before him, offering him their hands. Alma held John's lifeless body the rest of the way back to Saint Martin with Daniel sitting next to her.

Chapter 33

A small parade of boats used and captured in the battle slowly made their way back to Saint Martin. Cédric was on José's captured yacht with the rescued children. They passed the beaches filled with tourists drinking Heineken and *Presidenté* beer, listening to reggae music, playing volleyball and building sandcastles. They were all oblivious to what was passing in front of them: the survivors of the largest battle to have gone down in the Caribbean in decades. The vessels moored on the beach where the first sixteen girls of Sanctuary had been carried up the hill. There would be no landing in any official port, no need for authorities and their laws – justice had been the law of the day.

Two hours later, the second small flotilla – the one that had taken down José's cousin using the same sniper strategy – arrived at the beach. The 23 children they had rescued stayed on the boats until the wounded and the dead could be taken off. Rasmus had taken a bullet in his leg and another had nicked his hand. Another one of Sanctuary's militia, a schoolteacher named Ken, had taken a bullet to the shoulder. A man named Craig, a lobster fisherman from Saba, lay dead in the bottom of the cigarette boat with a blue tarp left over from Hurricane Irma covering his body. A bullet had gone through his neck and he had bled out within a minute.

Over the next few hours, the other teams would arrive back in St. Martin with their wounded and dead.

The two former apprentices of José working out of Trinidad had been taken down quickly after a short gun battle. Oscar died taking down the trafficker who operated out of Martinique. The scoundrel had been listening on the shortwave radio and knew something was up; he was ready when Oscar and the others came through the door. Another man, Julio, also one of the young men from Saint Barth's, also died before a SEAL buddy of Sam's dropped Julio's and Oscar's killer with two shots to the head. The freelancer working out of Turks and Caicos died quickly while lying around his pool. Except for the wounded who needed immediate attention, the Sanctuary members waited on the beach until all were home and accounted for. The group anguished over those they lost. Still, for the complexity and size of the operation, they all knew it had gone well.

Runners fetched four slabs of wood saved from the original slave ship while the women washed the bodies of the four who had fallen, John, Oscar, Craig and Julio. The bodies of the men were placed on the slabs of wood for their journey up the hill. After Pastor Eboune blessed the bodies, they were slowly carried up to Sanctuary. John's was the last body in the procession; it only seemed fitting, for ever since he was a small child, John had covered his friends' backs.

Finally, Pastor Eboune blessed the children as they were helped ashore, and the rest of the group escorted them up the hill to their new home.

Within hours, the news of what had happened spread throughout the island. By dinnertime, islanders were already bringing prepared food to nourish everyone and welcome the children. Within twenty-four hours, men were already at work, expanding the living and eating quarters of Sanctuary. By the end of the week, Sanctuary would look like a small village itself, with forty-eight young new residents.

Three local doctors were staying at Sanctuary tending wounds since none of the wounded wanted to be taken to the hospital. Marilyn and some of her social work friends were there to start the healing process for all.

Funerals had to be planned. It was decided there would be one large funeral for all who had fallen. Amid the swirling emotions, a decision had to be made. The group wanted a special place to bury their fallen members, but Sanctuary had been conceived as a slave cemetery, and these four were not slaves, but free men who made a brave choice to risk their lives for this cause. They decided to build another cemetery next to SANCTUARY, where any member of Sanctuary could be buried. All that was needed was for the landowner to give permission, which he did; in fact, he deeded over all his land on the hill to Sanctuary, with the stipulation he could live on the land until he died and be buried in the cemetery dedicated to those who are part of and believed in the cause.

In contrast to the respectful and solemn activity, there was another kind of work to be done. José Ravaia was escorted very unceremoniously that first night by Sam and Daniel to the city dump, where they stripped him naked, staked him out, and made small cuts on his genitals so the animals and insects would know where to start. They carefully skinned the tattoo of the naked lady under the palm tree from his arm, as Cédric wanted to give it to

Dominique. Then they walked away, leaving a guard to watch over José.

After three hours, the guard placed a cage over him, with openings too small for the rats to get through. They crawled on the cage, squealing angrily about not being able to get to the meal they could see and smell. Thomas had built the cage because he wanted the other smaller creatures – the mice, the centipedes and millipedes, the maggots – all to have their day feeding. As night fell, the guard removed the cage covering José so the rats could eat their fill. He died that night.

Two days later, they held the funeral service for John, Oscar, Craig and Julio on the largest beach in Saint Martin. Tourists were diverted to other beaches, baffled at the unusual inconveniences on this hospitable island as hotels, restaurants, souvenir stores were closed or short-staffed as so many people skipped work to attend the funeral. It was an entire island funeral.

Even with a megaphone, the voices of Pastor Eboune and the others who spoke could not reach the edges of the crowd, where mourners simply bowed their heads and prayed to the accompaniment of the soft waves washing the beach. Oscar's family decided to bury him in the new cemetery along with his fallen friend instead of taking him back to St. Barth's; they knew their son would prefer to rest near the place, idea and dream he died for. As a sign of respect, no word of any of this was reported in the newspapers, except for the regular obituary notices.

The day after the funerals, three empty French military transports and two more filled with gendarmes came lumbering down the road. They pulled away the barriers that blocked the road up to SANCTUARY and proceeded up to Cédric's home. Local men and women were there working on the expansion.

They stopped working when Lieut. Col. Claude Fleming got out of his vehicle and walked up to Cédric.

"I have come for the children, and this time I will not leave without them. I have brought my men."

Cédric looked him in the eyes, his voice barely containing his rage. "Leave. Leave now, while you can. Sacrifices were made!"

"I am not leaving without the children. None of them have papers. There are many immigration issues, and who knows what diseases they may have. I hear some of them came straight from the jungle. We're going to shut this place down."

Cédric motioned for the top law enforcement officer in French Saint Martin to step off to the side with him. "I know why you're here. Your masters have told you to retrieve the cocaine. All I have to do is call out one word, and it will all be scattered to the wind. I don't care about their cocaine. They can have it back. I'll gladly give all it to them, but I want to meet face-to-face with your master and talk."

Cédric raised his hand, and the Lieutenant Colonel looked up to the top of the hill where ten men appeared with long rifles and the machine gun recovered from Roberto's boat. Some of the men working on the building, and even some other women, pulled pistols and stood at the ready. Cédric said, "Look down at the road." Lieut. Col. Claude Fleming looked down and saw more than one hundred people standing on the road with two-by-fours, baseball bats, tire irons, machetes, guns and some with rifles.

Cedric continued, "This is a fight you cannot win. Have your master call me. After we talk, I'll tell them where they can find their cocaine. You'll get paid and everything will be okay."

Fleming's veins were popping on his neck. "How dare you speak to me like this? Who the hell do you think you are?"

"I am Sanctuary. I speak for it. Now leave."

For the second time, Lieut. Col. Claudine Fleming left the hill empty-handed and humiliated. His authority had been shown to be empty compared to the conscience of good people. He was becoming more unstable with each encounter.

Chapter 34

Two days later, there was a message, "Next Tuesday there will be a yacht anchored a quarter-mile off Oyster Bay in the Atlantic. You wanted to talk; let's talk. I guarantee you your safety. Bring whomever you want. Paco Mandelaze."

It was not hard to check out Paco Mandelaze. Anyone who had anything to do with cocaine knew that Paco Mandelaze was the man running operations for one of the invisible cartels operating in Columbia and throughout the Caribbean. He was known as a "takes no prisoners" kind of guy, working his way up the food chain during the days of the Norte del Valle Cartel from delivery boy, to assassin, to handling the cartel's business in the Caribbean. Paco had grown up with Luis Enrique and Javier Antonio Calle Serna, the heads of the Norte del Valle Cartel. As the heydays of the cartels ended and drug lords became invisible, Paco was one of those who came out on top.

Since Ramus was still recovering from the bullets he had taken to his right hand and thigh, it was left to Thomas to accompany Cédric; the group's policy was to never let Cédric go alone.

When the sun rose that next Tuesday, a beautiful 70-foot yacht was anchored about a quarter mile out from Oyster Bay. Around ten-thirty in the morning, Cédric and Thomas motored out to the yacht and were graciously welcomed aboard.

When Paco invited them into his main dining cabin for an early lunch, Cédric asked, "Do you mind if we sit on the deck?"

Paco looked up into the hills and smiled. "I don't mind a bit. Which one of the hills is your sniper on?" he laughingly asked, knowing he would not receive an answer. "That's why I told you would be anchored a quarter of a mile offshore, within firing range of your men. I mean no harm to you. I'm doing everything I can to show you that, and I thought it was brilliant the way you used snipers to take out José's big guns that he was so proud of. He never had a chance from the beginning with that strategy. But you've cost me in delays, and you have quite a bit of something that's mine."

Cédric was **absolutely** sure that Sam and his friends had Paco in their crosshairs at this very moment, as was Mr. Mandelaze. As Cédric stared at the man sitting across the table from him, facing the bluffs of Saint Martin, he tried to size the man up. Cédric was trying to sense whether Mr. Paco Mandelaze was an evil man to his core, or just a businessman in a dirty business. He decided he was a bit of both. He carried himself well; he presented himself as sophisticated and powerful. He wasn't crude like José and his group, but Cédric could sense the deadly seriousness of the men around him; this man was at least as dangerous – perhaps more dangerous – than José. Just as Sam's sniper was trained on Paco, Paco's men stood ready to kill Thomas and him in a heartbeat.

"I want you to know that I believe the trading of flesh is a dirty business, especially when it involves the young ones," was how Paco started off the conversation.

"Then why were you in it?"

Paco leaned over and very seriously looked at Cédric. "I was not in that business. I want to make that perfectly clear: I was not in that dirty business. I was using José because of his connections, which I needed. The man he dealt with in Puerto Rico was a very competent conduit for getting our cocaine to the United States, and he did a good job for us. In disrupting that connection, you have caused problems for us. But you need to understand that we do not deal in flesh; we deal in cocaine."

"He was a slave trader. He even sold Colombian children. Does that not matter to you?" Cédric challenged.

"You probably think I'm evil, but if some parent wants to sell their daughter, that's none of my business. That was José's business. Just as I don't care if someone wants to snort a deadly powder up into their nose, but supplying *that is* my business. And I'm good at it. I make no apologies, just like I'm sure you make no apologies for torturing those men. By the way, how did he do, staked out on that garbage heap? We can all justify what we do, but I will grant you that what you're doing and what you stand for is much better than what I stand for. I do respect what you're trying to do, but I don't want you getting in my business." Paco sat back in his chair, watching, waiting for Cédric's response.

There was a silence for a minute or so and then Cédric spoke up. "We have no desire or intention to interfere with your business. That's why I made it clear that I am totally willing to give you back all of your cocaine. Our cause is a righteous cause; slavery – and especially young children being turned into sex slaves – is something no one should condone."

Paco interrupted. "On this, we can agree, but it is a sad reality that this goes on."

Cédric angrily looked Paco square in the eyes and said, "But because of your dealings with José, scum like him, you were condoning it. It's clear you're a very smart man; you could have found ways around working with José, as I'm sure you're doing right now. You either condoned it more than you say, or you were very lazy using José." Two of Paco's men stepped forward. Paco raised his hand and Sam, watching from the hills through the scope of his sniper rifle, relaxed the tension on his trigger finger when he saw Paco's men step back.

Mandelaze responded with a laugh, "I was lazy. I like you. You're honest and you've got balls. You're right, José was easy and simple. And you're also right that we're making those connections as we speak. If you give me back my cocaine, it will be in the United States by tomorrow, on its way to all those Americans who like their nose candy. You know what I want from you.

What is it you want from us?"

"I want your guarantee that you will not be involved in sex trafficking in the Caribbean or anywhere. You will not sell anyone into slavery. That's all I want from you. And I suppose I must add I don't want you in it even by association with men like José. I would ask that you leave them to us to deal with."

"Done. As I've said, we're not in that business, so it's easy for me to agree to this. In fact, if I hear about it – and I have many sources – that information will quickly become yours."

"Good. I do know that your word is good; that is your reputation."

Cédric raised his hand, then he looked at Paco. "You see that barren island over to my left? A man is right now planting a flag where your cocaine is buried. It's all there." They all looked over at the island. After a minute or so, a man got into a small boat and motored away, leaving a small red flag waving in the wind on the backside of the island, visible from where they were but not from Saint Martin.

Paco smiled, and then looking at Thomas, he pushed a briefcase toward him that had been resting beside his chair. "This is for your children. We can see that you're doing a lot of building."

"What is it?"

"One million dollars US currency. Consider it a finder's fee – after all, you did find and return a lot of cocaine."

Thomas accepted the briefcase with a glance at Cédric and a nod to Mandelaze.

Now, let's have a good lunch. Oh, and by the way, Lieutenant Colonel Claude Fleming may be returning to France soon. We have a friend working on that. He's become a nuisance not just for you but for us. He's untouchable, but not indispensable."

Cédric felt a great relief hearing that, as his confrontations with Fleming were getting worse with each encounter.

As they sat eating lunch, another boat approached the island from a different direction, and after a few minutes, they could see Paco's men carrying the cases of cocaine to the boat. Then it sped off.

Their lunch conversation was almost pleasant as the men sized each other up and agreed to some rules for their peaceful coexistence. As the visit was wrapping up, Paco cocked his head and said to Cédric, "Some information for you. You have created a vacuum. The Russians are already moving in to fill the space. They are much more ruthless than José. They are racist, not liking anyone of my color or especially of yours. You'll need to send them a message – a strong message – if you don't want them here. I'm sure they will aggressively let you know they don't want you here and that they are in charge. I'll be sitting on the sidelines watching, as they say. I have no dog in this fight. But I do appreciate the good that you're trying to do. You and I know there is much evil in this world; we are actually part of it, both you and me. But some evils are worse than others. These Russians are the worst kind. Be careful."

Chapter 35

The flag flew high the next day at El Capitan. Cédric's wounds were healing well, but he walked with quite a pronounced limp. Gingerly, he trekked up the hill, watching out for the many boulders strewn about the trail. When he reached the summit, he found no note, but tucked under the boulder was a plane ticket to Martinique, dated two days hence. He could feel himself smiling and excited; he was going to see his ally and good friend Madame Dominique Bute again. It had been way too long.

He informed the group he had a business trip that would take him off the island for a few hours that coming Thursday. The entire group was very reluctant to let him go alone. "Please, Cédric, let me go with you. I won't be a nuisance. And you're still healing." Thomas did his best to convince Cédric to accompany him. But Cédric made it very clear to all that he would be going alone.

Cédric enjoyed the view out the plane's window on the short flight to Martinique. The puffy white cumulus clouds seemed to symbolize the calm now in the air for all those involved in Sanctuary. The good people of Saint Martin were proud of the victory won. The news of it had spread faster than the winds of Hurricane Irma, which had been the first domino to fall in this journey. Many of the good people of Saint Martin had long been tired of the ugliness they all knew surrounded them. They had felt powerless in the face of this evil, but the events of the last couple of years changed that and their attitudes. They were proud that, for at least a moment, justice seemed to win out.

The new dormitories of Sanctuary were coming along well, for, as they say, many hands make light work. Many of the good women of Saint Martin, who would have never thought of selling a child provided care and mothering to the little ones. No one wanted them to feel like orphans; they truly were children of the island now. The children were responding well to the care and love that constantly surrounded them. Those that had been wearing necklaces would need more than love and care, so Marilyn and her social work friends were in charge of healing and tending to them. Of course, Mirabella and Monique were helping by telling the girls of their own survival. They were Marilyn's most effective co-therapists.

Cédric's plane landed smoothly at the airport on Martinique, and as he emerged from the airport, he saw Ms. Dominique Bute standing next to a car, waiting for him as before. Smiles of pride and gratitude filled their faces. They had not seen each other face-to-face in well over a year; it had not been safe. It still wasn't, but it seemed less unsafe. Ms. Dominique Bute ran to him and hugged him, not wanting to let go. She had so few true friends, and she counted Cédric as one of those. He felt the same way about her.

As Dominique released Cédric and stepped back to look at him, she said, "When I heard there were casualties and you were hurt, I could hardly catch my breath until I heard that your wounds were not life-threatening. It's so nice to see you! I've longed for this day since the last time we met on this island."

"Me, too!" Cédric said, staring into her eyes, looking to see how the events may have changed her. She looked older and tired.

She touched his wound. "How bad is it?"

"Actually, it's not that bad. Doc says I should have full use of my leg in about a year if I do my exercises."

"I must tell you, I'm so happy about what's taking place up on the hill. I drive by the hill to see the building going on and the children talking and playing in the yard, some hand in hand with good people who all clearly care for them. I get a tear in my eyes when I drive past; I wish there had been a place like Sanctuary for me. Perhaps my life would have been very different." She didn't let herself stay in that thought too long. "Oh well, it wasn't meant to be."

Cédric pushed. "Please, woman! For God's sake, know that none of this would happen without you. I know – and I wish others did, too – that in many ways, you were the general behind the scenes. You are Sanctuary as surely – even more so – than I am. I long for the day when you can step out of the shadows and people can hear your story. Your life is a great book that sits on the shelf, waiting to be read."

Dominique Bute got a tired look on her face. "I long for that too, my friend. I'm tired of being a whore and a madame of whores. It's been so long. But enough about things that cannot be, at least for now. Let's go to lunch at our restaurant; the chef promised to have a wonderful meal waiting for us. I told them I was bringing a member of Sanctuary– in fact, I was bringing Mr. Cédric – for lunch. I'm sure that will get us a good table. They, like many in the islands, have heard a lot about this little war, and they are so proud. They were surprised to hear that you are coming; it's as if I'm bringing royalty to the island for a visit!"

Arriving at the restaurant, they were surprised to find it was closed – closed, that is, to everyone but them. In the center of the dining area overlooking the ocean, there was one table set up. Somewhere they had found fine china and sterling silverware, which they used to adorn the table. The owner of the restaurant came and bowed, thanking Cédric for everything he had done, and for honoring him by dining at his restaurant. Cédric did everything he could to make it clear that his dear friend, Dominique Bute, chose his restaurant as a special treat. Cédric put his hand on the owner's shoulder and whispered, "I want you to know something, but you can't tell anyone – if you do, I'll tell everyone the food was bad here, but if you keep the secret I will tell everyone the finest meal I ever had in my life was at your establishment. She, the woman standing before you, is the one who allowed Sanctuary to be victorious. She actually deserves more praise than I." Dominique smiled; it felt good to hear his kind words, which she knew had some truth in them.

The food was exquisite; Cédric had never tasted foods this delicious before. The service was impeccable. They couldn't take a sip from their water glasses without a waiter being there to refill it. They already knew he liked *Presidente* beer, and it was chilled to the perfect temperature. Dominique sipped a glass of the restaurant's finest wine. The waiter and the chef kept a close eye on them, ready to spring into action to serve them.

"I wanted to see you before I go. I'm going to France to visit my girls. Would you like to see the latest pictures from them?" Dominique handed Cédric her phone and showed him all the latest pictures her girls had send to her from their visit to the Palace Versailles.

"My God, they're so grown and beautiful! How long will you be with them?"

"Just a week. If I'm gone any longer, the brothel goes crazy. The girls start to argue with each other about every little thing – mostly about who gets the best customers – there's always some drama going on. A bunch of crazy women getting screwed by crazy guys… hey, what could go wrong? Sometimes I feel like I'm much more den mother than madame. That's probably what *Madame* means in French – den mother for crazy women!" They were talking like they were old friends who had just seen each other yesterday. But Cédric had to add something.

"We're not done, though," Cédric threw into the conversation.

"I know, I know – the pesky Russians! But I think if we do something with them, send them a message – a strong message – we can keep them from trying to fill in the void that José has left. If we can do this, we've got half a chance of keeping the Caribbean safe from these parasites."

Cédric was thinking the **same thing**, but he also remembered that Paco Mandelaze had said the same thing to him, using almost identical words. He wondered if he and Dominique had a connection. He thought about asking her but then decided she was entitled to her secrets.

"Also, I've got to ask you, Dominique, what do you think I should do about Lieutenant Colonel Claude Fleming? Each confrontation is getting a bit crazier. I'm afraid next time he'll come driving up the hill in a tank blasting away with an army of men behind him."

Dominique smiled, stretched her hand across the table, and patted Cédric's hand. "Cédric, leave Fleming to me. While I'm in France, I'm going to speak to some former customers and ex-lovers who may be able to help; many owe me favors. You can't open yourself up to almost all the politicians on both sides of Saint Martin and not expect to have some favors in your pocket. Your hands are so busy shepherding Sanctuary; let me worry about Lieutenant Colonel Claude Fleming."

They sat for the next two hours talking strategies, for they both knew their work wasn't done. Cédric sipped on his Presidente and Dominique on her wine. When they had talked about the work until there was no more to say about it, Dominique turned the conversation to their relationship.

"You know, I've never had a friend like you. I have all these special feelings for you; sometimes, I get a sense that you have them, too. Yet I'm so glad nothing will ever become of them; a friendship like this is so important in my life. I've had plenty of lovers– or at least sex partners – but I've never had a friend or a friendship like this before. You're like the big brother I always wished I had. Who knows; maybe I have one I've never met! I can't remember much from those long-ago days; I can't even picture what my home was like. I only remember being sold – that moment is still as clear to me today as it was that day on the beach. It was that day and that night that I stopped being whoever I was, and instead, I became a whore. But thanks to you – what you did – and our friendship, now there are days when I don't feel like a whore. I feel like a human being. When I'm with you, my friend, or with my daughters, I even feel like a *good* human being. You'll never know how important you are to me."

Cédric's face registered satisfaction as he shared his thoughts with Dominique. "We have completed each other in many ways, haven't we? Through your courage and your bravery, I found my own. When I find my resolve wavering, I think of José smiling his evil smile as he fastened that necklace around your neck many years ago, and my resolve is renewed. Your courage becomes mine. Yes, ours is a special friendship, and I long for the day when we can walk through the streets of Saint Martin and everybody knows we're good friends. I look forward to the day when you can come to my house and sit with us –Marie, the girls and me – and we will laugh, joke, eat a good meal together and you can tuck in the girls at their bedtime – the girls that you saved. It is a good friendship and it creates love."

They learned that the chef had spent two days preparing their lunch; he wanted everything to be perfect, and it was. After an exquisite meal and heartfelt thanks to the chef and the staff, Dominique drove Cédric back to the airport. On the way, Dominique said, "You remember your promise to me. If something happens to me, you'll teach my girls about me – all of me."

"Of course, I promise. Do you know something I don't know?"

"No, I don't. I guess it's that I'm getting more worried as I get older, and I would like someone to know who I am or who I was. Mine hasn't been a bad life; some good has come out of it. At least, that's what I tell myself. And I want my girls to know my whole story. I know someday they'll find out that I was a whore, and I want them to know how I became one, and to know I was more than that. At least, I think I am."

"I promise, and you are."

Their hug at the airport was sweet. What they were doing with Sanctuary was dangerous, and they didn't know when they would see each other again. They also both knew that their cause –with the responsibilities, duties and commitments to others it entailed – was more important than their wish to spend more time together. They sensed that their mission was guided by holy principals more important than personalities and personal desires; they knew that better than most.

As Cédric's plane took off, he could see Dominique standing near her car watching, smiling, waving goodbye, and blowing him a kiss he would never receive. That was the last time that Cédric ever saw his dear friend and ally alive.

Chapter 36

Everything was quiet for the next couple of months. Then, one day, Cédric picked up *The Daily Herald* and smiled to himself. The headlines read, "Lieutenant Colonel Claude Fleming Returns to France," and the article reported that Colonel Baudion Couture had replaced him. He could sense Dominique Bute's hand in this, and he knew that Paco Mandelaze was involved somehow; he just didn't know how deeply. Cédric slapped the paper down in front of Marie. "Fantastic!"

"Well, we don't really know, until we meet the next one – this Colonel Baudion Couture – and get a sense of what kind of man he is."

"It would be hard to be any worse than Lieutenant Colonel Claude Fleming."

"With that, I agree."

Things within Sanctuary were going well: the girls' sleeping quarters were finished quickly, despite the tendency for projects on the island to be often delayed by shortages of materials and just the slower pace of life – 'island time', as they say. They also built a small school where all the lessons were taught in both French and English, and they were free to teach each other their native languages. That worked out pretty well; within a few months, their daughter by birth knew conversational French, English, Spanish, and Portuguese.

New girls settled into life at the compound fairly quickly, helped by their sisters. They were most comfortable with each other and the female volunteers, though they became less skittish around the men as they saw them working around the compound, building and fixing things, making a nice home for them. For some reason, they didn't seem afraid at all of Cédric, Thomas, Ramus and Daniel; maybe it was from what the other girls told them, or maybe it was the compassionate and gentle respect they showed the girls.

Alma and Daniel came every day to John's grave to bring fresh flowers, talk with him, and say prayers. Often, Cédric and others of Sanctuary would join them. More often than not, Daniella prayed with them, too. John was Daniella's godfather, and he had taken a special interest in Daniella. John and Daniella often went for a hike together, and what Cédric and Marie learned after John's death was that John took his responsibilities as godfather very seriously. Neither he nor Daniella had ever told them about their ritual of stopping to read a Bible passage, then talking about it as they hiked. Sometimes now, Cédric would look over at John's grave and see Daniella reading to John from her Bible.

Sam Dresser had not been seen for a while, even by Daniel. There was some talk he had gone through the Panama Canal over to the other side of South America to verify rumors of the Asian pedophile smuggling rings they had first heard about from **Darryl Harrison**, but no one knew for sure. The only thing they were sure of was that if he was needed again, he would appear, perhaps along with some of his friends.

Then one day, a very official-looking car pulled up at the bottom of the hill and two gentlemen stepped out. One went to the back of the car, opened the trunk, and picked up a large box full of bouquets of flowers. They walked up towards Cédric and Marie's home and Sanctuary. Both were dressed in military uniforms. The whole of Sanctuary went on alert, and the children disappeared into the dormitories. By the time the two men reached the top of the driveway, a small committee was ready to greet them: Thomas; Alma, who was drawn to the work, but also to sitting at her husband's grave; Cédric and Marie were ready to welcome or confront the visitors.

The older man, who was **clearly** in charge, stuck out his hand and smiled. "My name is Colonel Baudion Couture. I am now in charge of the French gendarmes on Saint Martin. I've been on the island just a couple of days, but I so wanted to meet all of you and pay my respects to Sanctuary. I know things have been a bit tense with my predecessor; that is over. There is no reason anyone should have anything but respect for what you've done; perhaps he was ashamed that he did not do what you did, and what he should have done all along. I have many friends in France and a few on the island who greatly respect what you have done."

Cédric immediately thought of Madame Dominique Bute and smiled; she said she would take care of it, and she did. He briefly wondered if she and the Colonel had been lovers, but then he reminded himself that was none of his business.

"Again, I apologize for my predecessor. I would be honored if you would take me to SANCTUARY and teach me what's taken place here. I hear that there are 16 innocents in the slave cemetery, so I brought 20 bouquets. I would ask your permission to place one on each of the graves of the innocents. The others are for soldiers lost. It is their sacrifice that has brought some small degree of justice and decency to a small part of this cruel world."

Introductions were made, and Marie guided Colonel Baudion Couture up to SANCTUARY, telling him all the details from that first day when they discovered the horror in José Zavaia's yacht. At each grave, the Colonel placed a bouquet, saluted each unknown hero, and said a brief prayer.

Sanctuary was getting a sense these men were not dangerous. The children came out of their dormitories, and everyone was standing around the slave cemetery watching as this man in full uniform placed flowers on the graves, saluted and said prayers.

As Colonel Baudion Couture was leaving the cemetery, a small girl around ten years old walked up to the Colonel, pulled on his pants leg, looked up at him and asked, "Are you a policeman?"

"Yes, young lady, I am. And who are you?"

"I am Maya. I live here; this is my home. Why are you here? We've been taught to be afraid of policemen. Have you come to take us away? That's what the other policeman always wanted to do – he always wanted to take us away!"

The Colonel got down on one knee, and looking directly into Maya's eyes, he said, "Oh, sweetie, I am not here to take you away. This is clearly your home, and it seems to be a very loving one. Truthfully, Maya, the last policeman was not a good man; his job was to protect you and he didn't do it. My job is to protect you, and I will. I have a daughter about your age; her name is Valerie, and I will protect you like I would protect her. Maybe someday, if your parents let me, I can bring her over here to play with you."

Maya looked up at Cédric. He shrugged his shoulders with a questioning look on his face and replied, "Maybe someday, Maya, maybe."

The Colonel thanked everyone for the tour. Once more, he told them how much he respected their work and their mission, and that he hoped they could work together more in the future. As he was leaving, he turned to Cédric and said, "I know it's not much, but our government will begin putting 10,000 euros a month into an account for Sanctuary to help with its maintenance and to provide food for the children. Consider it partial payment for our falling down on our duties. He then handed Cédric and the others his personal card with his private phone number. "Call if there's anything you need; otherwise, we'll leave you alone. You seem to be doing quite well without our help."

Chapter 37

Late one morning after returning from an early exploratory dive, Cédric sat outside his home, enjoying the view from his hillside location. He was thinking appreciatively that things were going well, and life was relatively calm. Life at Sanctuary was developing a rhythm, and he was grateful.

The new relationship with the gendarmes under the command of Colonel Baudion Couture was working out well. He did indeed bring his daughter Valerie over to play with Maya, and they liked each other immediately and began frequently begging for adults to drive them to each other's homes for playdates.

Every now and then, the French military trucks showed up, the soldiers dressed in bathing suits, ready to take any willing children over to Orient Beach to swim, make sand sculptures, and play beachball games. Some of the children chose not to go because hanging around a beach brought unpleasant memories of the last time they saw their parents, while they unknowingly awaited the arrival of the slavers who bought them and ended life as they had known it, introducing them into hell on earth.

Lately, though, some rumors were bubbling up that Russians had been buying children in Brazil. The Sanctuary group was actually meeting to discuss what to do. They were near deciding to send out a boat to explore the area and the rumors.

Suddenly, the air was filled with the noise of sirens – not just one siren, but many. People around Cédric stopped whatever they were doing, just as he had, wondering what was going on. Marie casually walked over and said, "There's been a murder up on Butte point. That Madame from El Capitan – you know, the one I had issues with – has been killed. I'll bet it was one of her disgruntled and crazy customers who did it."

Cédric shot up out of his chair, raced down to his car and sped away, leaving everybody wondering why this news was upsetting him so. He parked his car where he always had and ran as fast as he could with his bum leg up the trail to the boulder where he'd always received messages from Ms. Dominique Butte. Colonel Baudion Couture was already there. Dominique was sprawled across the boulder, their exchange point; her dress up and her panties pulled down to her knees and the word "whore" written across her stomach. There was one bullet hole to the side of her head. As soon as Cédric saw her, he yelled out, "For God's sake, cover up the good woman!"

A gendarme said, "We need to leave her like this to take crime pictures for our forensic investigation and report."

Looking to Colonel Baudion Couture, who seemed to be in shock, Cedric requested, "Please, cover her up. There's no need for an investigation; you and I both know who did this. It was the Russian traffickers sending a message to me."

Colonel Baudion Couture looked at one of the female gendarmes and directed, "Pull her panties up, erase that word from her stomach, and straighten her dress. Make her look presentable. She's a wonderful, beautiful woman." It was clear to Cédric by the Colonel's tone that his relationship with Dominique had been more than just friendship; he was clearly painfully distraught.

Cédric moved close and put his arm around the Colonel as the gendarme was returning Dominique's body to some form of modesty. Later, Cédric learned that Dominique and the Colonel had had a long-standing relationship. He was the one who had helped her get papers, French citizenship, and passports for her daughters. Whenever she went to France, she spent time with the Colonel. He had taken the assignment in Saint Martin after his wife's alcoholism had taken her life. He wanted to be next to Dominique and was planning that when his tour of duty was over, to retire in Saint Martin so they could be together. Later he would share with Cédric that he had known everything about Dominique's and Cédric's relationship. He knew how they had worked together and how much Dominique respected him, and how Sanctuary's mission had awoken a spark of compassion and responsibility that had lain dormant inside her for many years.

"I want to arrange her funeral. She will be buried in SANCTUARY; she has earned that right," Cédric announced matter-of-factly. Colonel Baudion Couture instantly agreed.

"They have sent their message; in time, I will send mine. But first, we have a courageous woman to bury with honors."

Cédric gave the Colonel the name of the mortuary where he wanted Dominique's body delivered. Then he left to start planning his friend's funeral.

Cédric's first stop on his way home was at the Tabernacle Methodist Church on Rue Du Quarter D'Orleans to see Pastor Eboune. As he was pulling into the parking area, the minister came out of the church. Cédric stopped him. "Pastor Eboune, I don't know if you've heard, but Ms. Dominique Bute has been murdered on top of Butte Point. I would like your permission to hold her funeral here a week from Saturday."

"I'm sorry, Cédric, but I must refuse this. Both you and I know what type of woman she was; my congregation would not approve of her funeral being held here. Her body does not belong near our sacred altar."

"Pastor Eboune, I think I have earned the right to ask this of you. She is a very special woman, and her story needs to be told from a sacred place. I know many good, decent people are part of your congregation, and I believe they will understand and approve when her story is told. Please. I haven't asked much from you, and you need to trust me on this. You've been such an important part of Sanctuary."

"You're right, my friend – you've earned the right to ask this of me. I will see that it happens, even if that means my congregation decides to get a new pastor."

"Thank you, my friend. I guarantee you they won't."

Cédric called Colonel Baudion Couture to tell him he would next call Dominique's daughters and arrange for them to come for the funeral. He would tell them that their mother was gravely ill and ask them to come right away. He didn't want to tell them over the phone she was dead, that she had been murdered.

The Colonel offered to make the flight arrangements and get all the necessary documents so the young women could arrive on Wednesday or Thursday at the latest. He would pick them up at the airport; with him, they would bypass Customs and Immigration red tape. The Colonel would provide a villa for their stay. If they arrived on Wednesday, Cédric could take them to Sanctuary and teach them about their mother's life and work.

The Daily Herald published her death announcement and an abbreviated obituary, stating that her funeral would be held at Tabernacle Methodist Church on the Dutch side, with Cédric performing the funeral ceremony.

Soon after the obituary announcement appeared, calls and complaints from church ladies flooded Pastor Eboune. It wasn't right that a woman of ill repute would be buried out of a respectable church, they complained. All he could reply was, "Please come to the funeral. Your concerns and complaints may change as you learn her story, and in any case, this is the decision I have made and I'm OK with it." Pastor Eboune was worried, assuming that the only ones attending the funeral would be a few ladies who worked at *El Capitan*, himself and Cédric. And he was sure from the calls he was getting that his parishioners had already started talking among themselves about getting a new pastor.

That second night, Cédric sat with Marie, Alma, Rachelle, Thomas, Ramus, Margaret, Daniel and Gloria to tell them about his relationship with Ms. Dominique Bute. They were all aghast to learn her personal history, her work, courage, and dedication to helping the cause of Sanctuary; of the intelligence she had provided as she acted as a general behind the scenes; of her two daughters whose freedom she had bought. Cédric told them she was the one who provided the name José Zavaia. All sat in quiet reverence, listening, many feeling ashamed of their attitude towards their unknown comrade.

Then Cédric looked at his wife. "Marie, she was so sad for what she put you through during Carnival. I want to read one of the notes she had left for me. It came after the news conference we held, which was her idea. She didn't want our movement to be stolen by the righteous people who saw all prostitutes as evil. I've thrown away all the other notes for her safety and ours, but this one I think best shows Dominique's nature:

> "Perfect! What the two of you said to the press, and what all of you did, it was absolutely perfect! Thank you! My God, how I wish I could have met the others and Marie in another world. How I wish she could have been my mother. She honored all of us yesterday, especially your daughters. I can see why you love her. I wish I could have been her friend; I think we would have gotten along well, but we never know where fate will take us."

Marie crumbled into tears. The tension of the last days, and now her remorse for having judged and scorned this brave ally, set her emotions reeling. Cédric moved to stand behind his wife as he continued, "It is my wish that Ms. Dominique Bute will be buried in SANCTUARY. I believe she has the right. You and I don't have the right to be buried in a slave cemetery, but she does;

she was a sex slave like our sixteen daughters and nieces buried there." Stunned silence was followed by murmuring.

Everyone agreed. Thomas and Rasmus said they would have her grave ready for the funeral. Marie spoke up. "I would like to help them. Each stone placed and embedded in her burial box should be placed there by someone who loves her." They decided they would all work together to create her burial box. It would be higher than the others so she could look after her grandchildren.

"I want her body in a white robe placed on a colorful silk-covered slab of wood and carried from the church to SANCTUARY, as we did with our daughters. We of Sanctuary and others true to our cause will take our turns carrying her. The sun will be hot. Colonel Couture has reassured me the road will be free for us to use. He will work out the details with his Dutch counterparts."

Chapter 38

Early Thursday afternoon Cédric, Marie, and Colonel Couture met the plane on the tarmac, and the girls were the first ones let off the plane. Esther and Frieda were **clearly** nervous, but glad to see Cédric and Colonel Couture, both of whom they had met before: Cédric on Martinique, and Colonel Couture in Paris.

"How is our mother?" Esther asked.

Cedric lovingly grabbed Esther's hand. "Dear Esther, there was no way I could tell you and your sister over the phone, but your mother – your dear mother, is no longer with us." The girls broke down, and Frieda reached for Esther and held her tight as they cried on each other's shoulders as Marie's arms encircled them.

Finally, Esther stepped back and asked Marie, "Can we see our mother?"

Marie answered, "Absolutely. We will take you directly to see her." Colonel Couture escorted them into his car, and they all drove to the funeral home where Dominique was laid out. The girls cried and kissed their mother's dead body, telling her how much they missed her and how much they loved her, begging her to come back to them to no avail. They all sat there for four hours, helping the girls get used to the fact and the sad reality that their mother – with whom they never got to spend as much time as they needed or wanted – was gone.

"Esther and Frieda, I made a promise to your mother that if anything were to happen to her, I would tell you her story – more than you already know about who she truly was. She wanted you to know. You're going to hear things about her, some of them painful, that are important for you to understand; you need to know the whole truth. The Colonel has arranged for you to stay at his villa while you are on the island. I would like us to go there, share a meal to refresh you after your very long and difficult journey, and share our stories about her. Let me tell you the story of your mother as she told it to me, and as I saw her live it; you need to hear these things first before I tell the whole island on Saturday at her funeral."

They all went to the villa and found the rest of the members of Sanctuary awaited them, as was Alfred, whom the girls had met many times before. Esther and Frieda ran to him and threw their arms around him, as Frieda exclaimed, "Oh, Alfred! How wonderful it is to see you! Mama's sweet companion! We always knew she loved you as much as she loved us."

He had been nearly inconsolable and filled with remorse ever since Dominique's body had been found. As the two young women clung to him, the giant of a man fell to his knees, sobbing. "I should have saved her! It should be me who is dead, not her!"

Esther shook off her own tears and took Alfred's face in her hands. She looked him square in the eyes. "Don't you dare say that. As our mother said a thousand times over, there is no room for self-pity. It is as it is, and we now have a task to do. We need to bury her. She still needs your strength. We need your strength. We want to hear about our mother – the whole truth."

Cédric and Alfred shared Dominique's life story, as they knew it, with Frieda and Esther. Together, the men unfolded the account: how she was born in Venezuela and sold into slavery, decided to survive, became a prostitute, and survived with Alfred's help. Alfred told story after story of how Dominique protected the women of *El Capitan* and taught them to live with as much integrity as they could.

Finally, Alfred gently looked into each girl's eyes and said, "You need to know that your mother didn't exactly adopt you. She bought you both at a virgin slave auction, saving you from the life that had enslaved her. You would have had more sisters, but your mother only had enough money to support the two of you. She often cried about that, all those girls she didn't have money to save.

"That's always what she wanted."

Alfred spoke, "When Cédric pulled those slave girls from the bottom of the sea and created SANCTUARY –she came up with a plan to help him."

Cédric told of how he had met their mother. She had contacted him after the sixteen girls were buried in SANCTUARY to set up their first meeting in Martinique. That meeting was when Cédric met Esther and Frieda for the first time. He told them how it was Dominique who had found the man José

Zavaia, who had bought her and taken her innocence, then sold her into slavery. and how she helped Sanctuary defeat him.

"What happened to him?" Esther asked.

"Justice," Cédric responded.

"What kind of justice?" Frieda asked.

Alfred spoke up. "The justice of hundreds of rats, centipedes and other animals eating at his skin, devouring his body until there was no more of him."

Both the girls simultaneously said, "Good! Thank you!"

It was around two in the morning when the girls went to bed. Thursday they would rest at the villa, eat well and visit with Alfred and get to bed early, anticipating their planned visit to Sanctuary the next day to see what their mother had helped create.

Chapter 39

The Colonel's housekeeper cooked a hot breakfast for him and the girls that Friday morning, and at 10 o'clock, they got into the Colonel's car and they drove to Sanctuary, parking at the bottom and walking up the hill. The place was busy with activities: the children playing, and many women and men busily sewing the gowns that all members of Sanctuary and all the saved children would wear at the funeral tomorrow – simple white gowns identical to the one Ms. Dominique Bute would be buried in.

Esther and Frieda, accompanied by the Colonel, were met at the top of the hill by Cédric and all the members of Sanctuary. Young Juliana had asked to be the greeter to welcome them. She had two large bouquets of white lilies. She curtsied in front of Esther and Frieda. "Welcome to my home, Sanctuary. My name is Juliana. I was brought here some time ago; I can't remember when. I didn't speak a word for many months because of the bad things done to me. But finally, my father, Cédric, convinced me it was time to speak. He tells me that if he's my father, then your mother is my grandmother, so we're all related! These bouquets are for you." Juliana gave Esther and Frieda each a bouquet of white lilies. "Dad thinks it should be one of us children that shows you around and teaches you about Sanctuary. I volunteered. I like to talk now."

Esther got down on her knees, hugging the bouquet of lilies. She kissed Juliana on both cheeks and explained, "This is how we greet relatives in France where we live."

Juliana giggled. "They do that here, too! It always seems a little funny to me, but I like it."

"I know I speak for my sister. We would be honored to have you show us around. I bet you're a wonderful little guide!" Esther said, a twinkle in her eye.

"If we need an adult, we can grab one. There's a lot of them around here too."

Juliana took Dominique's daughters by their hands and walked them directly up to SANCTUARY.

"All of this area is called Sanctuary, but this is actually the real SANCTUARY." They were standing in front of the archway gate to the cemetery, with the large sign overhead that Thomas had carved out with his blowtorch telling everyone who entered this was SANCTUARY. "The fence is made from the chains and shackles that were around the girls. Dad also found more in the slave ship." Esther and Frieda had always wondered what those scars around their mother's wrists and ankles were from, and she had always brushed those questions to the side. Now they were staring at the instruments that had created them.

.

Juliana continued, "This is a slave graveyard. Only slaves can be buried here. The stones in the graves came from the walls made by slaves hundreds of years ago on the island. My sisters are buried here, and I'm going to be buried here someday. I was a slave, you know."

Frieda added, "No, I didn't know that. I'm sorry."

"That's okay. The lady who helps us here, Auntie Marilyn, tells us it wasn't our fault. It took a while for me to believe it, that it wasn't my fault. I used to think I did something wrong to make me get sold. But she says that's not true. She's been very helpful to many of us. I'll introduce you to her later. You know your mother is going to be buried here. "Would you like to see her grave? My mother and my aunts and uncles finished her grave this morning. It's the most beautiful one in the whole graveyard! Here, let me show you."

Juliana walked them up to the grave that their mother would rest in. It was higher than the rest of them and more beautifully decorated than the others. Dominique's daughters fell to their knees and cried all over again.

Standing between them, little Juliana gently rubbed their backs. "It's okay to cry. Auntie Marilyn taught us that, too. We all cry here at times, even Dad. Would you like to say a prayer? We do lots of that here." Juliana got on her knees and all three said the Our Father, wrapping it up with weak smiles and a hug.

"Come! There's so much more of Sanctuary to show you. I want you to meet some of my sisters." Juliana continued the tour, introducing them to all girls willing to meet them; some were hiding in their rooms as they were still afraid of strangers. Juliana introduced Esther and Frieda to Daniella. "This is Dad and

Mom's first daughter – the one who came from Marie's tummy. She's the best! Daniella, would you like to come with us on the tour?"

"No, little sister. You're doing just fine! I'll talk with them later. Let them meet the others."

Juliana introduced them to the girls as "Grandma's daughters." The other children eventually followed them around, adding things that Juliana might not point out in her tour. She showed them the dormitories, classrooms, and the dining hall. "This is where we'll have lunch in a little while. It gets crazy noisy with all of us girls! I feel sorry for the boys."

"There's boys living here in Sanctuary?" Esther asked, a tone of surprise in her voice.

"Yes, I have five brothers living here. You know, those bad men sell boys too. All my brothers were bought to be sold again to people who do bad things to boys, too. But Dad and his friends save them. They're not bad at all, but they *are boys*, and you know how that is. It's not like having sisters, but they're good."

Frieda just squeezed Juliana's hand a little tighter she looked down at her. "I just met you and already I love you. You're a little angel."

"That's funny! Dad calls me his little broken angel! It's funny that you both say I'm an angel! There are lots of angels here. My sister Daniella can see them and talk to them. Anyway, I love you, too."

Cédric, Marie, and the others watched from where they stood waiting. Nothing like this had ever taken place before at

Sanctuary; there was an instant bond between Esther, Frieda and all the children. It was as if Ms. Dominique Bute was finally getting to walk through Sanctuary.

Esther and Frieda stayed all day, talking and playing with the children. Eventually, even the ones who were still afraid of people came and joined the group around the two nice ladies.

Towards the end of the day, Mirabella asked the two sisters, "Are you going to march with us?"

Esther looked puzzled and said, "I don't know anything about this. Let's call Cédric over."

They motioned Cédric over; it was one of the few times during the day he got to talk with Esther and Frieda. "The children say they are marching tomorrow, and they want to know if Esther and I are going to march with them. What is this?" Frieda asked.

"We were going to ask you later. All of us are reverently marching in silence from Sanctuary to the church dressed in white robes like your mother is going to be buried in. I believe it will get the whole community interested and make them pay attention to your mother's story. They need to hear it; both your mother and I knew that it could only be told after her death. It's also my way to honor my dear friend."

Esther and Frieda listened intensely.

"After the service, we will carry her on our shoulders from the church back here to SANCTUARY, where she will be buried. We will sing as we carry her, and we hope people will dance as she joyously goes to her resting place. We would like you to march with us. In fact, we would like you to lead us. Mirabella and Juliana know the way, and they can walk beside you and guide you. The children will follow you, and then the rest of us from Sanctuary will follow them. It will be a long hot day. Or, we can have a car drive you from the Villa to the church."

The sisters looked at each other, then back at Cédric. "We march! Of course, we march! Can we sleep here tonight?"

"After watching you with them all day, we've already got beds made up for you in the girl's dormitory. I think they would love to have you stay with them."

"And we would love to stay with our sisters."

With plans agreed on, the rest of the day and evening was spent visiting among themselves and learning about Dominique as a mother, from her daughters' viewpoint.

As the stars appeared and the crickets sang their rhythmic song, they all drifted to bed, for they had a long hard day ahead of them. The only one who didn't was Daniella; she was sitting out back in the SANCTUARY talking with the spirits, who were happy and ready to greet the new arrival.

Chapter 40

As the day of the funeral dawned, everyone was up early, gathering in the dining hall for an especially hearty breakfast and drinking lots of juice to prepare for the long walk to the church from Sanctuary. There was an air of excitement and fear – two sides of the same coin – among both children and adults. Today was not only a day of mourning and tribute for Dominique; in a sense, they were inviting everyone on the island to join in their Sanctuary community.

Pastor Eboune stopped by, as he often did, to say a prayer over the meal and bless the children. He also wanted to meet Dominique's daughters Esther and Frieda before the funeral. He decided he would march with them – and the other members of Sanctuary – as he allowed himself to join with them even more deeply, accepting that indeed he was proud to be one of them. They always considered him one of them; now, he decided to step in with both feet. Pastor Eboune would be wearing the robes of his religious calling, a strong symbol and message to the people.

After breakfast, everyone scurried to get dressed, preparing to leave for the church in an hour. Colonel Baudion Couture checked in to let Cédric know that his gendarmes would stop traffic on the road in both directions, providing the group smooth entry to the main road as the procession marched down the big hill. Detour routes were mapped and marked; they would be attended by gendarmes in their finest dress uniforms. They would clear the processional route in each direction to the church and back to the SANCTUARY cemetery. Dutch military and police would also be attending and helping out when borders were crossed. They also would be wearing their dress uniforms.

Other precautions included white water bottles for everyone to sling over their shoulders, for it was almost an hour march to the church, and the Caribbean sun would be rising higher in the sky. The only vehicle would be a medical van following behind with extra water and a doctor on board if needed.

At 9:30, Esther and Frieda led the march down the hill, holding hands with each other and with Juliana on one side and Mirabella on the other. Next came the children: older children walking with younger ones. Every child had been sold into slavery. Every child had faced a life of bondage, soul-wrenching abuse and misery. And every one of them had been rescued with the absolutely necessary help of the woman they were honoring and burying today, who they now called Grandma Dominique.

Even by the time Esther and Frieda and their child guides reached the bottom of the hill, people were paying attention and wondering what was happening. As the last of the party – the adult members of Sanctuary – exited the driveway and entered the road, out of the brush came Sam Dresser, the crazy white guy they all loved who was as much a member of Sanctuary as any of them. He was wearing the same white robe as all the other members of Sanctuary. He joined the procession, marching alongside Daniel and Gloria, their daughter was up with the other children.

Sam whispered to Daniel, "My friends are in the mountains, making sure this parade is safe. There's somebody up there watching, but they are not armed. We'll follow him and see where he goes."

"Nice to see you, brother! Where did you get the robe? Or do all you Texans just have your own white robes for special occasions?"

"I snuck down out of the hills the other night and stole it. There was no way I wasn't going to be part of this. I think I've earned the right to walk with all of you."

"You have, my brother, you have!" They walked in silence.

People watching from their houses lining the road were now on their cell phones calling others; the news was spreading that Ms. Dominique Bute had been a member of Sanctuary. The procession grew as people fell into step. Clouds drifted in to shield the marchers from the hot sun and a cool gentle breeze blew, almost as if the ancient ones were using their influence to comfort the mourners.

People were now coming from every direction to find out what was going on. At the church, people were gathering but held back from going into the church by the Dutch Marines until the children and members of Sanctuary had arrived and taken their seats.

By the time the children reached the church, over 700 people had joined them to find out what was going on and what would happen next. The only people in the church when the marchers from Sanctuary arrived were fourteen prostitutes dressed in their most colorful dresses, sitting in the back with Alfred. He had brought them over from *El Capitan*. He was still their protector, more so now than ever, as Dominque had left them. The women of *El Capitan* had come to honor her; for many of them, Dominique was the closest they had to a mother figure. There were also two reporters from *The Daily Herald* taking notes; they, too, sat in the back of the church. The "ladies of ill repute" were surprised and confused at the commotion now enveloping the church; what was all this commotion about? It was just a whore they were burying today.

Slowly and silently, Juliana, Esther, Frieda and Mirabella, filed into a front pew and sat down. Cédric, Marie, their daughter Daniella and all the rescued children – now also children of Cédric and Marie – filed in behind them, filling in nearly a quarter of the church, with adult members of Sanctuary scattered amongst them. Cédric and Marie sat in the same pew with Esther and Frieda. Daniella sat next to Mirabella and held her hand. Pastor Eboune walked to the front of the church and said an opening prayer, asking God to bless the woman they were burying today, and asking for the angels, all their ancestors and saints above to welcome her and watch over her and all those attending today's funeral. He then announced that Miss Sunflower from *El Capitan* would play the piano and sing *Amazing Grace*.

Miss Sunflower sauntered up to the piano in her Sunday best: a tight-fitting, bright red dress. She was incredibly nervous, for the Dutch Marines had now let the crowd gather around the church, the front door and windows of the church open so everyone outside could hear. She had **certainly** not expected to sing to a growing crowd of well over seven hundred.

She took a deep breath and addressed the assembly. "This was my friend Dominique's favorite song. I often played it for her when she was troubled or had trouble falling asleep. If you know the words, as I'm sure many of you do, feel free to sing along. She always did!"

Then this woman of low reputation, with just a little too much makeup on her face, played the piano and sang. Her voice was beautiful; it was as if God had sent one of his angels to sing. By the end of the song, nearly all the people gathered there were singing along, and the music bounced off the hills and valleys. People who weren't at the church, even tourists on the island, stopped whatever they were doing to listen, wondering where the music – the sweet, sweet music – was coming from.

When she was finished, Miss Sunflower sauntered back to her seat, a tear running down her cheek. She was feeling emotions she hadn't felt in years – feelings like pride, being respected, being a member of a real community, and grief. She missed her friend. She hadn't felt this pure and peaceful in years.

When she sat down, Cédric stood, walked to the front of the church, and took a place behind the pulpit. There was a still quietness in the air; it was as if even the birds had hushed, wanting to hear what Cédric was going to say.

"Thank you, Miss Sunflower. I've never heard that song sung so beautifully – God has clearly given you a gift. I can see why my friend sought you out in times when she was troubled." He paused, looked over the crowd, and said, "Before I start, I would like to introduce everybody to Dominique's two daughters, who live in France. Esther and Frieda Bute, please stand up." The two young ladies stood, turned and smiled at the sea of people, and sat down again.

Then Cédric started to speak again. "I'm sure that none of you knew Dominique had daughters. They are not hers by birth. She bought them at a virgin slave market auction years ago when they were ten and eleven years old. She bought them with money she had made by lying on her back. She did it to save them from the fate she knew all too well. Yes, let me be clear: we are here today to bury a prostitute, a whore, a Madame, my dear, dear friend, Ms. Dominique Bute.

Today I look out at my children – these beautiful young children – and I know that if it weren't for her and the way she helped Sanctuary develop from an idea, a hope, a dream, that these children would not be here. They would have been sold into sexual slavery, and in 10 or 15 years, if they were still alive, most likely, the world would be calling them whores and looking at them with disdain.

What you don't know – what even her daughters didn't know until yesterday – is that Dominique's life, the one so many of us good people look down upon –started out in Venezuela, where she was sold into bondage to two slave traders decades ago. Her family sold her, probably in order to feed their other children. That first night when she lay without hope in a little hut on a beach – her first night as a sex slave at eight years of age – she was dragged to the center of the room and her innocence was taken by the evil man we just killed months ago. Then he turned her over to his crew, and the rest of the night, they had their way with her over and over."

In one hand, Cédric held up the necklace with Tammy's name on it. "I took this necklace off one of the girls I found in the wreckage of the slave ship that many of you have heard about – the sunken yacht that held sixteen dead girls. It says *Tammy*, for those of you who can't see it." Then in his other hand, he held up another necklace. "This other necklace says *Kitty*; it was placed around Dominique's neck after they spent hours raping her. She told me they did this so they could tell the virgins and non-virgins apart when it came time to sell them again. These necklaces are sacred objects created by the untold suffering of a small girl and a great woman. She gave me her necklace, the only thing left from her childhood – if you could call it a childhood – the day she showed me a plan and explained how we could take down the sex traffickers. She was the general; my friends and I are the foot soldiers. She is as much Sanctuary as my sweet wife and I, my dear friends and my children are. She deserves credit for the small community that lives on the side of the mountain near my home. She found a way to survive with the help of dear Alfred, who sits in the back of the church with the women he protects. He was Dominique's protector and only friend for most of her life. Bless you, Alfred.

She told me she made a decision that night. At eight years old, violently soiled and debased by those men, she decided to survive. And survive she did. She did it better than any of us here could have, in her circumstance. She had no choice in becoming a 'whore', yet she decided to care about herself and others despite this isolating label. She became a madame, to care for and watch out for the other women who are part of this profession for whatever reason. She made sure nobody at *El Capitan* was under 21. She watched out for and guided the women who sit in the back of this church in their colorful dresses. Oh, but that's right; we can't talk to them or take their life seriously. They are just whores. We use them and pretend they don't exist. We make fun of them when we see them, or at worst, we even spit on them.

When Miss Dominique Butte came to honor the girls of SANCTUARY, my wife and I would not let her in because of our pre-judgements. We did not see past them to learn who she was. Today, when we leave here, she will finally be welcomed to enter Sanctuary, and all she had to do to get there was to be murdered. Yes, we will bury her in SANCTUARY. She will now have more young girls to look after, sixteen of them.

"Dear friend, Dominique Bute, I will miss you. Thank you for opening my eyes. Thank you for showing me the way that my friends and I could be victorious with the cause that was given to us that day when God directed me to that wreck at the bottom of our beautiful Caribbean Sea. Thank you for my children – all of them – who sit before me. Thank you for your two daughters, Esther and Frieda, who I've only known for a brief time but will be part of our family from now on.

I know today that throughout the hills of Saint Martin, our ancient ancestors – our slave ancestors – are welcoming you, proud to have you in their communion of saints. May we all strive to make our hearts as good as yours. Rest well my friend, and be sure to dance, for I know our ancestors like to dance! We all hear them sometimes, on those quiet nights in the summer. Please walk with us and guide us from where you are now, as you did when you were alive. And know you will be avenged."

Cédric stood silently until after a minute he said, "Miss Sunflower, if you would close this funeral by singing another of Dominique's favorite songs?"

Miss Sunflower walked to the piano again. Looking around, she invited the crowd to join in the song. "Dominique loved that old slave song used to communicate messages about the underground railroad during the times of slavery in the United States. The song is "Swing Low, Sweet Chariot." This time, when Miss Sunflower and the people sang, the music reverberated beyond the churchyard into the hills as the spirits of the slaves buried in the hills of the island rose up and sang along.

When the song was over, Alfred walked to the front of the church and picked up the slave who had finally found her freedom. He lifted the slab of wood that supported Dominique's body and carried her out of the church. The crowd outside parted as Alfred led the long march towards Sanctuary cemetery. Freida and Esther, with heads high and tears in their eyes, walked behind their mother. All the members of Sanctuary and the children followed. The women of *El Capitan* kicked off their high-heeled shoes and walked behind the children, many with their colorful umbrellas twirling as they walked proudly. Then all the others that had gathered to see and hear the truth about Ms. Dominique Bute followed behind.

The members of Sanctuary were there to offer Alfred relief if he needed help, but he carried his dear friend on that slab of wood all by himself from the church to her grave up on the hill now called SANCTUARY. Part of Alfred was wishing he would die as he carried his friend – he so wanted to join her – but he knew his work wasn't done.

As the word spread about what was happening, people came out of their houses with instruments. They played sweet, joyful, festive music, singing and dancing all the way to Sanctuary, as was the old tradition when a slave was buried. It was a celebration for a slave's heavy burdens were finally lifted; finally, there was rest, and no more suffering – just peace behind the golden gates of heaven where there were no masters and no slaves, only God's grace and mercy. And now that was where Dominique rested.

Chapter 41

It seemed like nothing else was talked about on the island over the next week. It was still a time of celebration. Folks brought food and flowers to SANCTUARY and even to the women of *El Capitan*. Sunflower, Rose or one of the other flowers were always there to receive the gifts and to chat. The women of *El Capitan* were starting to be seen as women with tough jobs, instead of as "whores." Many people were checking their own moral compasses after what they had learned about Ms. Dominique Bute. There was a lot of humble pie being eaten. Murmurs about replacing Pastor Eboune had quieted.

Suzanna Rodriguez, always an outspoken critic of Ms. Dominique Bute and *El Capitan*, even brought over a big soup pot of her famous Cajun stew. She was met at the door by Miss Sunflower. After a pleasant exchange, Miss Sunflower said, "You're Suzanna Rodriguez, aren't you?"

Suzanna was quite startled, but she knew that Miss Sunflower and her husband Robert got together about once a month at *El Capitan* over the past year or so. "How do you know who I am? We've never met before."

Miss Sunflower smiled compassionately at Suzanna. "Oh, sweetie, I'd recognize you anywhere. Robert, your husband, you're all he talks about. He has described you to me in great detail, always showing me pictures of you. He talks about how much he loves you and misses having relations with you since, you know..." Miss Sunflower's voice faded off.

Suzanna had been stricken with cervical cancer, and after that, she didn't feel like much of a woman. She had cut off sexual relationships with Robert.

"I know when he's having relations with me, he's actually reliving memories, moments he's had with you," Miss Sunflower continued.

Suzanna cried as she put her pot of stew down on the ground and sat down on the bench outside of the door of *El Capitan.* "I don't feel like a woman anymore! I miss him so, and I feel bad about what I can't give him anymore. That's why I never complained when he goes to see you." Miss Sunflower sat next to Suzanna, stroked her head and let her cry. For Suzanna, it was the first time she had talked about what happened to her because of the cancer.

As Suzanna's upset wore itself out, Miss Sunflower took Suzanna's face in her hands and looked her square in the eyes. "Dear sweet woman, you're still beautiful and sexy, and your husband loves you and wants to be with you, not with me. I know that better than anyone else. There are some things I can teach the two of you, if you'd like. He really needs to be with you, not me – and you really need to start seeing yourself as the beautiful, sexy woman you are. Just because certain parts don't work the way they used to doesn't mean there aren't options for the two of you to have a wonderful, vibrant sex life. Next time he comes here, why don't you come with him? I can teach the two of you how to have some damn good fun! I'd much rather be your teacher than be your substitute. We could surprise him! When he comes over, you could be here and the two of us could greet him and I'll teach you two how to be funky again."

Suzanna smiled. "I'd like that a lot! But instead, why don't you come to our house to have supper with us and teach us there?" Suzanna smiled, hoping the young lady would accept her offer. Suzanna added, "Now I know why you have the voice of an angel – it's because you are one! Next Saturday night, about seven – or are you working?"

Miss Sunflower smiled. "I'd love to have dinner at your house. I'll make sure I have the night off. But don't tell Robert; let's let it be a surprise! Let's keep it between us ladies." It was the first time in years that Miss Sunflower it felt like a person or a friend, instead of a whore.

As Suzanna left, she kissed Miss Sunflower on the cheek, as was the custom with friends. "I look forward to Saturday night. Do you have any favorite dishes? I love cooking."

"No, it will just be lovely to have supper in a nice home."

Suzanna added, "…with friends.

Miss Sunflower picked up the stew and quickly turned, hiding the tears in her eyes as she went inside *El Capitan.* Being treated with respect and decency was having an overwhelming effect on her heart.

Albert visited Dominique's grave every day. He was still watching over her, though he didn't need to anymore, because the ancient ones were. Daniella often saw Dominique play and dance, sit and talk with her arms around the girls of Sanctuary. She was their grandmother now. Whenever Albert was going to leave, she would kiss him on the forehead, for she knew that his suffering was much greater than hers. Albert was worried, for he hadn't seen his sister, the one who ran the fruit stand, in days now.

Then the sad news came. She was found up in the hills, dead. All her bones had been broken, as was a custom of the Russians. She was buried under a pile of pineapples. Another message was being sent to Cédric and the members of Sanctuary.

Albert became a broken man that day. Everything he had loved in life was now gone. His sister was buried in the cemetery next to Sanctuary, where all of them would be buried someday. The group built a small house on the property, where Albert would live and they could all look after him, and he could be close to the two women he loved and looked after in life.

Cédric decided that something needed to be done with the Russians. Otherwise, he was afraid of what the next message sent to get his attention might be.

Chapter 42

Cédric contacted Paco Mandelaze, the Colombian drug cartel lord, and asked him to get a message to the Russians saying he wanted to meet. There was no answer until one day, a huge yacht, *The Palladium II,* came sailing toward Saint Martin and moored outside the port, for it was too big to make its way into the harbor. It was flying a Russian flag. The yacht sat there a half-mile offshore for three days; just its presence sent a message.

During that time, Cédric learned that the yacht was owned by a Russian oligarch named Grigori Bobrov, his last name meaning "the beaver." Grigori was a cousin of the late leader of Russia, Vladimir Putin, who had died of an assassin's bullet right before he was to meet with President Donald Trump of the United States. Everyone suspected that it was the CIA sending a message, more to President Trump than to Russia, but Chechnyan rebels took responsibility for the assassination. Trump, however, received the message; he did not attend the funeral of his good friend and mentor Vladimir Putin, and after that, he stopped tweeting.

Grigori made his fortune in Russian steel, owning most of the steel mills in Russia. But on the side, just for fun, he ran the biggest prostitution and sex trafficking ring in Russia. He saw himself as quite the ladies' man, when in reality, he owned every woman who had anything to do with him.

After three days, a black sedan pulled up in front of Sanctuary and two large men emerged, walked up the hill, and asked to speak with Cédric. The man in charge looked at Cédric with disdain in his eyes.

Without introducing himself, he said, "We've received word that you want to talk with our boss, Mr. Bobrov. He's on his yacht having a party with some of his lady friends. He's willing to meet with you in two days. There will be a boat to taxi you out to the yacht, but he doesn't really have much to say to you." This man's mannerisms and every word he spoke sent a message of intimidation to Cédric.

At night, screams of young girls could be heard coming from the yacht moored not too far off the island. Grigori was making it clear to anyone within hearing range he didn't respect or give a damn about Sanctuary and what it stood for.

Two days later, a small craft waited at the dock, and Cédric boarded it alone, which was a break in Sanctuary's protocol. The decision that Cédric would go alone to meet with the Russian criminal was a tough one, but in the end, the group decided to comply with Bobrov's terms. The craft slowly motored its way among the boats and yachts anchored in Simpson Bay. Music coming from the restaurants filled the air; few people knew or suspected the important meeting about to take place. The tourists relaxing on the beach were clearly oblivious. But the three men positioned on the top of the hill with sniper rifles knew exactly what was happening.

When Cédric arrived at the yacht, he was ushered up to the main sitting area. Encircled in bulletproof glass, it offered anyone sitting in there a 280° view of the harbor, island and the blue Caribbean Sea. A bodyguard motioned for Cédric to sit on the leather couch directly across from Grigori. On either side of this Rasputin's tattooed body were two young girls no more than twelve years old, both totally nude and cuddling up to Grigori. Cédric had heard that the Russians were big into tattoos, and they always had a coded meaning to them, but even so, he was surprised by the extent of Bobrov's tattoos. His entire chest and arms were covered.

"So nice to meet you, Mr. Cédric. I'd like you to meet my friends. This young beauty just starting to bud, her name is Dominique; and the other one's name is Sandra. As you can see, she's just a bit older." Sandra was the name of Albert's sister who owned the vegetable stand where Cédric left his messages for Dominique. He was clearly telling Cédric what they both already knew: that he was responsible for Dominique's and Sandra's deaths.

He didn't want Cédric to feel any sense of power in their negotiations. He wanted to humiliate Cédric and everything he stood for. "Mr. Cédric, let's have lunch." Grigori clapped his hands, and a table was brought out and set between them. Then two more young girls in tiny micro bikinis brought out two beautiful salads, bread, champagne for Grigori and a glass of water for Cédric. "I hope you don't mind salads, but I'm eating light. I must watch my figure; my girls like me looking good for them." His eyes never left Cédric.

Cédric didn't want to be adversarial. He kept his affect contained, even submissive because he didn't want to give any clue that might disrupt what was going on around them. Cédric complimented Grigori on the wonderful lunch, and how fresh the bread was – perhaps better than the excellent French bread on the island. Grigori told him the flour was brought from Russia and the bread was made fresh every day. Halfway through the meal – and probably because Cédric was showing enough submissiveness – one of the young girls brought out a *Presidente* beer and poured it into a frosted glass for Cédric.

At the end of the meal, the table was taken away and Grigori smiled at Cédric. "Usually, I enjoy one of my little darlings here after lunch, but I suppose you wouldn't want to join me in that," he said, laughing. The girls snuggled into Grigori as he stared at Cédric. Then Grigori pushed the girls aside and leaned in toward Cédric. His mannerisms and expressions changed, and he became as cold as any Siberian winter.

"Mr. Cédric, you wanted to talk to me. But I'm going to talk to you and tell you the way it is. You will listen and not interrupt me." Grigori leaned in even more, locking his stare into Cédric's eyes, trying to look into his being. "You're not dealing with the likes of José anymore. I actually thank you for getting rid of that piece of scum. You people created a vacuum that I'm going to fill. I have no real competition. Ravaia thought he was a prince, but he was a petty commoner. I am the King.

"I'm going to make you an offer and let you think about it for one day – just one day. There is a huge need for fresh young innocents (he paused as he stroked Dominique's right thigh), and

I am going to fill that need. My associates and I will procure young girls from Africa, and from some of the islands, and up and down the South American coast where José purchased them. I know that slavery – especially sex slavery – disgusts you, what with your background – being black and everything – but it is a reality. It is my reality.

"I have $12 million in gold coins in two vaults on this ship. It is yours if you agree to my terms, which are: I *do not want you or any of your friends involved in that thing called Sanctuary to meddle in or disrupt my business in any way.* This is all I want, and if you don't agree to it, well, I have a boat not far from here that holds fifty highly trained soldiers at my disposal. In addition, I have another thirty on this ship. We will come on to Saint Martin, destroy your home, take all of "your girls" including your biological daughter – Daniella, I think her name is – and she will become my personal whore for me and my crew members to use until there's nothing left of her. Then I'll send her to a cheap brothel where men can have her for $20. I will send your wife and your friends' wives into the filthiest brothels I own in Siberia, where they will be used by dirty coal miners day in and day out for the rest of their lives. The rest of you pathetic do-gooders and vigilantes will be killed – hung in trees. That's something they always did to slaves, and I know you people find it disgusting. I will dig up the bodies of your slave daughters, burn them, and scatter their ashes so there is no trace of them. You and what you tried to do here will just be a bad memory.

"If you accept my offer, the gold is yours. All the young girls you saved will not be touched, as long as you don't try to save any more. I want you to stay out of my business. Don't test me, or I will take you to one of the slave markets in the Middle East and sell you just like your ancestors were sold."

Grigori had clearly thought about how best to intimidate Cédric, threatening every person in the world he cared about and debasing him and everyone in Sanctuary because of their values and the color of their skins.

Cédric kept his rage under control. He knew there were things more important than his anger and desire for vengeance. Though there was not a drop of fear in his body, he worked to look nervous and scared because he wanted Grigori to believe he would get his way. He planned to use Grigori's prejudices and preconceived notions against him.

"I'm truly sorry about your good friend, that madame woman. She was a saucy woman, very strong. I hear she did not die easily. But a message needed to be sent, and she and the pineapple lady were handy. And, after all, she was just a whore, so I hope you can forgive me for their deaths. What say you?"

"You make quite a compelling argument, but of course, I'll have to talk to the rest of the members of Sanctuary."

"Remember to tell them what will happen to them if you don't accept my offer: that they are dead, and their wives and children... well, you know..."

"I think I understand you loud and clear. I can tell by your eyes you're a man of your word, even if your word is despicable."

Grigori laughed, as did his bodyguards.

"Again, I'll have to think about it. I do want to use that one-day window you offered to confer with my associates. You promise me that my girls – the ones we've saved – will not be harmed in any way. That you will not harm my daughter, my wife, my friends or their families. Do you give me your word on this?"

"I do. And, as you know, I'm a man of my word. To show that I do have some decency in my heart, and to sweeten the deal for you, when you leave today you can take my little playthings with you. You can take Sandra and Dominique and the five other girls I have with me. They can be additions to your Sanctuary. I want you to see that I do have compassion. But first and foremost, you need to understand I'm a businessman and my business is flesh."

Inside, Cédric was overjoyed to hear Grigori's offered to give him his young sex slaves. He had been racking his brain about how to bring them into the negotiations. Cedric wanted this monster to believe that the negotiations were going his way and that he was more interested in the money than the girls, so he asked, "So, you'll give us $12 million in gold coins to leave you alone? How would the gold be delivered to the island?"

"Don't you worry about that. If you agree, you just tell us where you want it and it will be there, a pirate treasure. You know, you and your friends are just pirates stealing what wasn't yours. José had worked hard and paid good money for those girls and boys. And you stole them. You're just common pirates who've been lucky. But your luck has run out. I don't deal in luck."

Cédric was thinking to himself, "…*and neither do I. Neither do I, you evil racist bastard!*"

"How should I let you know my answer?" Cédric asked.

"I will be moving my vessel this afternoon. I will meet with my other men, preparing for the onslaught we are preparing for you if your answer is 'no.' When I arrive back tomorrow evening, I will anchor over near Philipsburg. Mooring on that side of the island, I will be able to see the flag post of *El Capitan* from my yacht." Grigori smiled. "If your answer is 'yes', just go to *El Capitan* and tell my man who will be there to raise the flag like Dominique used to do when she wanted to send you a message. And if the flag isn't flying high by the end of the day tomorrow, all hell will rain down upon you and your little piece of ground you call Sanctuary."

Chapter 43

Because of Sam's scouting, Sanctuary already knew about the other two boats carrying Grigori's small army of fifty Russian mercenaries. They were anchored off on a small uninhabited island about ten miles from Saint Martin, where people sometimes paused just for a day or night to enjoy its sandy beaches while sailing through the Leeward Islands. That's where Grigori's mercenaries were hanging out, awaiting his orders to engage on St. Martin or to stand down and head back to Russia. Sam and Rasmus were keeping track of them with a high-altitude drone.

Cedric was angry at Grigori and also glad. The Russian mobster was not taking Sanctuary very seriously. They were leaving themselves exposed. He and others like Sam were sure it was part of the racism that the Russians were notorious for directing toward blacks, always seeing them as inferior. They soon would be proven wrong. Their prejudice was going to get them killed, and rightfully so.

Cedric thought to himself, *"How dare you disrespect us after all we've been through, but if you're going to, then you're going to pay; you're going to pay with your lives."* The small army of mercenaries would be easily neutralized. Two high-powered long-distance drones armed with missiles sat at the ready in a tin hut just off the Grand Case airport, their batteries constantly charging to be ready for the upcoming assault. The drones would effectively take out the two boats quite easily. Then the mercenaries would be stranded, sitting ducks to be picked off one at a time by the snipers arriving in cigarette boats.

Meanwhile, the Russians were treating this interlude like a party. There was plenty of vodka, and young girls and ladies provided for the men's use in a tent on the small island. They were just waiting for Grigori's instructions, which they knew would be coming in a few days.

Also, the three days Grigori spent anchored off the island using his yacht to announce his presence, believing it would intimidate everyone, had been another stupid play. It had given Sanctuary plenty of time to come up with what everyone believed was an effective strategy, and time to put it in place. Clearly, Grigori had not come prepared. He really had no idea who he was dealing with; there was not a member of Sanctuary that could be intimidated. His personal racism and inflated ego clouded his judgment and created fatal flaws in his normally sound thinking.

Grigori's world was predicated on and organized around raw power: might makes right; to the winner belong the spoils. In Grigori's world, greed, prejudices and ego ruled. In Grigori's world, loyalty was something he bought and paid for. Grigori did not understand that dignity and decency generate a different type of strength and loyalty; he did not comprehend that the essence and strength of Sanctuary was that it radiated from ethical power.

The strength of Sanctuary did not radiate from one man but from a set of principles that its members believed in, sacrificed for, and would die for knowing these principles were more important than any one individual.

Had Grigori done his homework, he would have known the backgrounds of those in Sanctuary. He would have learned that many in Sanctuary were divers, and he might have considered the implications of that fact; but again, he was underestimating his opponent. The three days had given them time to assemble sixteen magnetic mines – mines that divers attached to the underside of Grigori's yacht as he and Cedric talked, negotiated and ate lunch.

Margaret had formed a very good relationship with Colonel Baudion Couture, who had joined Sanctuary as a silent member, following Dominique's example. He was not surprised to learn that the Russians wanted to move into the vacant space. Margaret was his liaison, keeping him informed, for he would play a small but crucial role in the events of the day.

Couture agreed to assist with the operation against the Russians in a subtle yet effective way. Margaret provided him a set of coordinates and requested that he ensure the French military frigate on Saint Martin would be practicing maneuvers in that area, effectively blocking Bobrov's yacht from its most direct route into deep water. As he headed out to meet with his mercenary force, his large yacht would need to make a slight shift in its route, passing through an area that was much shallower but still easily navigated.

Towards the end of their meeting, Cedric asked Grigori, "May I see the gold? Sanctuary will want verification that you are actually prepared to pay it. And I have to admit, I've never seen that much money." Cedric raised an eyebrow and allowed a hint of a smile, planting the impression he was, after all, lured by the prospect of wealth being offered.

"Of course. I was expecting that you'd want to see it. That's why I brought it along." Grigori led Cédric through the ship down to the vaults. Cedric took in all the details, making a mental map of the yacht and where men were stationed, in case he and his team needed that information. They entered a room next to the engine room, where there were four large gun safes. Grigori spun the tumblers and he pulled open the doors on two vaults filled with bags of South African Krugerrands, American Buffalo, American Eagle, Canadian Maple Leaf and British Britannia in one-ounce coins. "I'm leaving you coins instead of bars. They are much easier to exchange and use for purposes that a group like yours may have. Plus, I have so many of them." Grigori said, flaunting his wealth and talking down to Cedric. "I like the coin that hangs around your neck. I've been in admiring it. Where did you get it?"

Cedric was just about ready to tell him how he got it while diving, but then he changed his direction before responding; he didn't want Grigori thinking anything about ships, gold coins, wreckage, and divers. Instead, he quickly said, "I got it from a pedophile named Henry Crane. You know those pedophiles always have cash and gold; that's their currency. Well, you know that better than I do. It's your business. You probably got a lot of your coins from guys like him."

Grigori didn't respond. He took a small bag of the coins and gave them to Cedric. "Here, so you can show your friends what's waiting for them. These should help you convince them. If you double-cross me, I'll just get them back when I murder all of you."

Grigori led Cedric to the skiff with one of his men walking behind them. As they got to the skiff, seven girls were brought from the other direction. Cedric hadn't known, but it was becoming clear to him that Grigori was a pedophile, since all the girls appeared to be younger than fifteen. Perhaps that's why he got into this business – so he could have access to an endless supply of young innocents. One thing that Cedric had learned about pedophilia was that it wasn't so much about sex; rather it was that sex was the knife used to cut out and kill off the innocence – drain the souls – of the young ones. Their innocence was the food that fed the pedophile. These seven girls had that sad look about them that Cédric had come to recognize; it came, he knew, from seeing things and being part of things they were way too young to make sense of. Cédric realized that Grigori was giving them to him not out of compassion, but because they were used up, it was time for him to dispose of them. He knew that if he wasn't stopped, Grigori would soon have more young ones to feed on like a vampire in the dark of the night.

"My yacht will be back tomorrow on the Philipsburg side of the island, and I will watch for your decision. Choose wisely, or many will die. But I do get the sense that you're seeing the situation correctly; I was told that you are a smart man, and I'm getting that sense myself."

As Cedric stepped into the skiff, he thought to himself, *"You're absolutely right! Soon, many will die. It's time for you to receive a message – one written in your own blood. And yes, I am smart, but it's mainly because of my friends."* He looked to the skies said a small prayer and said in a soft voice, "Dominique it's time to send them to hell."

On the short ride back to the island, Cedric tried to comfort the girls though he realized that many of the girls did not understand his language and probably couldn't hear him clearly over the sound of the motor. He knew that no matter what he wanted to convey to them, they would not **really** understand for a while, and it would be the women and children of Sanctuary who would help them to feel any **degree of safety**. It would take time, and for some of them – hopefully, a rare few – there might never be healing and recovery.

Chapter 44

The French frigate D641 Dupleix, stationed at Saint Martin, was on maneuvers nearby. From the dock where he and the girls had been dropped off by the Russians, Cédric smiled. He saw The *Palladium II* head west instead of straight out into the Caribbean. The captain was taking the route Cédric had hoped he would because the D641 Dupleix was blocking the more direct route. Once the ship was out of sight, Cédric dialed up Colonel Baudion Couture to thank him. He reported that the vessel wasn't needed anymore, and it could return to port. "Baudion, please stop over on Sunday for a barbecue. We would love to host you and your men. The girls love it when they come and play games with them. You can meet my seven new daughters."

Over in Grand Case, two large drones equipped with missiles sat on the runway, waiting for the call. When the phone rang next to Rasmus, he hit the button. "Hello."

"It's time. Let those sweet birds fly! May the ancients guide them. I'll let you know when we're ready for the drop," Margaret said to her husband. She was coordinating everything from Sanctuary.

Margaret was tracking the course of *The Palladium II* and the drones at the same time. The drones were in position, and *Palladium II* was just entering the small red circle she had placed on the map. She nodded to a group of people headed up by Pastor Eboune; they were all on phones, communicating with different parts of the team. In unison, they all gave the word. "Now! Let it begin!"

Pastor Eboune added, "Let the fury of the heavens descend upon the wicked." He had always wanted to say that, even though he knew it was a bit showy.

Marie tapped Alfred on the shoulder, and he pressed the button. Even though the *Palladium II* was far enough away for safety, a small rumbling could be heard as the bottom of *The Palladium II* was blown out, and it immediately began to sink in 100 feet of water. Two cigarette boats rushed up upon it, and as men started swimming about, searching for any piece of wood to hang onto for survival, shots rang out. Bodies quickly drifted towards the bottom of the Caribbean. Sam saw Grigori frantically trying to make it to one of the lifeboats; it was an easy shot for Sam. Within five minutes, the *Palladium II* rested on the bottom and all the men who had been on board were gone. Including Grigori.

The cigarette boats sped off to the barren island, where Rasmus had destroyed two more vessels with direct hits from the drones. The fifty men they had carried were stranded, and soon the two cigarette boats met up with two Sanctuary boats already circling the island, picking off Grigori's men. The fierce gun battle left all fifty dead, with only one casualty and three wounded from those helping Sanctuary.

Within two hour, Cédric, Marie, Thomas, and Rasmus were on the site diving. They quickly found the *Palladium II's* safes, still intact and lying on their sides. Using their underwater cutters, they opened them and brought up the $12 million in gold coins.

They found Grigori's body. They **decided to use** the flesh of this powerful criminal to send messages to some of his associates and competitors. Thomas cut off his head and his hands laden with rings; he would deliver the body parts to the Colombians, who had agreed to help.

The Colombians took pictures and spread the word of what had happened on Saint Martin. They sent the hands and rings to another Russian oligarch named Alimzhan Churbanov; he was the son of Yuri Churbano, who the Colombians expected might be next to step in where Grigori had tried and failed. A week after the body parts were sent out, the Columbians reported they had heard **back** from Alimzhan in a simple note. "Message received. Will not bother you! Stay on your fucking island!"

For now, the Caribbean was off-limits to sex trafficking and slavers.

Epilogue

After goodbyes were said, Sam was not seen again, though there were lots of rumors about some small white guy and his friends on the other side of South America hunting pedophiles. And he was always remembered by the stories to group told of the crazy little white killing machine who talked so funny and who made you nearly instantly love him by his good heart.

The day of the funeral for the last member of Sanctuary who died in the battle with the Russians, most of French Saint Martin was closed. Many businesses and church bells rang on the Dutch side of Sint Maarten, joining in observing a day of respect and honor for all the members of Sanctuary who had put their lives on the line for their cause.

The gold was stored safely in the vaults of the banks around the island.

More small dorms were built at Sanctuary to accommodate the new girls and to prepare for the new children they expected would continue to find their way to them every now and then seeking an escape and a new safety. They knew there were many more victims out there – often victims not of cartels and traffickers but of their own families. All were welcome.

Esther and Frieda decided to move to Saint Martin and live at Sanctuary to be close to their mother's grave, and to continue her work of taking care of women and girls. They invited Alfred to live with them. Cédric was glad when he accepted the offer; it would allow the girls to know their mother through his stories. And the arrangement gave Alfred a sense of purpose in taking care of and protecting Esther and Frieda. He died about a year later of natural causes and a broken heart.

Daniella stopped seeing the spirits of the girls and Dominique. Dominique had said goodbye for all of them, explaining that it was time for them to walk on in their journeys and rest with the ancients. But their singing voices could still be heard some nights when the moon was bright, and the trade winds swept across the island.

Every Sunday, rain or shine, Cédric and Marie hiked the trail that Cédric used to hike to receive messages from Dominique. They sat on the boulder where Cédric retrieved so many important notes. They felt peace in their hearts when they sat there, knowing they had honored Tammy and all their children who shared her suffering. They had responded to the questions she had haunted them with, and their souls had been changed in the process. Tammy's death was not for nothing. Her death had not been meaningless.

As they sat there, Cédric and Marie always felt two spirits with them. They knew Tammy and Dominique were there, blessing them and letting them know their work was done. At least for now.

CPSIA information can be obtained
at www.ICGtesting.com
Printed in the USA
LVHW050844231220
674954LV00016B/308